"Tired?"

"*Nee*. Just thinking that I really enjoyed myself."

"*Gut*." They left the restaurant and she chose the long road home.

He shot her a knowing glance. As they rode along, the full moon floated above them, casting light, then shadows, over the strong bones of his face. He was at once the man she'd known for years, then the mysterious one she learned more about each day that she spent with him.

She stopped beside a field. "Do you remember this spot?"

"We stopped here the first night you let me drive you home from a singing," he said slowly. "Honeysuckle was blooming along the fence and fireflies were dancing over the field."

"*Ya*."

"I wanted to kiss you but it was too soon."

She turned and smiled at him. "It's not too soon tonight," she said, a little surprised at her boldness.

The AMISH BABY FINDS A HOME

ALSO BY BARBARA CAMERON

The Amish Midwife's Hope

The AMISH BABY FINDS A HOME

BARBARA CAMERON

A Hearts of Lancaster County Novel

FOREVER

NEW YORK BOSTON

Copyright © 2021 by Barbara Cameron

Cover design and illustration by Elizabeth Turner Stokes
Cover copyright © 2021 by Hachette Book Group, Inc.

Forever
Hachette Book Group
1290 Avenue of the Americas, New York, NY 10104
read-forever.com
twitter.com/readforeverpub

First Edition: August 2021

Forever is an imprint of Grand Central Publishing. The Forever name and logo are trademarks of Hachette Book Group, Inc.

The publisher is not responsible for websites (or their content) that are not owned by the publisher.

The Hachette Speakers Bureau provides a wide range of authors for speaking events. To find out more, go to www.hachettespeakersbureau.com or call (866) 376-6591.

ISBN: 978-1-5387-5164-0 (mass market), 978-1-5387-5165-7 (ebook)

Printed in the United States of America

CW

10 9 8 7 6 5 4 3 2 1

For Steph, Justin, and Rachel.
You are such good parents.

The AMISH BABY FINDS A HOME

Chapter One

Gideon Troyer unlocked the door to Gideon's Toy Shop and stepped inside.

His heart always beat a little faster when he entered his shop and looked at all the shelves of wooden toys. His *Englisch* customers—especially the older ones—sometimes teared up when they picked up a car or truck or knelt and looked into the windows of a dollhouse. More than once, people told him that his toys reminded them of the ones they'd received and played with as children…times when kids played with real, quality toys.

He'd no sooner walked inside, put his lunchbox in the back room, and started a pot of coffee when he heard a knock. It was March and business here in Paradise, Pennsylvania, was brisk with tourists who loved to shop for Amish goods while they were on vacation. When they browsed his shop, they often bought birthday and Christmas gifts for the children and grandchildren in their lives.

But when he walked back to the front of the shop he found he didn't have a customer. It was Hannah Stoltzfus, the owner of the quilt shop several doors down from his. And the woman he'd grown to love these past months.

He opened the door he always kept locked until he was ready to change the sign on it from **Closed** to **Open**.

"*Guder mariye*," she said, smiling as she stepped inside. "I thought you might like a donut." She held up a bag from the coffee shop nearby.

"I never turn down a donut."

She smiled. "I know." Her hazel eyes sparkled as she pulled off her knitted shawl, revealing a dress of a pale robin's-egg blue that made her look like spring. Her face was oval with creamy skin and her dark blond hair was tucked neatly under her *kapp*. She was slender and petite, and her small size often brought out a protective feeling in him. But she was stronger than she looked and a hard worker. He'd learned she had an independent nature and didn't want him to treat her as some delicate *maedel*.

"The coffee's almost ready."

They shared coffee each morning before they opened their shops. Sometimes she brought a treat; sometimes he did.

Gideon carried a stool from behind the counter and placed it in front of the counter for her and then went into the back room for coffee. When he returned, Hannah was perched on the stool, looking so fresh and pretty on a cold winter morning. He'd always thought she was the prettiest *maedel* at *schul*. Now that she had opened her own shop and it was doing well, she had a lovely air of quiet self-confidence about her.

When she'd stopped in at his store one day last year looking into renting the shop space a few doors down from his that he'd told her about, he hadn't believed his good fortune. He'd been interested in her and had asked her to a few singings and other church events, but since he was only in the second year of owning his business he hadn't been able to ask her out as often as he wanted to.

So these early morning coffee get-togethers were a time he cherished. He'd always heard that God set aside a mate for you, and he'd come to believe Hannah was his. He thought Hannah felt the same about him, and he was working up his courage to ask if that was true.

They chatted easily about their plans for their shops for the coming months, and all too soon they had to part. Gideon walked her to the door and after he said goodbye, he flipped the sign on the door to **Open**.

An older *Englisch* couple walked in a few minutes later. The man immediately moved to the shelf of wooden trains. "This reminds me of my childhood," he said, lifting one to admire it. "We lived near railroad tracks and I ended up going to work for the railroad. Just retired a few years ago."

His wife stopped beside him and gave him an indulgent smile. "Are you buying that for our grandson or yourself?"

He chuckled. "Maybe a little of both. These are the kind of toys that make you get off the sofa and play. Kids today sit around with electronics and never play, never use their imagination."

They were all Gideon had played with as a *kind*, so he didn't really know how to respond to statements like that. So he'd learned to just nod and smile and enjoy having something he'd made appreciated by someone who would take it home to play with their *grossdochder* or *grosssohn*.

The wife wandered off to the section that featured dollhouses and toys Gideon associated more with girls. While Amish *dochders* and *fraas* helped care for the farm animals and helped with field work when necessary, they still had more traditional roles than the *Englisch* and played with dolls and such.

"Oh, Henry, come look!" the woman called. She could be heard opening and closing doors on the biggest dollhouse he'd made. "Henry!"

"Women," Henry muttered as he put the train down on the counter in front of Gideon. He ambled off to find out what his wife wanted.

Gideon heard a lot of murmured conversation as he took a toy he'd been working on over with him to place on a shelf. "I just finished that the other day," he said, showing them how the walls inside could be moved to make the rooms larger or smaller. "We're having a special Spring sale this week. Ten percent off purchases over $50."

The man patted his wife's shoulder. "Honey, let's get it for Amber. She'll love it."

She beamed. "You're the best husband."

Gideon carried it to the counter and rang it up along with the toy train the man had chosen. Then he locked his door and carried everything out to their car, which was parked a few spaces down from his shop. The big sale was a nice start to the morning.

He waved to Hannah when he saw her standing inside her shop near the big front display window. She beckoned him to come in, so he did.

"Sold the big dollhouse."

"I knew you would. It turned out so nice."

"Your display window looks so much better than mine," he said, studying it.

"*Danki*. I'd be happy to help you with yours. Katie Ann is here today, so I can come by later."

"That would be *wunderbaar*."

Another opportunity to see her and get the benefit of her help as well. He usually just put a few things in the display window, but he didn't have the gift for arranging one the way she did. He went back to his shop and worked on painting several smaller toys at the counter as customers came and went. He enjoyed working on them during shop hours. Some days when he had a lot of customers he didn't get a lot done, but when business was slow it filled in the time.

And he'd discovered that customers enjoyed seeing

that a real person made them—that he didn't get them from some factory. Occasionally he got a male customer whose hobby was woodworking, and then it was great fun to compare notes on favorite types of wood and stains and such.

All in all he was glad that he'd chosen to open the shop, despite also having to help his twin *bruder* with the small farm they'd inherited when their *dat* died a few years before. Eli enjoyed farming, so he never begrudged doing much of the daily chores on his own, but lately Gideon sensed some unhappiness in him that his *bruder* denied. He and Eli shared what his *mudder* called the *zwillingbopplin* bond—the twin bond. So he'd sensed that Eli was unhappy even when Eli acted like nothing was wrong. Gideon wondered if it had anything to do with Emma Graber moving away. He knew Eli had been seeing her, and Eli had been moody after he came home the last time they'd been out together. The bell over the shop door interrupted his thoughts.

* * *

Hannah stopped in the doorway and blinked at the man sitting at the counter. He was staring at a paper in his hands, his dark eyebrows drawn together in a frown.

"Hi," she said a little hesitantly.

He looked up and smiled.

For a minute there he had looked like Eli. She knew some had trouble knowing which twin was which, but she'd always known the difference. *Schur*, they were identical, with dark brown hair and eyes. But while Gideon had an open, friendly look about him, he was usually quieter than Eli, who tended to use his charm on *maedels*. But for months now Eli had been quieter, almost...broody the past months.

Ironically, some *maedels* liked that distant sort of manner. Once a friend of hers had happened on a copy of *Wuthering Heights* at the library and said Eli reminded her of Heathcliff. Well, Hannah had tried to read the novel to see what her friend meant, but she just didn't like that sort of behavior. Seemed to her it was just a person who needed to lighten up. She smiled at the silly thought while Gideon stood and grinned at her, dimples appearing in his tanned cheeks. He wore a navy cotton shirt with his black broadcloth trousers and suspenders. Such a handsome, hardworking man, she mused. Her heart beat a little faster.

"You're *schur* you have the time?" he asked.

She nodded. "You helped me so much setting up my shop. I'm glad there's something I can do to help you."

Gideon took the box she carried. "What's all this?" he asked, looking inside as he set it down on the end of the counter.

"I had some decorations I thought you could use." She pulled out a little wooden fireplace. "What do you think about making the window look like a living room where a *kind* just had his or her birthday party?" she said. "Like he or she got all the toys wished for."

"I like it."

He walked over to a shelf and found a number of wooden cars and trains, then watched as she set them about in front of the fireplace. It made her feel *gut* that he trusted her advice about the placement and the type of toy. She had him take one of the dollhouses he'd built and set it in the middle of the display, then she stepped back and narrowed her eyes, examining the finished look critically.

"Needs one more thing," she said. "Be right back."

She left his shop and hurried to hers, where she poked in the back room and found what she wanted. She returned carrying some birthday wrapping paper she kept for times when customers wanted gifts wrapped. She took several sheets and ripped and crumpled them, then scattered them about to look like they'd been torn from the toys.

"Perfect," he said as he stood close to her to take it all in.

When she straightened and found him staring at her she blushed. "Perfect," he repeated as he stepped closer, his attention focused on her lips. She felt her heart race, and tension radiated between them. Her feelings for him had deepened over the past year. They were perfect for each other. She felt she'd learned how to be more patient and calm from him, and he'd relaxed and smiled more when they were together, so maybe she helped him not think about work and be so serious.

She hoped he would propose soon and tried to be patient waiting for him to do it. Marriage season was coming up. Couples would wed after the harvest ended.

Twenty-four was a *gut* age to marry. Couples were waiting to marry later these days. After all, marriage was forever in their community.

He bent his head and then jumped back when the shop door opened and the bells jangled.

Two women walked in. "We just noticed your window and had to come in and tell you how cute it is," one said.

"I just love the dollhouse," the other woman told Gideon. "I had such fun playing with one when I was a little girl. I think all of us girls did."

Her friend nodded and they chattered on about it. Hannah had never had a dollhouse when she was a *kind*. Her *eldres* wouldn't have thought of giving her such a thing. They'd believed strongly in practical gifts, and besides, she was usually too busy doing chores around the house to play.

The women wandered around the shop, and Hannah heard them talking about what they found. When they returned to the front counter a few minutes later they each laid toys on the counter.

"I just love the cradle," one said as she looked in her purse for her money.

"I thought I was finished shopping but the little red wagon is perfect to put my son's presents in," the other told Gideon. "I'm so glad we stopped in."

"I'm glad you found something for your children," he told her.

After the women left Gideon turned to Hannah. "*Danki* for your help," he said.

"You're *wilkumm*," she told him as she lifted the box she'd brought over. "I'll see you at lunch."

She walked back to her shop and found Katie Ann looking a little frazzled as she stood at the cutting table unfolding a bolt of fabric.

"I was about to call you," she admitted. "We suddenly got busy."

"A bunch of us came on a bus from Harrisburg to shop," one of the customers told them.

Hannah set the box under the counter and noticed a group of women walking by. She wondered if Gideon was going to get the benefit of the extra shoppers as well.

The morning was a whirl of activity as people streamed in and out of the shop, buying fabric and thread and craft kits. Some came in bearing bags printed with the names of Gideon's shop and others along the street.

When lunchtime came, the customers took off to eat at the Amish restaurants.

"It was a *gut* morning," Katie Ann said. She went into the back room and returned with Hannah's lunch tote. "Go have lunch with Gideon. We won't see any customers for at least an hour."

Hannah started to protest, but Katie Ann was right. Things were often slow during the lunch hour.

"What about your lunch?"

"I brought a sandwich."

"If you're *schur*."

"I'll call you if we get busy again."

Hannah grabbed her shawl, draped it around her shoulders, then picked up her tote and left.

She strolled over to Gideon's shop. When she walked in he was wrapping up a wooden train and tucking it into a shopping bag for an older woman, so she wandered over to the display window and tweaked the placement of a toy.

She was still eyeing the display when she heard a *boppli* cry, a thin, indignant wail. She glanced around. Someone else must be in the shop. When she didn't see anyone walk up from the back, she frowned. Maybe it had been her imagination. Or a toy. *Nee*, that didn't make sense. Gideon didn't have any toys that made noise.

She heard the cry again coming from the back of the store. Curious, she walked in that direction and nearly stumbled over a basket sitting on the floor. She stopped and stared down at it, her eyes widening. A *boppli*— perhaps five or six months old—looked up at her and waved its little hands.

Hannah glanced around for its *mudder* but there was no one around. She rushed up to Gideon who was closing his cash register.

"There's a *boppli* in the back of the store."

"A what?" he looked up at her, his attention clearly not on her.

"A *boppli*. Someone left a *boppli* in your store."

He stood. "You're joking."

"I'm not! *Kumm!* See for yourself!"

But as she retraced her steps, she wondered if she'd

11

imagined what she'd seen. Who would leave a *boppli* in a store?

Hannah heard the *boppli* cry again as she walked past the last of the display shelves and there it was.

"See!" she announced, turning to him. "Whose *boppli* is that?"

Gideon came to an abrupt halt beside her and gawked at it, looking shocked.

The *boppli* stared up at them and wiggled in its basket. And then it beamed a smile at them, revealing dimples in its cheeks.

Chapter Two

I'm checking the restroom. Maybe the *mudder* is in there." But Gideon wondered who would leave their *boppli* out here instead of taking it with her.

"*Gut* idea. I hadn't thought of that."

Gideon hurried to the back of the shop but found the door to the bathroom standing open. The adjoining break room was empty as well, but a diaper bag sat in the middle of the table. He picked it up and carried it back to where he'd left Hannah, praying he'd imagined there was an abandoned *boppli* in his shop.

But there it was, staring up at Hannah with wide blue eyes from its basket on the floor.

"This can't be happening!" He set the bag down, shoved his hand in his hair, and frowned.

The *boppli* jerked its head, looked up at him, and began crying.

"Ssh! Don't cry, *lieb*!" Hannah bent and unstrapped the *boppli* and lifted it into her arms. "Gideon didn't mean to frighten you." She looked at him as she rocked it gently. "Did you?"

"*Nee*, of course not," he said in a quieter voice. "But what am I supposed to do with it?"

"Him," she said. "I think it's a boy. See?" She turned the *boppli* to show him the pale blue cotton shirt.

The *boppli* began fussing again. Hannah rocked it and spoke to it quietly, and it settled down again.

"Look in the diaper bag and see if there's a bottle. I think he's *hungerich*."

He dug into it and found a zippered insulated bag that held several bottles. And then his hand touched a folded piece of paper. He unfolded it and read, "This is your *sohn*, John. It's your turn to care for our *boppli* for a while. I'll be in touch."

Appalled, he looked at Hannah. "This is not my *kind*. I swear it."

She gave him a long stare. "Then there's only one other person who can be his *dat*. You know who that is."

He shook his head.

"Gideon. Think." She held the *boppli* out to him and he jumped back, holding up his hands in defense. "Just look."

He stared intently at the *boppli*'s face. "You think it's Eli's," he said slowly. "How can that be?"

"I don't know. We need to ask him."

"I'll call him." He got out his cell phone and frowned when the call went to voice mail. "Eli, it's Gideon. Call me as soon as you get this."

He turned to Hannah. "He's at a horse auction today. He stopped in earlier on his way to say he wouldn't be back until late tonight."

The *boppli* began crying again. "We need to feed him," Hannah said. "We don't know when he last ate."

He held out the bottle to her and she just looked at him.

"Gideon, you don't give a *boppli* a cold bottle," she chided and shook her head. "Here." She held out the *boppli*.

He backed away, terrified, as if she were trying to hand him a bomb. "I can't hold him!"

"*Schur* you can," she told him firmly, stepping forward and putting the *kind* in Gideon's arms. "I'll be right back with his bottle."

Gideon stared down at the *boppli* in his arms. His was a small family. His *mudder* had borne twins and then never had other *kinner*. Knowing how ragged he and Eli had run her—especially Eli—he thought that had probably been best.

He walked over to the stool behind the counter and sat down. The more he looked at the *boppli* the more he saw the resemblance. Hannah had seen it almost immediately. He couldn't wait to talk to Eli.

"Who is your *daedi*?" he asked the *kind* in a low voice, not wanting to alarm him again. "And where is your *mudder*? Why would she leave you with me?"

The *boppli* stared up at him with big blue eyes, his cheeks wet with tears.

His lips trembled, so Gideon rocked him gently as he'd watched Hannah do. "She'll be back in just a minute."

"Here we go," Hannah said as she came back and held out the bottle. The *boppli* immediately became excited, waving his hands and making a cooing noise.

"Here, let me give him to you so you can feed him," he said.

"*Nee*, he's comfortable," she told him firmly and handed him the bottle. "You can do this."

The *boppli* reached for the bottle, so Gideon guided it to his mouth and watched the tiny hands latch onto it. Gideon felt panic rising up his throat. "Don't leave me with him," he begged.

"I wasn't going to."

"How old do you think he is?" he asked, looking up at her.

"Maybe six months. It's hard to tell with the way they grow sometimes. But my *schweschder* has a *boppli* about this size, and he just turned six months."

"You know, he doesn't just look like Eli," Hannah mused. "He reminds me of someone else, too—the way he tilts his head and looks at us. But I can't think who."

The bell over the shop door jingled as an *Englisch* woman walked in. She took one look at them and smiled. "Oh, my, what an adorable baby!" she cried.

Startled, the *boppli* let go of the bottle nipple and

16

jerked his head to look at her. Milk dribbled onto his chin. He grinned at the woman as she approached making cooing noises.

"How old is he?" she asked as she leaned on the counter to admire him.

They exchanged looks. "Six months," Hannah said quickly.

"So nice that you can bring your baby to work with you," the woman gushed. She glanced around at the shelves. "Imagine what fun he'll have when he gets older and he can play with all these toys!"

The *boppli* grabbed at the bottle and began sucking again now that the attention was off him.

"You're such a lovely young family."

Gideon felt a flush stealing up his neck.

"Can I help you with anything in particular?" Hannah offered quickly, as if sensing his embarrassment.

"I'll just browse if you don't mind. I have several young nieces and nephews, so when I'm in a toy shop I like to look for gifts." She walked over to the doll-houses in the display window. "This is my first time in this shop."

"Of course. You just let me know if I can answer any questions," Hannah said. "Gideon here makes all of the toys."

She waited until the woman wandered away then leaned over the counter. "Gideon, what if the *mudder* doesn't show up?"

Fear struck Gideon. "You think we should call the police?"

17

"If we do, they'll give him to Child Welfare Services. Then if it's Eli's he might have trouble getting him back."

Gideon sighed and shook his head. "You're right."

She walked to the shop window, looked out, then returned to the counter. After she glanced around to make sure the woman wasn't in hearing range, she leaned close again. "It's going to be interesting to see what Eli has to say when he comes home."

He nodded. "I can't wait."

The *boppli* drained the last of the bottle and let the nipple slip from his slack lips as he dozed off.

Hannah walked around the counter to take the bottle and set it down. Then she lifted the *kind* from his arms. As she did Gideon's hand brushed her arm and their gazes locked. She blushed and walked around to take a seat on the stool in front of the counter.

"Found some lovely toys," the woman who'd been browsing said as she placed the things she'd chosen on the counter.

Gideon rang up the purchases and handed the woman the bag. "Thank you for shopping with us."

"It was my pleasure," she said. She smiled at the baby. "You enjoy him. Time goes so fast, he'll be grown before you know it."

Hannah turned to Gideon as soon as the woman left the shop. "I need to get back to the shop."

"You can't leave me with him!"

"You could put him back in his basket."

"And what if he wakes up again?"

18

She bit her lip. "All right, I'll take him back to my shop. He can take a nap in the crib I keep for when my *schweschder* helps out at the shop."

"*Danki*, Hannah!"

He sounded so relieved she couldn't help smiling. "Get his diaper bag."

When he returned with it she slid it over one arm along with her lunch tote.

"You didn't get to eat your lunch."

"I can eat at the shop."

"I'll walk you down." He stood on legs that felt weak.

"I can manage, *danki*."

"I'll see you at closing then, then?"

"You will," she said definitely. "Be thinking what you're going to do if the *mudder* doesn't show up."

He swallowed hard as he watched her walk out and down the sidewalk. He'd be doing nothing else but thinking.

* * *

Hannah's shop was just a short stroll from Gideon's. When she entered, she realized she should have spent the time coming up with what she was going to tell Katie Ann about the *boppli* in her arms.

The woman stared at her as she stepped inside and headed toward the crib in the corner.

"Who is that?" Katie Ann wanted to know as Hannah lay the *boppli* down in the crib and then began poking in the diaper bag.

"Hmm?" she said, playing for time as she pulled out a fresh diaper and a box of wipes. Her faith didn't believe in lies and prevarications, but the situation wasn't one where she could simply offer an explanation.

"This is John," she told Katie Ann as she bent over the crib. "Isn't he darling?"

The *boppli* smiled up at them sleepily.

"Whose *boppli* is it?"

"A friend's. I ran into her at Gideon's and offered to babysit so she could do some shopping."

Hannah glanced up and looked pointedly at the clock on the wall. "Time for you to go. You said you had an appointment with the loan officer at the bank about the bakery."

"*Ya*, but—" Clearly torn, Katie Ann looked at the clock, then sighed. "I can reschedule and stay if you need me."

"We'll be fine. He's going to take a nap. And that appointment is important." Hannah knew Katie Ann had been planning on opening her own bakery for some time.

Katie Ann went to the back of the shop and got her sweater and purse. "You're *schur* you don't want me to stay?"

Hannah tucked a blanket around the *boppli* and looked up with a smile. "He didn't even wake up when I put him in his crib."

"Well then, I'll see you tomorrow," Katie Ann said as she walked to the front door and left.

Two women strolled in, regular customers, so she

walked over to say hello and see how she could help them.

"Well, so who's this?" one woman asked as she stopped near the crib. "It's not yours, Hannah."

"Sssh," the other woman hissed. "Don't wake the baby."

"I'm just babysitting for a friend," Hannah said. "I got some new fabric in since you last visited. Let me show it to you."

What had she gotten herself into? she wondered. It felt like she'd had nonstop questions since she'd brought the *boppli* back to her shop.

The two bought several yards of new fabric each and left shortly afterward. Hannah was grateful for a lull.

After they left she sat in the chair beside the crib and watched the *boppli* sleep. It was so peaceful watching the gentle rise and fall of his chest, to see the flutter of eyelashes as he dreamed.

How innocent he looked, she thought. Sadness swept over her. How could a *mudder* just leave her *kind*? How did she know he would be cared for properly? Had she lingered nearby to make *schur* someone else didn't pick it up and walk off with it?

She stood and looked out her window. What if the *mudder* had spied on them and seen her carry her *kind* to the shop? Would she come to see why Hannah had taken him? Hannah stood looking out the window but didn't see anyone watching.

Restless, she roamed about, putting a few bolts from the cutting table back on their shelves, straightening items on display tables, and checking the *boppli* every few minutes.

Fortunately, a customer came in—an older woman who reminded Hannah a lot of her late maternal *grossmudder*. She browsed the selection of quilt and craft kits. Then she stopped abruptly and her eyes grew wide.

Turning, she stared at Hannah, her eyes wide. "Oh, my! There's a baby in there."

Hannah nodded and smiled. "I know."

The woman chuckled. "Well, of course you do. He's sleeping so soundly, I almost missed him," she marveled. "How I wish I could sleep like that. I lie awake half the night and after I finally fall asleep I wake at the least little noise."

She selected a quilt kit with a Christmas theme and walked to the counter. Hannah rang up the purchase, tucked it into one of the shop's brown paper shopping bags, and tied the handles with a scrap of fabric.

The woman hesitated. "You know, I really should pick up a kit to make a crib quilt. I have a grand-daughter who's having a baby in March."

Hannah set the bag aside. "Which one did you want?" she asked as they walked over to the shelf that held them.

"I think this kit with the multicolored blocks. It would be appropriate for a boy or a girl." She stared down at the baby in the crib. "I just can't believe that I'm going to have a great-grandchild. It's my first."

"How wonderful. You must be so excited."

The woman nodded. "My husband's happy as a clam in his workshop building a cradle for it." She smiled at the *boppli* again. "Family's so important, isn't it?" she said, not bothering to wait for a reply as she waved and sailed out the door.

Hannah pulled out her lunch tote and ate her sandwich and drank her tea. She found herself thinking about what the woman had said. Oh, not the great-grandchild part. But having a *familye*. Her relationship with Gideon had grown so much this past year as she opened her shop and they'd spent more time with each other. She'd loved him for such a long time and sensed he felt the same for her, but he was a quiet man who moved slowly. Well, that was fine. It was one of the qualities she loved about him, so she could wait for him to ask her to marry him. She smiled wryly. Well, as long as he did it before the marriage season ended.

Gideon had talked about how he wanted to make *schur* that his shop was a success and hinted that it was important for a couple to start out with a stable foundation. He and his twin *bruder* shared the family farm but Eli did most of the farming, with occasional help from Gideon when he wasn't at his shop.

She walked over to sit near the crib after her customer left. There was really no doubt in her mind that Gideon would be the first to marry. Eli had made it clear that he enjoyed being single. There was a time when she'd thought that he and Emma Graber were seeing each other, but then Emma moved away and Eli seemed like he was back to dating many *maedels*.

The *boppli* whimpered in his sleep, then shifted a little and slept on.

"Who are you, little boy?" she whispered. "Who is your *mudder*? Your *dat*?"

Her gaze was drawn to the diaper bag sitting on the table in front of her. Maybe there was a clue inside besides the note Gideon had found. She pulled out the insulated bag with the remaining bottles and put it on the table in front of her, which was used for quilting. Diapers followed, along with a box of wipes, shirts, a pacifier. Jars of strained baby food. A note about John's feeding schedule.

She pushed her hand into the front pocket of the bag and there, at the bottom, her fingers encountered a small scrap of paper. She pulled it out and examined it. A piece of a bus ticket. The state listed was Ohio but the city was missing. She shoved her hand deeper in the pocket but there was no more of the ticket, just another pacifier. Thoughtful, she put the ticket in her apron pocket and returned the baby items to the bag.

It was just a piece of a bus ticket but it was a clue. She couldn't wait to show Gideon. A glance at the clock showed that there was just a half hour left until she could close. She bit her lip, then rose, and walked over to lock the door and turn the sign to say **Closed**. She took the day's receipts from the cash register, tucked them into a zippered bank bag, and retrieved her shawl, purse, and lunch tote. When she walked back to the crib the *boppli* was stirring and opening his eyes.

"Hello there, sleepyhead," she said smiling at him as he yawned and blinked at her owlishly.

She once again had the thought that there was something about the way he studied her, his head tilted a certain way, that reminded Hannah of someone. But she couldn't think who.

She was struck by how sweet and easygoing he was. What would she have done if he cried for his *mudder*?

"Let's change your diaper and go see Gideon," she told him and set about the task. When she was finished she went into the back room to dispose of the diaper and wash her hands.

She got her shawl and purse and walked back to the front of the shop. Then she shook her head and got out her cell phone to call Gideon. The least he could do was walk down and help her cart everything out when their driver came to take them home.

And while they waited for Liz, they were going to talk.

A knock sounded on the door. She glanced over and saw Gideon standing there looking in at her.

She walked over and opened the door. "I was just going to call you."

"I closed up a little early," he said as he strode in. "How has the *boppli* been for you?"

"*Gut*. He slept the whole time."

Gideon looked relieved. "I'm glad. I figured you'd have called if he cried or something."

She just stared at him. "And what would you have done?"

"I have no idea," he admitted. "But we'd have talked it over and come up with something together."

Speaking of which... She took a deep breath. "Gideon, we need to talk about what we're going to do with the *boppli*."

Chapter Three

Gideon gazed down at the little *bu*. When the *boppli* spotted him, he grinned and waved the rattle harder.

"I know. Eli hasn't returned my call." He sighed and shook his head. "I was hoping the *mudder* would come back. Every time the shop door opened I prayed it was his *mudder* coming for her *boppli*."

"I wondered if she was watching us and saw me bring him down here to my shop. I spent some time standing at the window looking out at people walking past," she told him. "I was hoping one of them would be the *mudder* and she would tell me she'd come for him."

She reached into her pocket and held out the ticket. "I found this in the bottom of the diaper bag. It looks like the *mudder* came here on a bus from Ohio. Do you know anyone who lives in Ohio?"

He frowned. "I have an *aenti* in Middlefield. My mother's there visiting her now."

She smiled when the *boppli* tossed the rattle down, and she picked it up to shake it for him. "Gideon, maybe we need to call the police."

"*Nee!* We can't call the police!" he said quickly.

She studied him for a long moment. "Because you think like I do that he's Eli's."

"I don't know. But like you said, if we call the police they'll take him to Child Welfare Services, and if he's Eli's then he'll have trouble getting him back."

She glanced at the clock. "Liz will be here soon. We should decide what to do before she gets here."

He sighed heavily. "I don't know what to do. The whole time you had him, I kept wondering what I'd do if you called me for help. I don't know how to take care of a *boppli*."

"And I do because I'm a woman?" she asked with a touch of asperity.

"*Nee*, but women do get more experience with *kinner*, don't you think?"

"So what are you saying?"

"I'm saying I don't know what to do."

"Well, I guess we have to take him home until we figure it out. Or until the *mudder* shows up."

"But whose home?"

As if sensing the tension in the room the *boppli* began to cry. Hannah picked him up and walked him around the shop. "It's *allrecht*, little man. We will take care of you." She looked at Gideon. "Won't we?"

28

He nodded. "We will."

A van horn honked outside the shop. Hannah put John in his basket and popped his pacifier in his mouth when he fussed. "Going for a ride," she told him. "It'll be fun."

She didn't blame him for not being happy at being put in his basket. It was likely he had ridden in it for hours on the bus.

Gideon gathered up her things and walked with her out to the van.

"Well, well, who do we have here?" Liz, their *Englisch* driver, asked with a big grin when Gideon slid the van door open.

"This is John, a friend's baby," Hannah told her. "We don't have a car seat."

"No problem. I keep one in the back of the van for my little passengers."

Soon John was buckled safely in the car seat between Hannah and Gideon, and the basket was safely stored in the back.

They were the first passengers Liz picked up in the afternoon. As the van filled with other Amish going home from work, they were the object of a lot of curiosity. Hannah kept her answers brief. She was grateful when Gideon interrupted Ada, who wanted to know who Hannah's friend was, and distracted her with a question about her shop.

Hannah's house was the third stop on the way home. Gideon stepped out and helped her with her things after she got herself and the *boppli* out. "I'll be right over," he whispered as he handed her the diaper bag, her purse, and her lunch tote. He prayed this would prevent fellow passengers from talking about the *boppli*. Gossip could race through the Amish grapevine faster than the internet.

He climbed back in, rode the short distance to his house, and waited for the van to drive out of sight before he walked to Hannah's house.

By the time he arrived at her house she had removed her sweater and that of the *boppli* and was seated at the kitchen table feeding John as he sat in an infant carrier.

"Where'd that come from?" he asked, gesturing at it.

"We have a few *boppli* things here since my *schweschder*'s visit."

John greeted him with a wide grin smeared with strained orange carrots. He shoved his fist in his mouth then held it out to Gideon.

"I think he wants you to have a taste," Hannah teased.

"*Danki*, John, but I'm not *hungerich*."

"*Nee?*" Hannah asked him as she offered John another spoon of carrots.

"Not for baby carrots." He pulled up a chair and watched her. "Something smells good and it isn't carrots."

"I put together a chicken and broccoli rice casserole before work this morning. It's in the oven. You're welcome to stay for supper."

"Well, John, I'd say this is our lucky night." He glanced around. "Where are your *eldres*?"

"*Daed* is out of town on business. He'll be back tomorrow evening. *Mamm* left me a note saying she's staying at my *aenti* Miriam's tonight. My *aenti* is feeling a little under the weather."

"Well, I'm sorry to hear that, but it did save us from some awkward questions."

"Eli hasn't called you back, has he?"

"*Nee*. How did you know?"

"You would have said so when you walked in." She scraped out the last of the carrots. After John swallowed, she wiped his face with a damp washcloth. "Distract him for a moment while I warm his bottle."

"Distract? How?"

She gave him a disbelieving look as she rose. "Are you saying you don't know how to make a silly face at a *boppli*?"

"*Nee*, of course not. I just wasn't *schur* what you meant." He made a silly face at John and got a gurgle of laughter, then made another and got more. "I guess I've felt off balance—helpless, really—all day since we got this little surprise." He picked up the jar and studied it. "How many of these were in the bag?"

"Six. We may need to get more supplies if his *mudder*'s not back in two or three days."

She got up and set the bottle in a pan of hot water to warm it, then checked the casserole in the oven. "Needs a few more minutes. Get John out of his carrier. His bottle's nearly ready."

Gideon wanted to protest, to beg her to do it, but it didn't seem right after all she was doing. He told

31

himself John wasn't a newborn and easily breakable. Still, he held his breath while he unstrapped the wiggly *boppli* and lifted him in his arms.

"Sit and feed him his bottle while I finish supper," she said briskly, handing the milk over to him.

"He likes to hold it himself," Gideon informed her as he sat at the table watching John. "Is that normal for his age?"

"It is." She warmed the contents of a jar of canned corn from the previous summer harvest and poured glasses of water.

"That was fast," Gideon said when John drained the bottle.

"He's a *gut* eater. Put him back in the carrier and he can keep us company while we eat." She used pot holders to remove the casserole from the oven and set it on the table along with the bowl of corn, then got out dishes and silverware.

"John, it's too bad you had to have strained carrots," Gideon told him as he sampled the casserole. "Hannah is a *wunderbaar* cook."

"And Gideon is a *gut* eater like you, John," Hannah said. Then she blushed. "I didn't mean that to sound like I believed he's yours."

"I know you didn't," he reassured her.

They were just finishing their meal when Gideon's cell phone rang. He looked at the display then at Hannah. "It's Eli."

"At last," she said.

Chapter Four

You called?" Eli said and yawned in Gideon's ear.

"Hours ago. Why didn't you call me back?"

"I was busy. What do you want? I've had a long day. I want to go to bed."

Gideon frowned. Eli sounded more than tired. His words were slurring. Gideon knew that when Eli went to a horse auction with his friend Naiman they sometimes indulged in a beer, which church rules said was *verboten*. The two had enjoyed it during their *rumschpringe*, and though they were baptized now Eli had admitted they occasionally had one while out of town.

"We've had a long day, too. You need to come over to Hannah's. Now."

"Can't it wait?"

"No. Now, Eli."

"This better be important." Eli broke the connection.

Gideon sat there for a long moment staring at the phone before putting it down on the table. "He's coming over."

"From what you said it didn't sound like he wanted to."

"*Nee.*" He reached for her hand and looked deep into her eyes. "Hannah, I haven't thanked you enough for believing me about John. And for helping me the way you have today. I don't know what I would have done without you."

She squeezed his hand. "You have thanked me. And I wanted to help." She glanced at John, who was looking around the room with avid interest. "Who wouldn't want to help with a sweet little *bu* like this?"

Just then, there was a rap on the door that startled John. He threw his hands up and his mouth trembled.

Eli walked in but stopped abruptly when he saw Gideon and Hannah sitting there holding hands. "You didn't call me over to tell me you two are engaged, did you?" he asked, looking put out. Then his gaze fell upon John. "Who's that?" he asked.

"Close the door, Eli."

Eli did as Gideon asked, then stood there gawking at John.

John stared at Eli then Gideon. Then he looked at Eli again and frowned. He babbled as if to say, *Two of you?*

"Someone left this *boppli* at the shop today," Gideon told him. "Know anything about it?"

"Why would you think that?" he asked indignantly.

Hannah rose to rummage in the diaper bag on the counter. She pulled out the note, handed it to him, then backed away. "Sit down, Eli. I'll get you some coffee."

Eli looked sheepish for a brief moment, probably realizing that he smelled like the beer he'd drunk while out of town. "*Danki.*" He then read the note and a gamut of emotions ran through his face. "He isn't mine," he finally said flatly. He put the note down on the table. "You can't think he's mine."

"Look at him, Eli," Gideon told him. "He looks just like you."

"If he looks like me, he looks like you, too," Eli pointed out.

Gideon met his gaze steadily. "I know he's not mine. Can you honestly say the same?"

Hannah set a mug of coffee in front of Eli. "Gideon? Want some coffee?"

He nodded. "*Danki.*"

"I'm going to take John in the other room and change his diaper," she told them. "*Kumm*, John, let's get you changed and into a sleeper." She unstrapped him and held out her arms. John giggled and leaned forward so she could scoop him up.

"Look at him, Eli," she said quietly. "You can't deny what you see." She touched John's cheek and he grinned at her. The dimple in his left cheek deepened. Turning on her heel, she left the room.

Gideon waited a moment before turning to Eli. "She's been taking care of him most of the day."

Eli stared at the note in his hand. "What are we supposed to do?"

"You mean what are *you* supposed to do?"

"I'm not accepting that this is my *boppli* just because someone says he is."

"There are ways to prove it. When the *mudder* returns she can demand that you take a test."

Eli rubbed his hands over his face, then his hair. "What am I going to do?" he muttered. "I can't take care of a *boppli*."

"We have to until the *mudder* shows up," Gideon told him bluntly. "If we call the police they'll have him sent to Child Welfare Services. Is that what you want?"

"*Nee— ya—*" Eli stood so abruptly he knocked over his chair. "I don't know what I want. I don't know what to do." He picked up the chair and sank into it. "What a mess."

Gideon rose and topped off Eli's coffee. "Get some more of this in you and sober up."

"I only had one beer," Eli muttered, but he drank the coffee. "I just didn't eat much today at the auction. And I'm tired. We left before dawn."

Hannah walked back into the room and turned the flame on under the teakettle. "You're welcome to some supper."

While her tone wasn't the friendliest, it was her nature to take care of others. Eli looked up at her and smiled gratefully. "*Danki*, I would appreciate it. I'm sorry for the trouble this has caused you today."

She got a plate from the cupboard and scooped some

chicken casserole and corn onto it, then placed it before him with a fork. "He's a sweet *boppli*." While the water heated she dug some cookies out of the cookie jar, spread them on a plate, and set it on the table. "Sorry there's no pie," she told Gideon.

"This is great," he said, taking a big bite out of a cookie.

When the teakettle whistled she poured a mug of boiling water and sat at the table to dunk a tea bag in it. "I can take care of John tonight. We have a crib in my *schweschder* Linda's room for when she visits with her *boppli*. He's already sound asleep."

Hannah stirred a teaspoon of sugar into her cup, then sipped it as she studied Eli. "Hopefully the *mudder* will show up tomorrow. Then the two of you will need to talk and figure out what to do."

"And what if she doesn't show up at all?" Eli asked as he pushed aside his empty plate. He watched Hannah and Gideon exchange a look. "You've thought of that, too."

"All day," Gideon said.

"Let's not think that way," Hannah told them firmly.

Gideon rose and cleared the table. "I'll wash and you dry," he told Eli. "Hannah's done enough today."

With the kitchen cleaned up it was time for them to head home. Eli thanked Hannah again for the meal and waited on the back porch while Gideon said good-bye to her. Then they climbed into the buggy and started home.

Gideon looked at Eli, then stared at the road ahead and wondered what was going to happen next.

* * *

Hannah woke, not sure what had awakened her. Dawn light filtered in through the windows.

She blinked and realized she wasn't in her own room. And then she heard babbling noises. Sitting up, she saw the crib a few feet away and remembered she'd gone to sleep in her *schweschder* Linda's old bedroom.

The babbling turned to whimpers. Hannah slipped from the bed and went to lean over the crib. "*Guder mariye*, John. You slept all night! What a *wunderbaar boppli* you are!"

He grinned up at her and waved his arms.

"Let's get a fresh diaper on you and get you some breakfast."

She wished she could be a fly on the wall and hear what the *bruders* were saying this morning. As she changed John's diaper and replaced his onesie, she studied his cheerful face. He had such dark blue eyes and the sweetest grin.

"You're a charmer for *schur*," she told him as he waved his fists and jabbered at her. "Are you trying to talk me into making you a big breakfast?"

When she was done, she put him back in the crib. "I am going to change really quick," she told him. She dressed as quickly as possible, then fixed her hair and pinned on a fresh *kapp*.

"There!" she exclaimed as she leaned over the crib rail to pick him up. "You were such a *gut* boy and so patient."

She carried him downstairs and distracted him while she pulled a bottle from the refrigerator and set it in a pan to warm it. Bouncing him in her arms, she walked to the back door and opened it. "Look John, there's a robin!"

His eyes grew wide as he followed the path of the bird walking along the porch railing. By the time the bird flew off she figured the bottle was warm enough. She closed the door, plucked the bottle from the pan, and smiled as he chortled his happiness at seeing it. His feeding schedule said he ate rice cereal in the morning, but he seemed too hungry to wait for her to fix it, so bottle first.

She sat in a kitchen chair feeding him the bottle and gazed ruefully at the percolator sitting on the stovetop. She craved a cup of coffee as much as John did his bottle. With a sigh, she looked down at him. "This is what *mudders* do, John. They put beautiful *bopplin* like you first."

Then she frowned. How could his *mudder* have left him alone with his *dat*? How could she trust that Eli would take care of their *boppli* as he deserved to be?

Well, hopefully today John's *mudder* would show up and all would be explained. In the meantime she needed to get moving if she was to be ready when her ride came.

John went into his carrier without complaint while she filled the percolator and set it on the stove, then made him a bowl of rice cereal. Once he was fed he watched her as she drank her coffee and ate a quick bowl of cornflakes. Then she packed her lunch, put John's bottles in his diaper bag, and set them on the bench by the door with her shawl and his sweater.

"There, ready." She took a deep breath. With just minutes to spare.

Then the kitchen door opened and her *mudder* walked in just as Hannah was ready to scoop everything up and head for the front door.

"Well, well, what's this?" Mary asked as she came to a dead stop.

"This is John." Hannah slung the diaper bag over her shoulder.

"And where did John come from?" She bent to chuck him under the chin and John responded with a delighted squeal.

"I'm watching him for a friend."

"What friend?"

Hannah drained her coffee cup and set it in the sink. She'd have loved a second cup but there just wasn't time. She picked up her purse, looped it crossbody, then grabbed the diaper bag and picked up John.

"Hannah?"

"Hmm? Sorry, *Mamm*, I'm running late."

Mary followed her to the front door. "Hannah, whose *boppli* is that?"

"It's a long story," she said. "We'll talk later."

"You're taking him to work with you?"

"*Ya*. My ride should be here any minute." She opened the front door and walked out onto the porch hoping her *mudder* wouldn't follow her.

Mary stepped out onto the front porch and blew that hope away.

"Bye, *Mamm*. I should be home by six thirty."

"I'll be waiting. Have a *gut* day, both of you." She waved at Liz as she pulled up.

Hannah didn't have to look back to know her *mudder* was staring after her. She didn't have any idea what she was going to say to her when she got home tonight. The only thing she could do was pray that John's *mudder* would show up and take him.

Gideon stepped from the van. "*Guder mariye.* Let me help you strap him in."

"*Danki.*" She handed John to him.

John babbled happily at him and patted his cheeks.

"Well, *guder mariye* to you, too." Gideon laughed and looked at Hannah. "He's quite a talker."

"He hasn't stopped since he woke up," she told him with a smile. "Good morning, Liz."

"Good morning to you, too." Liz turned in her seat and grinned widely at them. "Gideon put the car seat in. Said you still have your little visitor."

"Yes." She watched Gideon struggle with the seat belt.

"Makes me miss my grandchildren," Liz said. "Can't wait to see them next month when they visit."

Gideon finished strapping John in and looked relieved. He gestured for Hannah to take her seat and walked around to the other side of the van to take his.

"Liz! Wait!"

Hannah glanced out her window and saw her *mudder* hurrying down the sidewalk. She rolled her window down.

"You forgot your lunch!" Mary handed it to her. "Good morning, Liz," she said, poking her head in. "Thank you for waiting." Her glance slid over to Gideon, then John in his car seat between him and Hannah. She paused and looked back at Gideon. "*Guder mariye*, Gideon."

"*Guder mariye*, Mary," he said.

She stepped back from the vehicle. "Everyone have a good day," she said cheerfully. "See you when you get home from work," she told Hannah.

After a quick wave to Mary, Liz checked for traffic and then pulled out onto the road.

Hannah glanced at Gideon and found him looking at her. Then, feeling like someone else was watching her, she looked up and saw Liz's eyes on her in the rear-view mirror. Liz quickly shifted her attention back to the road but Hannah felt warmth rush into her cheeks. She gazed out the window at the passing scenery.

Liz stopped and picked up more passengers. Greetings were exchanged, and then silence reigned as they approached town and the van stopped to let off passengers.

Gideon and Hannah got off at his stop as usual—but this morning they entered the shop with John.

"I'll make coffee," he said as he did every day. But today he hurried to the back as if he didn't want to talk right away.

Hannah put her things down on the counter then sat on the stool with John.

He came back a few minutes later with a mug of

coffee fixed the way she liked it and sat behind the counter with his own cup. "So what did you tell your *mudder* about John?"

Hannah winced. "She came home from my *aenti*'s just as I was leaving. I told her we'd talk later."

"What are you going to tell her?"

"The truth. What we know of it. What else can I do?" She looked at him. "I'm hoping John's *mudder* will show up today and everything will work out."

When he didn't answer and simply sat, staring into his coffee, she took a deep breath. "Gideon, what did Eli say after you went home last night?"

Chapter Five

Gideon stared into his coffee, searching for words. He looked up at Hannah. "He swears the *boppli*'s not his. No matter what I said to him I couldn't get him to say any different. As soon as we got home, he went in his room and locked the door."

He glanced over at John and smiled when he saw the *kind* watching him with owlish eyes. "Eli's always been the moody one. You know that. But something's been really bothering him for months. I usually know what he's thinking—my *mudder*'s always said that that's because of our *zwillingboppli* bond. But I don't know what the problem is this time and he won't talk to me about it. For the last year, maybe last year and a half, he's stayed in his room a lot, and doesn't go out with friends like he used to. I talked to my *mudder* about it a few weeks ago but she couldn't get anything out of him, either."

He shoved his hand through his hair. "Last week I suggested Eli speak to the bishop and he's barely talked to me since."

Restless, he stood and paced. "He wasn't in his room when I got up this morning. I don't know where he is."

He looked out the window, then turned to her. "I couldn't sleep all night. What do we do if the *mudder* doesn't come back?"

As if he knew they were talking about him, John screwed up his face and began crying.

Hannah rose and walked around, bouncing him a little in her arms. "There, there, *lieb*. Your *mamm* is coming soon." She swayed from side to side but still he cried. "Look, look at all these toys," she said as she walked down an aisle. "Soon you'll be a big *bu* and have toys like this to play with."

The tears dried up as John stared at the brightly painted wooden toys.

"I'm *schur* she'll come soon," Hannah said. "She has to be missing him. He's such a *gut boppli*."

"But she might not. We have to think what to do."

He saw Hannah glance at the clock on the wall. "All we can do is take it one day at a time. As for today, I can take care of him."

"*Danki*, Hannah," he said fervently.

Gideon gathered up the diaper bag and her lunch tote. He lifted her purse and draped the strap over her shoulder. "I'll walk the two of you to your shop."

"You don't have to."

"It's the least I can do." He held the door open for her then turned to lock it.

The sidewalks were already beginning to fill with locals and tourists. One *Englisch* woman smiled when she saw them and lifted her cell phone to take a photo but changed her mind when Gideon frowned. No doubt she was a tourist and wanted a souvenir.

"She didn't mean any harm," Hannah murmured.

"How would she feel if someone did that to her?" he growled.

She shifted John and dug in her purse with one hand for her shop key. Gideon took it from her and unlocked the door, then held it open so she could walk inside. He closed the door and took her things into the back room.

When he returned, she was taking off John's sweater as he lay in the crib. She glanced up and tilted her head. "Why the frown? Are you still upset about that woman?"

"*Nee.* I'll see you at lunchtime unless you need me to help with John."

She nodded. "*Danki.*"

He stood there for a long moment, staring at her and the *boppli*. Then he turned on his heel and left her to walk back to his shop. He wasn't just worried John's *mudder* might not come back for him. Hannah was being *wunderbaar* about the situation, but it wasn't right that she was the one doing all the work. Exposing herself to questions from her *mudder*...perhaps even gossip from those in the community.

Before this happened, he was getting ready to ask her to marry him. He didn't want anything to change that. But John's sudden appearance was going to change things a *lot*. If John was Eli's he needed to marry the *mudder*, and if he married her that meant Eli would take over the farmhouse. He and Eli had made a pact that whoever got married first got the house... Then where would he and Hannah live if she agreed to marry him? He unlocked his shop door and flipped the **Closed** sign over.

When he turned around, he saw the mirror image of himself sitting behind the shop counter.

Their gazes locked.

"What are you doing here?"

Eli shrugged. "I promised to give you a few hours today, remember?"

"It would have been nice if you'd let me know *you'd* remembered. You weren't in your room when I checked this morning."

"I had something to do." He shoved himself to his feet. "I'm getting some coffee."

Frustrated, Gideon followed him into the back room and watched him pour a mug from the percolator on the stove.

When Eli turned he didn't look surprised that Gideon had followed him. "Look, I'm going home if you're going to hassle me."

Gideon stood there and folded his arms across his chest. "I want some answers and I want them now."

Eli slammed the mug on the table and started for the back door.

"Where do you think you're going?"

"Home."

Gideon grabbed at his arm and Eli swung around and hit him in the jaw. He saw stars for a moment, then he shook his head and rushed at Eli, pinning him to the wall by the door. They glared at each other, their faces just inches apart.

"Hit me!" Eli yelled. "Go ahead! You know you want to!"

Gideon shook his head and backed off. "*Nee.* I just want you to take some responsibility. You can't deny John is your *sohn.*"

Eli dragged out a chair and slumped into it. He shoved his hands in his hair. "I'm not ready to be a *dat!*"

"Well, that's too bad because you are." Gideon sat at the table. "Who's the *mudder*?"

"Emma. Emma Graber."

Gideon frowned. "She left town a year or so ago," he said slowly. "So that's why?"

Eli nodded but didn't meet his eyes. "Go ahead and say it. I'm a jerk. I've never been as *gut* as you."

His eyes widened. "What?"

"You know it's true. You've always been the *gut sohn*, never getting into trouble, always knowing you belonged. Well I might look like you but I'm not you! I'll never measure up to you!" He put his head in his hands. "Only one person has ever understood me, and she's not here anymore."

Eli jerked to his feet and slammed out of the room before Gideon could stop him. Shocked, Gideon could only stare at the door.

He didn't know how long he might have sat there, but he finally became aware that someone was banging on the shop door. He hurried to it and had his second shock of the day.

"Emma!"

Chapter Six

W here is he?"

Gideon stared at the woman who strode into the shop and glanced around.

"Emma," he repeated. Now it was so clear why Hannah had said he reminded her of someone. John had Eli's big blue eyes but the way John always tilted his head and studied him reminded him of Emma. But while John's gaze was nearly always happy, Emma's was now filled with anger.

"John's—"

"I know where John is," she said in a testy voice. "I wouldn't have left him if I'd thought Eli would get someone else to watch him."

"So you've been watching what's been going on?"

"Of course. Where is Eli? I saw him come in."

Gideon touched his sore jaw. "He just stormed out of here. You can check the back room if you don't believe me."

He watched her hurry into the back to do just that. She returned moments later.

Emma frowned at him. "He hit you? Why?"

"I was talking to him about taking responsibility for John. He didn't like it."

She stood there, arms crossed over her chest, tapping her foot impatiently as she appeared to think about what he'd said. Then she heaved a big sigh. "Where did he go?" she asked finally.

"I don't know."

There was a loud rapping on the door. Gideon glanced over and saw a woman peering in the glass.

"I need to open up," he said. "Give me a minute. Please." He walked over and unlocked the door. "I'm so sorry, I'm a little late opening up."

"No problem. I heard you have some wonderful dollhouses," the older woman said.

"Let me show you where I've got a display of them," he told her, leading the way. "They're all handmade. I have *Englisch* houses and Amish houses."

"Oh, they're lovely!" she exclaimed, bending to peer in the window of one of the rooms in a two-story wooden house. "I think I'm going to find it very hard to decide."

"You take your time and let me know if you have any questions," he said, keeping a wary eye on Emma as she stood by the counter.

He walked back over to her, thinking she'd changed since he'd last seen her. She was just nineteen—twenty by now, he remembered, but she seemed to have matured. He supposed she'd had to grow up fast since she'd been responsible for a *boppli* all by herself.

"We can't talk right now," he said in a quiet voice. "Do you want to have some coffee, wait until my customer leaves?"

She frowned and shook her head. "I'll walk down and see Hannah. I miss John and I need to thank her. It isn't right that she took care of him when I meant for Eli to."

Gideon reached out and touched her arm, then quickly withdrew it when he realized he'd startled her. "Don't leave again, Emma. Let me help you."

Her eyes filled with tears. "You're a *gut* man, Gideon. Why did I have to fall in love with the wrong *bruder*?"

Her words hit him like the blow he'd taken to his jaw. "Emma" was all he could manage.

Then he realized his customer was approaching him. "Give me just a minute, Emma."

"*Nee*, I'm going to go see John and talk to Hannah."

"Promise you won't leave again."

Emma sighed. "Promise."

"Hannah and I have been having lunch while things aren't too busy. Can I pick you up something from the coffee shop? I can bring it and we'll talk."

She nodded. "I like the turkey sub." She reached into her purse but he waved his hand.

"My treat."

"See you in a while." She left the shop.

Gideon turned to his customer.

"I think I have to have the yellow house," she gushed, her face pink with excitement. "It's more than I should spend, but my oldest grandchild is going to think I'm the best grandmother in the world!"

He grinned, his spirits lighter now that Emma had shown up, and pleased with the easy sale. "Did I tell you there's a ten percent discount for grandmothers?" he asked and was reminded of his own late *grossmudder*'s sweet smile when she beamed.

It took some time to complete the transaction, carefully box the dollhouse, and then carry it to her car. When he returned to his shop he had a spurt of customers. Sometimes he'd sit and wonder where they were, and then it was as though a half dozen would walk in at the same time and he'd wonder if a tour bus had unloaded outside. So it was more than an hour before he could pick up the phone and call Hannah.

But the shop's landline rang busy. He hung up. He'd see her soon.

* * *

Hannah walked around the shop carrying John as she helped answer a customer's questions.

When the bell jingled over the shop door, John quivered in her arms and squirmed, making happy jabbering noises. She smiled. He was such a people lover...But then she realized there was something about his movements that seemed even more vigorous than he'd been with other visitors.

Even before she'd seen the person who'd entered the shop Hannah knew it was John's *mudder*. She felt it in his movements, felt it in her bones, as she turned around. He held out his arms and his face lit up like a sunbeam.

"Emma. Emma Graber," she breathed. "You're John's *mudder*."

Emma walked forward and held out her arms. Tears were running down her cheeks as she took John and held him close. "Oh, my *boppli*, I missed you so!"

Tears rushed into Hannah's eyes as she watched their reunion. "He missed you, too. Oh, he didn't cry," she said quickly. "But I could tell he wanted his *mudder*."

"*Danki* for taking such *gut* care of him. You must think I'm a terrible *mudder*."

Hannah shook her head. "It's not my place to judge." She saw a customer approaching with several bolts of fabric in her arms.

"Sit while I help her," Hannah told Emma. "Don't leave. Please."

She smiled and nodded. "I promised Gideon I wouldn't."

"This blue flowered fabric just came in," Hannah told the customer as she took the bolts from her arms. "How many yards do you need?"

The two of them chatted as Hannah unfolded each bolt and cut the yardage needed from each. She stacked the cut pieces, wrote up the sales slip, and helped the customer add some matching thread and quilt backing. Then she walked over to the counter, rang up the sale, and tucked everything in a brown paper shopping bag. The customer was local, so she added a flyer about quilting classes, and tied the handles with a scrap of fabric kept by the register.

"Thanks so much for stopping by the shop. Come again!"

"I sure will. You have a good day."

Hannah waited until the customer left, then walked over to where Emma sat beside the crib holding John.

"I love your shop," Emma told her as she glanced around at all the tables and shelves crammed with fabrics. "It's a happy place. I worked in a quilt shop in Ohio while I was waiting to have John. I really enjoyed it."

"So that's where you've been?"

Emma nodded. "I didn't feel I could stay here. You know my *dat*. If he knew I was pregnant he would have made me marry John's *dat* or he would have thrown me out of his house. I had a friend there who offered to let me live with her."

"That's a very *gut* friend." Hannah wanted to say she knew who John's *dat* was, but she couldn't think of any way to say it. "Emma, would you like some tea or coffee?"

"I'd love some tea."

As Hannah rose to get it she heard the rumble of someone's tummy. When Emma blushed and looked embarrassed she realized the sound wasn't coming from John.

"Would you like something to eat? It's also almost time for a you-know-what for you-know-who."

"I can wait for lunch."

"Well, maybe a cookie or two to tide you over."

Emma laughed. "I'd love a cookie."

Hannah busied herself making tea and warmed a bottle for John. She took the cookies she'd packed for her lunch and spread them on a plate. She always brought extra because Gideon loved cookies. Didn't matter what kind they were, the man couldn't seem to get enough.

When she returned with a tray Emma was talking to a customer about a bolt of fabric. When Hannah set the tray down and walked over, Emma surprised her by handing John to her and taking the bolt of fabric to the cutting table. Hannah watched her chat with the customer as she cut the fabric and wrote up the charge slip. Then with a grin she handed the charge slip to Hannah, took John back, and walked over to sit and give him the bottle Hannah had warmed.

"I hope you didn't mind," Emma said after Hannah finished ringing up the sale and said goodbye to the customer. "I miss working."

"*Danki* for helping." She glanced at the other woman. "How long are you staying?" she asked.

"I don't know. It'll depend on what Eli has to say." She frowned. "And how long my money will hold out." She bit her lip. "I went by to talk to my *eldres* but my *dat* shut the door in my face."

"Oh, Emma, I'm so sorry."

She shrugged. "I expected it."

But Hannah saw the sadness in her eyes.

John finished his bottle and Emma put him on her shoulder and patted his back. He obediently burped and she laughed. The sadness in her eyes vanished. "I never have any trouble getting him to burp!"

"Let me change him so you can drink your tea before it gets cold."

"*Danki*, I'll let you." She passed John over and sipped her tea while Hannah changed him and settled him in his crib for his nap. "Mmm, the cookies are *gut*."

Hannah felt some concern as she watched Emma eat. She hoped Emma had been eating properly. She couldn't have had a lot of money saved up for the trip just working in a quilt shop. And she'd have had to take time off after John's birth...Had the church community in Ohio helped pay the hospital bills?

"Emma, where are you staying?"

Emma bit her lip. "I found a room in a motel. I can't afford to stay there long but maybe I won't have to. Once I talk to Eli..." She trailed off. She took a deep breath and forced a smile. "It's so nice you have a crib here," she said as she watched John sleep.

"My *schweschder* Linda brought it in when I first opened the shop and needed help but couldn't afford to hire anyone even part-time. Her youngest is four now and she doesn't need it, so she left it in case a customer took a class and couldn't find a sitter." Hannah smiled at John. "It was *schur* handy when John came along.

My customers love saying hello to him. Especially the *grossmudders*."

Emma frowned. "I never meant for you or Gideon to take care of him."

"We were happy to," Hannah said firmly. "He's such a sweet *boppli*."

The bell over the door jingled and customers came in. Some browsed. Some bought. The morning passed quickly, and then Gideon was striding in with lunch. Hannah locked the door, turned the sign to **Closed**, and used her finger to push the big hand and little hand on the clock to show she'd be back in half an hour.

They went into the back room, and Hannah and Gideon unpacked their lunch totes. Emma sighed happily as she unwrapped her sandwich.

"I've missed the sandwiches from the coffee shop," Emma said. Then her eyes filled with tears. "I've missed home." She set the sub down and got up quickly. "Excuse me." She rushed into the shop restroom and shut the door.

Hannah looked at Gideon. Typical male. He sat there looking uncomfortable with a woman's tears. "She's had a tough time."

"Did you get a chance to talk much with her, or did you have too many customers come in? My shop was really busy this morning."

"Mine too but we did talk a little. She said she needed to speak with Eli."

"I see."

She nodded and started to say something but she stopped when she heard the restroom door open.

58

Emma walked out looking calmer. "I'm sorry. I didn't mean to get emotional," she said as she took her seat.

Hannah reached over to pat her hand. "It's *allrecht.*" Her gaze locked with Gideon's as Emma began eating. *Say something*, she wanted to tell him.

He must have gotten her silent message. "Emma, tell me how we can help you."

Hannah's heart melted at his words. *Ach*, what a man.

Chapter Seven

Liz turned and glanced back when Gideon and Hannah climbed into her van that evening.

"Oh, you don't have the little guy with you," she said, looking disappointed.

"No, he's with his mother." Gideon waited for Hannah to get in then took his seat.

"I was looking forward to seeing him again. Such a happy little baby." She waited for them to fasten their seat belts, then checked for traffic before she pulled back out onto the road. "Well, I'll get my baby fix when I see my grandbaby soon."

"Liz, I'm getting off at Hannah's today." Gideon turned to Hannah. "So nice of your mother to invite me for supper."

Hannah looked at him quizzically but didn't say anything.

"No problem," Liz said. "I hope you both had a good day today?"

"Business was good," Gideon told her. "For Hannah as well."

She nodded. "That's always nice to hear." A few minutes later she picked up her other passengers and chatted with them.

"Supper?" Hannah whispered.

He jerked his head at the row of seats behind them and Hannah nodded, understanding. Gossip traveled fast on the Amish grapevine. They sat without speaking as Liz drove. When she stopped in front of Hannah's home he felt a mixture of relief and apprehension.

"*Allrecht*, tell me why you invited yourself to supper," Hannah said as they walked up the steps. "Not that you're not always *wilkumm* but..." She trailed off with a smile.

"I saw the way your *mudder* looked at John this morning," he told her. "And I heard her say she'd be waiting when you got home. I'm not letting you face her questions alone."

She lifted a brow. "Gideon, my *mudder* is not going to give me a hard time."

"*Nee?*"

"*Nee.*"

He stopped. "Wait. What if your *dat* is back?"

"I told you last night that he's not expected back until after supper. He's been out of town."

"I just hope he didn't come back early."

"Gideon!" She smacked his arm.

"Hey, it was hard enough to think about facing your *mudder*." He grinned to show her he was teasing.

He opened the door and followed her inside.

"Gideon! Nice to see you!" Mary said as they walked into the kitchen. She stood at the stove, a tall, slim woman in her late forties, stirring something in a pot that smelled heavenly.

She looked past them. "Where is the *boppli*?"

He shot Hannah a look then turned to her *mudder*. "John's *mudder* came for him. It was *gut* of Hannah to watch him for her." He took a deep breath. "Mary, please sit down. I'd like to talk to you about something important."

She turned the flame down under the pot and looked at them curiously. "*Allrecht*." She took a seat at the table, while Hannah hung her bonnet and shawl on pegs and left her tote and purse on the bench under them.

"We have a…situation," he said slowly, searching for the words as he sank into a chair next to Mary. "I would ask that you keep what I tell you to yourself until it's resolved." When she nodded, he went on, "Up until a day ago my *bruder* and I weren't aware that he fathered a *kind*. The *mudder* left town and returned recently to talk to him. Hannah was watching John while they did that."

Well, he supposed that wasn't exactly accurate, but he didn't want to make Emma look bad for leaving John at the shop.

"I don't want to tell you the name of the *mudder*," he told her, thinking that was her next question. "I don't know if she's going to stay or go back to where she's been living. I don't want to see her be shunned by the community while she's here for having a *boppli* outside marriage."

"I see." Mary sat silent for a long moment. "*Ya*, she would be. What does your *bruder* intend to do?"

He lifted his hands, let them fall. "I have no idea. I know what I'd like to see him do. I'd like to see him marry the *mudder* and claim the *boppli*, but I can't make him."

Her eyes narrowed. "Is that a bruise on your jaw?"

"I...ran into something."

"*Ya*. I'm thinking it was a fist." She studied him. "I'm well aware of how *bruders* get along sometimes, even when they're as close as you and Eli." She sighed and shook her head. "Well, I'll pray for those young people. God has a plan for them and He knows best."

She rose, grabbed pot holders, and opened the oven just as the timer went off. She pulled out a roasting pan, nodding with satisfaction at the perfectly browned chicken. After she'd tossed the pot holders on the counter, she turned off the timer.

"I don't know why she sets the timer," Hannah said. "She always knows when something's done before it goes off."

Mary chuckled. "After you've cooked as long as I have, you'll know, too."

Hannah washed her hands at the sink and took plates from the cupboard. She was just finishing setting the table when the kitchen door opened and her *dat* strode in.

"His timing is also always perfect," she told Gideon with a grin.

"What?" he asked as he took off his hat and hung it on a peg by the door. Then he walked over to kiss his *fraa*'s cheek.

"Welcome home."

"It's *gut* to be back." He sniffed. "Something smells *wunderbaar*."

"Roast chicken."

"That too," he said and chuckled.

Hannah walked over and hugged him. "Glad you're back, *Daed*."

"*Gut* to see you, Gideon," he said, smiling widely at him.

Gideon stood up to shake Lester's hand and greet him. "You too." And he was very glad there were no questions about John as the man took his place at the head of the table. After the meal was blessed, plates were heaped with roast chicken, mashed potatoes and gravy, and peas. Gideon split a golden brown biscuit, inhaled the fragrant steam, then spread butter on it and bit in. Light as a cloud.

He ate it in two bites and realized Hannah was watching him and grinning.

"No one makes biscuits like you, Mary."

"*Danki*, Gideon." She held out the basket filled with biscuits. "Have another."

He took it and looked away from Hannah. She was lucky to have a *mudder* who baked like this. His own *mudder* was *gut* at many things, but her biscuits didn't always turn out like Mary's.

"So, Gideon, how is your *bruder*?" Lester asked him.

Gideon nearly choked on a bite of chicken. "Doing well."

"And your *mudder*?"

"Visiting a *schweschder* in Ohio. She should be back in a week or two."

Lester nodded and ladled more gravy on his potatoes. Gideon was grateful when the older man's concentration on the meal prevented further questions. He scraped his plate clean and tried not to overdo it when Mary urged second helpings on him. Fortunately, he managed to save room for a slice of her lemon icebox pie.

"Well, that wasn't as bad as I thought it would be," he said as he and Hannah walked outside after dinner.

"I told you my *mudder* wasn't going to give me a hard time."

"Your *dat* didn't say a thing."

"She probably didn't talk to him today while he was working."

He frowned as he looked out at the fields as dusk fell. "It's not going to be easy for Emma and Eli, whatever they do."

"*Nee.*" She sighed. "It's up to them now. You can't make your *bruder* do what you want," she said quietly. "He may be your twin but the two of you are very different."

Gideon met her gaze. "*Mamm* said it felt like the two of us fought even before we were born." He sighed deeply. "Seems like he always made things harder for himself. Something he said recently made me think he's not happy."

"You don't think he'd leave the community?"

He looked at her again, and rubbed at the ache at the back of his neck with one hand. "I hope I'm worrying for nothing."

"You're not your *bruder*'s keeper."

"Nee?"

"Nee."

"Emma seems like a *gut mudder*," he said in a quiet voice. "I watched her with John at lunch. I wasn't *schur* if she wanted to keep him after she left him at my shop. Did she say anything to you about it?"

Hannah frowned. "I don't think she wants to let someone adopt him, if that's what you mean."

"He's *familye*. I wouldn't want that."

He glanced at the front door to make *schur* no one was looking, then reached for her hand and squeezed it. "I don't know what I'd have done if you hadn't helped me with John." He hesitated then looked at her intently. "I intend on seeing to it that Eli takes responsibility," he told her. "And if he doesn't I—" He broke off and released Hannah's hand as the door opened and Mary stuck her head out.

"You two want some coffee?" she asked.

Gideon set his hat on his head. *"Nee, danki,* Mary. I need to get home and make *schur* the evening chores were done."

"I'll say a prayer for all to work out." Her voice was quiet but kind.

"Danki. Gut-n-owed."

* * *

"So, Gideon seemed a little different tonight," Mary said as she handed Hannah a plate she'd washed and rinsed clean.

"Oh, how so?" Hannah took the plate, dried it, and put it in the cupboard.

"I thought he looked a little nervous when he first came in."

Hannah couldn't help it. She giggled. "He thought you were going to give him a hard time about John."

"Why would he think that?"

"*Mamm*, you looked at him like he was the *dat* or something this morning."

"I did not." She laid her hands on the lip of the sink. "Well, you have to admit that I had reason to be curious when I walk in the house and see my *dochder* leaving for work with a *boppli* I'd never seen."

Hannah grimaced. "That was a little awkward. But I couldn't say much since I was rushing out the door to work and I didn't know much myself at the time." She dried another plate and put it in the cupboard. "Why didn't you say anything to *Daed*? He didn't bring it up at supper."

"I didn't want to bother him at work. And I decided to wait to talk to you first."

Hannah gazed out the kitchen window. "Gideon said he was going to go home to talk to Eli. I wonder what is going to happen."

Mary finished the last dish and handed it to Hannah.

She pulled the plug and watched the water drain in the sink then looked up at her *dochder*.

"Gideon is definitely the more mature of the two *bruders*. They might be *zwillingsbopplin* but they couldn't be more different in personality." She put her arm around Hannah and hugged her. "There is only so much Gideon can do. He needs to trust God with this." She kissed Hannah's cheek. "You need to do that, too."

"I know." She sighed.

"I will say I'm glad you're interested in Gideon, not Eli."

"Gideon and I are just friends."

Her *mudder* lifted a brow. "*Ya?*"

"*Ya.*" She wasn't ready to admit she hoped they were more.

"Why don't you sit in the living room with *Daed* while I finish?" Hannah said as she picked up the sponge and began wiping the countertops.

"I think I'll do just that." Mary poured two mugs of coffee and left the room.

Hannah finished cleaning up the kitchen then packed her lunch and put it in the refrigerator for the next day.

She climbed the stairs to her bedroom but ended up walking on to the room she'd slept in last night. John had been with her for such a short time, but as she stripped the sheets from the crib to put them in the dirty clothes hamper she found herself missing him.

She sat on the bed and stared at the crib. One day when she was married she hoped she'd have a *sohn* like him and maybe a *dochder*. Well, several of each. She'd love a big *familye*...if she dared to dream of marrying Gideon she wondered if they would have *zwillingbopplin*. She'd heard that the more children you had the more likely you'd have them especially if either of you had them in the *familye*.

Oh, she was getting ahead of herself. Hadn't she just told her *mudder* she and Gideon were just friends? But of course she wasn't being truthful with her *mudder*. She wanted Gideon to ask her to marry him this season. But such things were best kept private until a couple became engaged.

She and Gideon had known each other all their lives, and had gone to the same *schul*. Then one evening they'd attended a singing with other young people from the church and it seemed she heard only his rich baritone. Their gazes had locked. After the singing was over he'd asked her if he could give her a ride home in his buggy.

Maybe it was a *maedel*'s fancy that the moon beamed brighter that evening as he took the long way to her home. Honeysuckle scented the warm summer air, and he'd stopped the buggy when she cried out with delight at seeing fireflies dancing in a field beside the road. It had felt like such a magical night. And then he'd turned to her and asked if they could start seeing each other.

Gideon had been the one to come to her house one evening after work to tell her that a shop a few doors down from his was closing and the space was up for rent. During one of their dates she'd confided her secret desire to open a quilt shop and he'd remembered. He'd insisted on going with her the next day to see the rental owner and helped guide her through all the sometimes-scary, sometimes-frustrating paperwork that was necessary.

"I don't know if I can do this," she'd cried the day she had to sign the lease.

"You can do it," he reassured her. "I'm here to help in any way I can."

And he had been. He'd looked over the lease for her and helped paint the ugly, discolored walls and built shelves and a few display tables. He'd helped in every way. Well, he'd refused to assist in decisions on stock, holding up his hands and saying he'd never so much as walked into a quilt shop and she'd do better to talk with other women about that.

Apparently he, like many Amish men, felt it wasn't manly to be around fabric and quilting supplies. She chuckled at the memory. It was so silly. After all, Amish women went into hardware stores, she'd pointed out. He backed away if she brought up the subject of fabric and sewing supplies.

But he'd been the first one in the door the day she opened and had brought her a vase of flowers for her shop counter.

A routine slowly emerged. Every morning since then they'd started their day with a cup of coffee at his shop or hers. Several times a week they ate lunch together. Gradually they began having supper out one evening a week—usually Saturdays.

And soon things changed from their being friends to more. Although neither of them had put it into words, Hannah felt this was the man God had set aside for her and slowly revealed to her.

She wandered back to her room, changed into a nightgown, and after she unpinned her *kapp* she sat on her bed and brushed out her hair. Then she braided it, tied a ribbon around the tail end, and climbed into bed. She picked up the book she read each night but soon discovered it held no interest.

Her thoughts drifted back to Gideon and their conversation on the porch before he'd gone home. It was nice to know that if they had ever become intimate— she felt the heat rush into her cheeks at the thought— that he would have done the honorable thing and taken responsibility.

But Gideon couldn't force Eli to do anything. His *bruder* was a very stubborn man. Even if Gideon enlisted the help of the bishop to talk to Eli, Hannah didn't think Eli would do what they wanted.

As she lay waiting for sleep to claim her, she wondered what Gideon had been about to say to her just before her *mudder* had interrupted to ask if they wanted coffee. He'd talked about Emma and hoped she didn't want to give John up. He'd told her that John was *familye*.

Did that mean that Gideon would adopt John and raise him if Emma gave him up?

Chapter Eight

Gideon handed Hannah her morning coffee the next day. "Are you busy this evening? I'd like to take you to supper."

Hannah stared at Gideon. They'd been making it a habit of going to supper most Saturday nights for some time. "That would be nice." She sipped her coffee. "But today's Friday. We usually go out on Saturdays."

He shoved a hand in his hair and grinned. "I know. I've been a little distracted lately but I do remember what day of the week it is. I'd just like to go out tonight."

"*Allrecht*," she said, smiling at him.

"Let's go someplace nice. You deserve it after taking care of John."

"I loved taking care of him. He's a precious little

bu. And he was no trouble at all." She sighed. "The customers—especially the older ladies—really enjoyed seeing him in my shop."

Gideon stared into his coffee and wished it was suppertime already so he could ask her something that had been weighing on his mind. He had an idea about how she felt about him, where their relationship was heading. But he needed to know for certain.

They both looked over as they heard the sound of a key being used to unlock the shop door.

Eli walked in. "Where is she?"

"Who?"

"Emma," he said impatiently. "Don't play games with me. Where is she?"

"She's not here."

"I've looked everywhere for her. I went by her house but her *mudder* said she wasn't staying there. She said she didn't know where she was. Then her *dat* came to the door as I was standing there and shut it in my face."

Gideon frowned. "Such a stern man. No wonder she felt she had to leave town."

Eli turned to Hannah. "Do you know where she is?"

"I know she's in town," she said carefully. "But she wouldn't tell me where she's staying."

Eli moved closer. "I need to talk to her. Think hard. Maybe she said something."

Gideon leaped to his feet and came around the counter. "Don't be pressuring Hannah."

Eli held up his hands and gave Hannah a beseeching

look. "I just want to talk to her. If you see her, will you tell her that?"

She nodded. "I'm hoping she'll come by my shop this afternoon." She reached for one of Gideon's business cards on the counter and wrote her shop number on the back. "Call me at the shop this afternoon." She rose and gathered up her things. "I have to go open up. Gideon, I'll see you at lunch."

He walked her to the door, disappointed that she'd left early, then turned back to Eli. "What time did you come home last night?"

"Late. I went out looking for Emma after you told me she was back. Then I got up early and went looking for Emma some more." He paced. "I just want to get this settled."

"Me too."

"What if she leaves town again? I'd never be able to find her."

Gideon sat again and sipped his coffee while he studied his *bruder*'s face. Maybe it was encouraging that Eli was so concerned. "What do you intend to do when you find her?"

"I don't know. I won't know until we talk." He turned and headed for the door.

"Where are you going?"

"To look for Emma."

"Don't pester Hannah!" he called after him but Eli was already out the door.

Customers kept Gideon busy for the next several hours. When he called, Hannah told him that Eli hadn't stopped by, so he relaxed and concentrated on business. When there was a lull, he pulled out paperwork he'd neglected. It was never too soon to think about ordering supplies needed to make and paint toys for Christmas. It took time to make dozens of toys by hand and have enough stock for the holiday.

Finally it was lunchtime—his favorite time of the day. As they headed into summer when things got busier, he and Hannah wouldn't be able to close their shops for lunch even for a half hour. So he cherished the time he could spend with Hannah now. He quickly grabbed his lunch tote, locked up, and headed down to the quilt shop.

Hannah met him at the door with a smile. "We have company for lunch."

He walked in and found Emma sitting by the quilting table feeding John a bottle as he lay in her arms. "Emma, John, *gut* to see you! If I'd known you were going to be here I'd have brought you lunch."

Emma gestured at the paper bag sitting on the table before her. "We stopped and got a sandwich. And of course John always brings his own lunch."

At the mention of his name John grinned at Gideon and milk dribbled down his chin as he broke the seal on the nipple of the bottle. She laughed and used a tissue to wipe his chin.

"I told her Eli's been looking for her," Hannah said as he sat and opened his lunch tote.

"I was afraid he'd come down here and pressure you about where she's staying."

She shook her head. "Haven't seen him."

There was a sharp rap on the door. All eyes turned to it.

"Eli," Emma breathed.

"I'll send him away if you don't want to see him," Gideon told her as he stood.

"*Nee*, that's why I came back to Paradise."

Gideon strode to the door and unlocked it. "She's here. I expect you to be nice to her."

Eli's mouth turned down. "This is *my* business, not yours."

"You made it my business when you didn't take responsibility. John is *familye*."

Emma appeared at his side. She put her hand on Gideon's arm. "It's *allrecht*, Gideon. We need to talk." She looked at Eli. "Let's go outside. I don't want John to be upset."

"Fine."

They went outside and sat on the bench in front of the shop.

Gideon returned to the table and sat down, but his attention remained focused on the shop window instead of finishing his lunch.

"Let them settle it," Hannah said quietly.

He dragged his attention back to her. "Hmmm?"

"Let Eli and Emma settle it." She got up and put John in a stroller, then began feeding him from a jar of strained pears.

"Where's your lunch?"

"Haven't gotten it yet." She stood and handed him

76

the jar. "Finish feeding John his pears while I go get my lunch from the back room."

"I don't know how—" he began, but she was already hurrying off.

John gurgled and waved his hands. Gideon sat and dipped the baby spoon into the jar, then offered it to John. To his surprise John accepted it and made a silly face as he swished the pears around in his mouth as if testing its texture. Half of the fruit ended up on his chin. Gideon wiped it with the cloth Hannah had left and tried a second spoon. John gobbled it up and bounced in his seat while he waited for more.

Gideon glanced up and saw Hannah moving gracefully toward him. She caught him looking at her and smiled. He felt the warmth of her smile spread through him.

He couldn't wait to talk to her, tell her what he hoped for them. Tonight, he thought, couldn't come soon enough.

John babbled at him, forcing him to return his attention to him. Gideon stared at the *kind*.

"Little boy with eyes so blue, if they don't want you I do," he murmured.

Hannah walked up and set her lunch on the table. "What did you just say?"

Gideon blinked. "What?"

"What did you just say to John?" She sat down and looked at him curiously.

Stunned at what had slipped from his mouth, he shook his head and stared at her. "Just guy talk," he said, pretending a lightness he didn't feel. He wasn't ready to share what he'd said to John with her just yet. He couldn't explain why he'd felt so much for this little *bu* so quickly.

And even if he wanted to adopt him if his *mudder* and *dat* didn't want him, single men didn't adopt in his community.

"I see. I bet I can get it out of John." She reached over and tickled John's tummy.

John giggled and babbled and Hannah nodded and laughed. "I agree. Gideon's a nice man." She leaned over and kissed Gideon on the cheek. "Get the rest of those pears in him so you can finish your lunch."

Chapter Nine

Eli paced in front of the bench outside Hannah's shop. "I went looking for you last year. Why did you have to go tearing off out of town without telling me?"

Emma glanced around. "Keep your voice down, Eli. Everybody doesn't need to know our business." She smoothed her skirt over her knees. "I couldn't stay. I was throwing up in the morning and having more trouble hiding it from my *familye*. And you didn't appear interested in helping."

"I was messed up, Emma. I wasn't expecting you to get pregnant."

She let out a short bark of laughter. "You think I was?" She sighed and shook her head. "I never thought one night would change my life forever."

"You didn't have to leave."

"How could I stay? You said you weren't ready to get married. I thought you loved me. I never would have been with you otherwise."

Eli stared at the passing traffic. "I do love you." He stood and paced.

"Well you *schur* have a funny way of showing it. Telling me you're not ready to get married."

"I wasn't ready for marriage then. You know I had a hard time getting over *Daed* dying after the way we always argued about farming. I've always felt I disappointed *Daed*."

He took off his hat, ran a hand over his hair in frustration, then set it back on his head and looked at her. "You were the only one who cared about who I was, who understood me. Emma, I want you—"

"Emma? Is that you?"

Rebecca Miller rushed up to them. "Emma! I can't believe it! You're back!"

Frustrated at the interruption, Eli watched as the midwife and Emma embraced. They chatted quietly for a few minutes until Rebecca glanced over at Eli. She must have sensed his tension.

She turned back at Emma. "I'm sorry, I've obviously caught you at an awkward time," she said.

"Eli and I have some things to discuss," Emma told her quietly.

Rebecca's expression was sober as she nodded. "Stop by and see me. We'll catch up." She started to walk away then stopped. She stood there, biting her lip, looking indecisive.

"I brought my *boppli* with me," Emma said, understanding. "I'll bring him for a visit."

Her face cleared. "*Gut!* I'll look forward to it!" She hurried off.

Emma sat back down, but he was too restless, too unsettled, to sit beside her. He watched as people walked past talking with each other, carrying shopping bags. It was just another day for them. But here he was, standing there feeling a fool, unable to come up with one reason why she should listen to him when he knew he'd let her down in every way a man could.

"Can't we go somewhere more private to talk?"

She shook her head. "It wouldn't be fair to ask Hannah to watch John again. You can say what you want to here."

Well, he'd blurted out that he wanted her and hadn't gotten the reception he thought he would. Then before he could say more, they'd been interrupted by Rebecca. Frustrated, he sat.

"Look, I wasn't there for you the way you deserved," he said. He took her hand and after some initial resistance she let him keep it. "I don't know how to make it up to you. I probably can't. But I've had some time to think about it and I knew if I ever had a chance to see you again I would ask you to forgive me and give me another chance. Marry me, Emma, and let's be a *familye*."

Tears rushed into her eyes. "I don't know if I can trust you, Eli. You've hurt me so much."

He had to look away from the tears, from the pain

in her eyes. "Then stay and give us the time for me to earn your trust."

"How are we going to do that? I can't move back in with my *familye* and I can't stay in a motel for much longer."

The shop door opened behind them. Gideon walked out, nodded to them, and hurried down the sidewalk away from them.

"I should get inside," Emma said, as she pulled her hand free from his. "Hannah needs to open her shop. We've already taken advantage of her watching John. And he needs to go down for his afternoon nap."

"I'll take you out to supper. Tell me where you're staying."

Her hesitation told him she didn't trust him yet.

"Please, Emma."

She gave him the name of a small motel nearby.

"I'll pick you up. Five *allrecht*?"

She nodded, rose, and started walking toward the shop door.

"Hey, Emma?"

She turned. "*Ya?*"

"Does John like pizza?"

She laughed and went inside.

* * *

Eli felt in a lighter mood as he walked back to the toy shop. When he entered, Gideon was busy helping a customer while two others placed toys on the counter. Eli moved behind it and began to ring up their purchases as he chatted with them.

"Nothing better than a train set, right?" he asked the older man who was running the little wooden train along the counter much like a *bu* would.

"We thought this was a good choice for our grandson. He's two, and it looks sturdy and well-made."

Eli nodded. "My brother makes everything by hand and uses only child-safe materials. Did you see the train conductor hats?"

"No, we must have missed those."

"We have them in child and adult sizes. My brother doesn't make them, but a woman in our community sews them and she's very good."

The man glanced at his wife.

"Go ahead, dear," his wife told him with an indulgent smile. "You know you want one."

"I was thinking of Benjamin," he said but he grinned.

Eli sold him hats in both sizes.

"*Danki* for the help," Gideon said after the shop emptied. "You know...the shop's only going to get busier, and soon I won't be able to help you with the extra crops we planted."

"I realize that." Eli gestured at the paperwork he'd set on one side of the counter.

"I have to find time to do some planning for Christmas. The creches are already selling and it's only end of March." Gideon started to make his way toward the back room. "Want some coffee?"

"*Nee.* I need to get back home and get some work

done. By the way, I need the buggy tonight. Emma and I are going out to supper to talk."

"*Gut.* What about John?"

"We're taking him with us. I asked Emma if he liked pizza."

"Very funny."

He grinned. "She thought so. Of course she has a better sense of humor than you. See you, bro."

It wasn't just Gideon who would need more help with the shop as it got busier, Eli thought as he walked out onto the street. As the toy shop had grown more popular, Gideon didn't have the time to help him with the farm as much as he had before. Eli needed to think about hiring some part-time help for the farm.

But he'd think about that another day. He climbed into the buggy he'd parked behind the shop and used the time traveling home to think about what to say to Emma that night.

* * *

Emma was still smiling when she walked into Hannah's shop.

"You're smiling," Hannah said as she looked up from covering John with a baby quilt. "Everything went well?"

"We didn't get much time to talk. Rebecca—you know, the midwife—came up as we were sitting there. But after she left, Eli asked if we could go to supper and talk more. Just before I came in, he asked if John liked pizza."

Hannah laughed. "That's Eli."

"*Ya.* That's Eli." Her smile faded. "Oh, what a mess I've made of my life."

"You haven't made a mess of your life. Things are hard but they're going to get better." She gazed down at John. "And look what a beautiful *boppli* you have."

Emma bent to stroke a finger down John's soft cheek. Love swelled up in her. He lay in the crib, his eyes closed, smiling in his sleep as if he was dreaming of something *wunderbaar*. "He looks so sweet when he's sleeping."

"He looks sweet all the time. He hasn't had one cranky moment since I've known him."

The shop phone rang and Hannah rushed over to answer it. Emma watched her frown and look concerned. "It's no problem," Hannah said to the caller. "You take care of yourself. Bye."

She hung up and stood there staring off into the distance.

"Is something wrong?" Emma asked.

"Katie Ann—you know, Rebecca's *schweschder*— just called to say she can't work for me anymore. She was granted a loan, so she's decided to open up her own bakery. I knew this was coming. She's wanted to do it for some time and was making the arrangements for it."

Before she could say more, a pair of customers walked in chatting with each other. They greeted Hannah and went straight for the tables that displayed fabric.

Emma walked over to the counter. "I'm available," she said.

"Hmm?" Hannah stared at her, distracted.

"I said I'm available. I told you I worked in a quilt shop while I was in Ohio. I can give you the name of the owner and you can check my reference."

"Does this mean you're staying?"

"I think so. I'll know more after Eli and I talk later, but I'm hoping we can work things out. That's why I came back."

She held her breath while Hannah looked at her and considered her offer.

"It's just part-time for now, but I'd need you for more hours as we head into fall." Hannah looked thoughtful. Then she grinned. "I don't need to check your reference. I watched you when you helped customers yesterday. You're hired!"

Emma breathed a sigh of relief. "And to think, just minutes ago, you were reassuring me that things were going to get better."

"I did, didn't I?" Hannah chuckled. "I guess I must be pretty smart."

"Well, you hired me," Emma said and laughed as she walked over to see if any of the customers needed help.

The two women knew what they wanted, and soon Emma had her arms full of bolts of fabric to cut. It was such fun to be doing something useful again, she thought as she cut the lengths they requested. She had missed working while on maternity leave and then done fewer hours after John's birth.

Since the two women were the only customers in the

shop, she was able to spend time chatting with them, helping them choose the right thread and backing for the quilts they were planning.

She hadn't had time to quilt since John was born. As she looked at the quilts Hannah had hung on the walls for display and featured for sale, she hoped she'd get back to it soon. She loved the creativity of making something beautiful and useful for a home.

And she hoped she and John would have a home soon.

When the women left loaded down with shopping bags, she walked over to check on John. He slept blissfully, not disturbed in the least by the jangle of the bell over the shop door, the ring of the phone, or the influx of a group of women who swarmed in, obviously shopping after a late lunch at a local restaurant. Emma felt a twinge of hunger when one woman walked past carrying a takeout bag and she smelled its contents. She'd been so distracted with seeing Eli that she had forgotten to eat her lunch.

She glanced at the clock and Hannah saw her. "Go take a break in the back room. I just realized you didn't get to eat your lunch."

"Me too," she said with a chuckle. "Would you like me to fix you a cup of tea?"

"Maybe later. Shoo, before John wakes and insists on his afternoon snack."

Emma was just finishing up half of the sandwich when Hannah walked in with a sleepy-eyed John. "Look who woke up."

John held out his arms for her, and she took him and

sat him on her lap. He immediately spied the empty jar of pears on the table and began reaching for it.

"He really likes pears, doesn't he?" Hannah said as she took a bottle from the refrigerator, held it to her side so John didn't see it, and ran warm water over it in the sink.

Emma nodded. "They're his favorite fruit although he likes strained bananas, too. He's always been a healthy eater."

Hannah turned off the water, dried the bottle with a dish towel, and handed it to her. John wiggled happily when he saw it and soon was sucking milk down vigorously. Hannah picked up the empty jar and tossed it into the trash. "Gideon helped feed the pears to John while you and Eli were talking. He acted a little afraid to do it at first. I guess he hasn't had much experience with *bopplin* since he and Eli were the only *kinner* in their *familye*."

She leaned against the table and studied John. "I came back here to fix a cup of tea, and when I went back out into the shop Gideon had the strangest look on his face."

"What do you mean?"

"I don't know. I can't describe it exactly. It was almost like . . . yearning."

"Maybe he's ready for a *familye* of his own." She frowned. "Not like his *bruder*." She sighed. "Who knew *zwillingbopplin* could be so different?"

Hannah chuckled. "I wish you could have seen John's face when he saw the two of them together.

He kept looking back and forth like he couldn't quite figure it out. Then it seemed like he recognized Gideon since he'd been with him earlier that day."

Emma watched John grow sleepier as he drained his bottle. "I was always attracted to Eli, not Gideon. You could tell Gideon was the more mature of the two, but Eli … he's got this twinkle in his eye and he's such a charmer."

John finished the bottle, burped loudly, then laughed and laughed at what he'd done.

"Has a way about him just like his *dat*, doesn't he?" Emma said with a chuckle as John patted her cheeks. She bounced him on her lap. "I was terrified when I found out I was pregnant, but I knew I wanted him no matter what. I love being a *mudder*."

She looked up at Hannah. "Gideon can't keep his eyes off you when the two of you are together." She wondered if Hannah knew she was blushing. "And I see the way you look at him."

"Is it that obvious?" Hannah bit her bottom lip.

"To someone else in love." She felt her mood slipping. "Well, it's a clean diaper for you, my Johnny, and then we're going back to the motel for a nap before we go out to eat supper with *Daedi* and talk."

"I thought about moving the crib back here because I was afraid the noise from the shop would keep him awake," Hannah told her as Emma carried him to the crib to change him. "But I think he could sleep through a tornado. Besides, the ladies love him so much."

"*Ya*, he's just like Eli," she said and tapped him on the nose to make him giggle. "Mr. Charm."

Chapter Ten

Gideon stood before his dresser mirror and combed his damp hair. He was glad he'd asked Hannah out a night early. It had been a long, busy week at their shops and they'd had the extra work and concern over John's arrival.

He studied his appearance in the mirror. His best shirt had mysteriously disappeared from his closet again, so he'd been forced to wear his second-best. He suspected he'd find it on Eli if he went looking, but he didn't have time for that now.

Maybe he needed to start hiding it.

He grabbed his wallet, checked its contents to make *schur* he had enough cash for tonight, and started downstairs. He wasn't worried Eli had borrowed any money. His *bruder* borrowed his shirts but he never borrowed anything else. Eli just didn't like having to deal with chores like washing and ironing and cooking. With their *mudder* away he was forced to do his own cooking and laundry.

It was no wonder Eli had welcomed all the baked goods the *maedels* in the community dropped by. He'd have them do his laundry too if it wasn't considered improper.

Eli was settling his straw hat on his head when Gideon walked into the kitchen. He glanced back and had the grace to look guilty.

"I should make you take off my shirt."

"But the one you're wearing brings out your blue eyes so nicely," Eli told him with a big grin. "I'm out of here. Have a *gut* time with Hannah."

"I will." Gideon glanced at the clock and saw he had ten minutes to spare. He slapped his hat on his head and headed out the front door to wait for Hannah.

The crocuses and daffodils his *mudder* had planted years ago had burst into bloom. He wondered if Hannah would like some. Then he told himself every woman liked flowers. He picked a bunch and remembered the lecture he'd gotten from his *mudder* when he picked roses from her favorite rose bush to give to Hannah on her sixteenth birthday. Well, crocuses and daffodils weren't his *mudder*'s precious roses, and since she was away she wouldn't miss them.

Still he found himself glancing guiltily over his shoulder as he picked the blooms.

Hannah drove up a few minutes later, and she looked delighted with the flowers when he gave them to her.

"Feeling brave, are you?" she asked, obviously re-membering the roses incident.

"I figure *Mamm* won't be back for a while and miss them," he admitted with a grin.

"I love spring flowers. We don't have a long spring season here, so I enjoy them while we have them."

She put the flowers on the seat between them. When he saw her glance at them from time to time as she drove, the reins held easily in her hands, he told himself he needed to give flowers to her more often.

"You look pretty," he told her then grimaced. He didn't have the charm of Eli.

She blushed. "Why, *danki*. Violet's my favorite color." She smiled at him. "You probably noticed I wear it a lot."

"You look pretty in whatever you wear."

"You're being awfully sweet tonight."

He felt heat rise under his collar. "Well, I'm no Eli."

"That's *gut*." She bit her lip. "I'm sorry. That wasn't nice. But I'm not happy with Eli at the moment."

"I know. Neither of us are. You know he's out with Emma and John tonight."

"I do. She told me." She pulled over to the right of the road so a car could pass them. "I almost suggested you and I go to the same restaurant to see how it goes. But that would be nosy."

"It would." He chuckled. "But I suddenly feel a craving for pizza coming on."

She shook her head. "We can't do that. They would know we're spying on them. And goodness knows they're old enough to solve their own problems."

"One of them is. Emma, I mean." He sighed. "I'm just five minutes older but sometimes I feel five years older than Eli."

"I know. You've always been the more mature of the two of you."

"He got more of the charm."

"I'm surprised you'd say that. I think you've been pretty charming. Especially tonight."

"I should steal my *mudder*'s flowers more often," he joked. He reached for her hand. "We deserve a night away from Eli and Emma and their problems. Just the two of us. I've been wanting to take you out for supper in a nice place for a long time."

"I don't need fancy. It's nice just to spend time together."

Was there ever a doubt this was the woman for him? he wondered.

The fields along the road were beginning to show green. It wouldn't be long before passersby could see rows of corn and wheat and many types of vegetables.

Hannah pulled into the parking lot of the restaurant he'd directed her to, and he had to let go of her hand for a few moments until they were out of the buggy and strolling up the walk. The restaurant was busy tonight. He saw a lot of *Englisch* couples, but he also spotted several Amish couples they knew and said hello to them on the way to their table.

The hostess handed them their menus and wished them a good evening.

Fine linen covered the table and crystal glasses

glittered in the candlelight. Music played softly in the background, something classical.

"Gideon, the prices," Hannah whispered in horror as she glanced inside the leather-bound menu. "Let me split the check with you."

"We deserve a treat," he said firmly. "And *nee*, you will not split the check with me."

He found himself enjoying the way she looked in candlelight, her eyes glowing, her posture so relaxed and graceful.

They ordered and then talked about their week.

"Oh, I know we said we weren't going to talk about Eli and Emma, but I wanted to tell you I hired her part-time."

Gideon stopped, his fork halfway to his mouth. "You did? So she's staying?"

"At least for the time being." She sampled her chicken Oscar and it melted in her mouth. "Katie Ann is starting her own bakery, and this gives Emma some money for the motel. And it isn't charity. She's very *gut* with the customers. She worked in a quilt shop in Ohio while she lived there."

He frowned. "When I told her I wanted to help she said she didn't need anything. Why didn't I think about the cost of her staying in town?"

"It's *allrecht*. It worked out for everyone. And I have to say I love having John around."

She'd be a *gut mudder*, he thought, studying her. She was a quiet woman—not one to chatter but with a real interest in others. He'd found he could share his interest in carving and making toys with her. After his *dat* had died two years ago she'd listened to him pour out his grief and not offered the platitudes others had.

"Gideon?"

"Hmm?"

"Are you *allrecht*?"

He smiled at her. "Of course. Just thinking how lovely you look in the candlelight."

Her cheeks grew rosy and her eyes warmed. "*Danki*," she said and when he reached his hand across the table for hers, she let him take it even though she was shy about such gestures in public. "I'm so glad you asked me out tonight."

Gideon caught a movement at the corner of his eye and glanced over at the table in the nearby corner and watched a man pull a small velvet box from his suit pocket. He frowned. Maybe now wasn't a *gut* time to talk to Hannah about their relationship after all. He wasn't quite ready to propose and if she saw what was happening at the next table, wouldn't she think he was about to do so?

This was what he got for taking his time and not bringing up the subject of their relationship earlier in the meal. He sighed. Well, there was nothing else he could do. Maybe he wasn't supposed to talk to her about anything serious tonight. He'd just have to find another time and hope things worked out then.

* * *

Hannah had resisted the idea of supper at such an expensive restaurant when Gideon told her where they

95

were going on the way there. Now as they lingered over dessert and coffee she wasn't sorry they'd come here.

Such an evening would be a memory she'd tuck away for the future. It didn't take linen tablecloths, fancy food, and candlelight to make her happy. But it seemed that when a couple dressed up and spent time in a setting that was designed for intimacy, for quiet talks over an exquisitely prepared meal, and were encouraged to linger and make a meal an event, it couldn't help being romantic.

Hannah wondered if Gideon noticed that the man sitting with a woman at the table tucked in a private corner nearby had just held out a tiny velvet box to her. The woman was crying and nodding and allowing the man to pluck the ring from the box and slide it on her finger. They kissed and celebrated with glasses of champagne.

This evening would indeed be a special memory for them.

When Hannah looked back at Gideon, she saw that he'd seen the proposal and seemed thoughtful, but he made no comment. She wondered what he was thinking but was afraid to ask. Would he think she was hinting she wanted a proposal?

She took a last sip of coffee and patted her lips with her napkin as Gideon paid the bill. Time to go. She sighed.

"Tired?"

"*Nee.* Just thinking that I really enjoyed myself."

"*Gut.*" They left the restaurant and she chose the long road home.

He shot her a knowing glance. As they rode along, the full moon floated above them, casting light, then shadows, over the strong bones of his face. He was at once the man she'd known for years, then the mysterious one she learned more about each day that she spent with him.

She stopped beside a field. "Do you remember this spot?"

"We stopped here the first night you let me drive you home from a singing," he said slowly. "Honeysuckle was blooming along the fence and fireflies were dancing over the field."

"Ya."

"I wanted to kiss you but it was too soon."

She turned and smiled at him. "It's not too soon tonight," she said, a little surprised at her boldness.

He leaned over and took her face in his hands and looked at her for a long, long moment. And then he kissed her. The kiss was warm and sweet and *wunderbaar*. She sighed when he released her face and drew back. She wanted more, wanted him to hold her longer, wanted more kisses. But best to avoid temptation. They stared at each other and neither had to say what they were thinking. Eli and Emma wouldn't be in the position they were in if they hadn't let passion overtake them.

"No fireflies tonight," he said into the silence.

"No honeysuckle, either," she told him, chuckling as the pungent aroma of fertilizer drifted on the wind from the fields.

"I wish I'd had more time to help Eli with the farm. We talked about how he'll need to hire some help when it comes time for harvest." He sighed. "I wouldn't have started my shop three years ago if I'd known that *Daed* would die and leave Eli and me the farm. Eli is carrying more of the burden than he should."

"But you love making toys and working at the shop."

"I do."

"And Eli loves farming."

"He does. Always has, more than me."

"So don't you think the path the two of you were set on is the right one?"

He glanced at her. "*Ya*," he said after a long moment. "I don't know that I would have had the courage to start my own shop if you hadn't encouraged me."

"*Schur* you would have. You love quilting and you worked in a shop before you opened yours. You're a born businesswoman. It was only a matter of time before you did it. I just mentioned when the space came open."

"You did more than that and you know it."

He shrugged. "I'd do anything for you." He reached for her hand. "I love you, Hannah. It's time I told you that."

Emotion swamped her. "I thought... I'd hoped you did. I love you, too."

They kissed again, and Hannah knew she would remember this moment forever.

"We'd better go," he said at last. "Drive us to your house and I'll help you unhitch the buggy."

"There's no need—"

"Drive us to your house. Allow me to be a gentleman."

"Then you'll have to walk home."

"I know."

"Perhaps I'll be courteous and walk you home."

"*Nee*," he told her with some firmness.

She turned back to face the road. "Giddyap!" she called, and Daisy began pulling the buggy again.

He got his way. Well, she let him. She could be just as stubborn as he could, but she didn't want to argue with him on such a night. So she let him unhitch the buggy and put Daisy up in her stall, and they kissed one last time. She watched him walk down the drive and head up the road to his house.

As she carried the flowers he'd given her up to her bedroom, she knew they had taken a new step in their relationship that night.

She wasn't *schur* where it would lead. But it warmed her heart to think about it.

Chapter Eleven

Emma was sitting in the booth they often chose at their favorite pizza restaurant when Eli walked in. John sat on her lap, looking wide-eyed at everything going around him.

When Eli walked up and John caught sight of him, the *boppli* gave him a wide, gummy smile. "Hello, Emma, hello, John," he said and then his heart sank as he watched John's smile fade, his little face looking puzzled. "John, how are you, buddy?"

John puckered up and began crying.

"Oh, sweetie, what's the matter?" Emma crooned, rocking him in her arms. "That's Eli. You remember Eli."

But John continued to cry. Emma dug in the diaper bag that sat on the seat next to her. "Here, here's your pacifier."

John snuffled, accepted the pacifier and sucked at it while tears ran down his cheeks. He just stared at Eli as if he'd never seen him before.

"I don't know why he's acting this way."

"Maybe he's tired."

"He had a long nap and he doesn't usually go to bed for another hour or two."

Eli knew little about *bopplin*. Most Amish *kinner* grew up helping take care of others in the *familye* but he and Gideon had been the only two.

"Maybe he's *hungerich*?"

She shook her head. "I fed him just before we came."

Zoe, the owner's teenaged daughter, came to take their order. She stared at Emma for a moment. "Well, I haven't seen you in here in quite a while. And who's this?"

John perked up at the attention and smiled at her. Emma made a fast grab for the pacifier as it slipped from his mouth.

"This is my son, John."

"He's precious." She glanced at Eli, started to say something, then bit her lip. She pulled out her order pad instead. "Now, what can I get you two?"

They ordered their usual—a large thin crust with everything but anchovies and two soft drinks.

"I'll put this in and be right back with your drinks. Anything for the little man?"

"He'll have a calzone and a brew," Eli said.

Emma chuckled and shook her head. "No thanks, Zoe." She watched Zoe walk over and give the order to the cook. "Well, that was awkward."

"I should have thought about that when I suggested this place," he said, frowning.

"I suppose it's going to happen." She looked down at John then at him. "You said you wanted to talk."

Zoe arrived with their drinks. Eli waited until she walked away to respond.

"We had some good times here, didn't we?" he asked her, looking around the restaurant. Booths were painted a bright red, and candles stuck in empty Chianti bottles sat on the tables. Posters of Italian specialties the restaurant served decorated the walls. An Italian opera played over the stereo system. It was a fun, affordable place that both the *Englisch* and the Amish patronized.

She nodded. "We did."

"I looked for you, Emma," he said quietly. "Looked for you for the longest time. I wasn't prepared for what you told me, and I'll be the first to say I was a jerk. I want to make it up to you and John."

She eyed him warily. "How do you want to do that?"

He reached for her hand. "I want us to get married. I want us to be a *familye*. I started to tell you that when Rebecca interrupted us."

"Here we go," Zoe cut in, placing the pizza on a stand in the center of the table. "Be careful, it's hot!" She dropped a stack of paper napkins on the table and left.

Eli wasn't thrilled with the interruption but took it in stride. He served them both a slice of pizza then frowned. "Should we get a highchair for John?"

"He'll be fine. I can eat this way." She held John in the crook of her left arm, picked up the slice of pizza with her right hand, and bit in. "Mmm. *Gut* but hot." She put the slice down on her plate. "I should have let it cool off a little." She sipped her drink.

He blew on his slice then took a bite. "Ouch. You're right." Well, what was a little burn on the roof of your mouth when the pizza was so *gut*?

"How are you doing here?" Zoe stopped by to ask.

John bounced hard on Emma's lap and threw out his hands. He knocked the drink Emma was holding and soda splashed down the front of her dress. Emma gasped.

"Oh my!" Zoe exclaimed. She grabbed some of the napkins and mopped up the spill, then grabbed some more from another table and handed them to Emma to blot the moisture from her dress. "Why don't you go use the hand dryer in the women's restroom to dry your dress?"

"I think I'll do that." Emma slid from the booth and, before Eli knew what was happening, thrust John into his arms.

"Well, this is a surprise" he told John, as Emma hurried away.

They stared at each other. *Please, please, don't start crying*, Eli prayed. He shifted the *kind* to sit on his lap and debated picking up a slice of pizza but decided he'd better not. He figured he was much less experienced than Emma at doing two things at once when one involved holding a *kind* . . . and the consequences of dropping John were too great.

"So, John, help me out here," he said conversationally. "How am I going to get your *mudder* to talk to me about getting back together if we keep getting interrupted?"

John frowned and babbled.

"Hmm. A nice drive in the country in the buggy sounds like a really *gut* idea," he said. "Maybe we could try that this evening after we eat. If you could promise not to spill anything else on your *mudder, allrecht*?"

"Eli."

He looked up. An attractive *Englisch* blonde stood by the booth smiling at him. "Sally."

"Yes, Sally." She tapped her foot as she studied him. "Haven't heard from you."

"I've been...busy," he said lamely.

"I see. Who's this?"

"This is my son, John."

"You never mentioned that you were married. That little detail seemed to have slipped from our conversation when you asked me out."

"I'm not married."

"But—"

"It's a long story," he said, glancing around.

"I see."

He didn't know what else to say. Except maybe it was time to start making things right. "I'm sorry, Sally. I'm...involved with someone now."

Before he could say anything else, Emma returned to the table. The two women stood there staring at each other until Eli spoke up. "Uh, Emma, this is Sally. Sally, Emma."

Sally didn't bother to say anything, just turned on her heel and walked off.

Emma held out her arms for John but then didn't take her seat.

"I can explain."

"I bet."

"Emma, please sit down and finish your supper," he said. "Please," he repeated when she hesitated.

She finally sat.

"Months after you left, I finally began dating again. I didn't think you were ever coming back. Sally and I went out a couple times. She didn't mean anything to me." He stared at his plate, then looked up at her. "I think we were both just kind of curious about the way each of us lived."

Zoe set a fresh drink on the table in front of Emma. "Is everything okay? You two aren't eating."

"We're fine, thanks," Eli assured her. He waited until Zoe left them and then picked up his slice of pizza. "John and I talked while you were gone. He had a *gut* idea."

"He did?"

He felt encouraged that she seemed to be trying not to smile. "*Ya*. He thinks we should go for a ride in the buggy and get away from all these interruptions."

Emma glanced down at John as he bounced with enthusiasm. The *kind* never seemed to sit still these days. "You think so, huh?" She looked at Eli. "How did you know r-i-d-e is one of his favorite words?"

"Isn't it every guy's favorite word?"

* * *

Emma couldn't help thinking how different this buggy ride was from the last one she'd taken with Eli. Back then he'd been all about taking her for a romantic drive.

Emma had been in love with him for years. He was twenty-four and graduated from *schul* years before her, so she'd thought that he had never really paid attention to her. The day she'd turned eighteen she'd walked up to him after church and asked him out to lunch. He'd been surprised. She'd told him she was tired of waiting for him to notice her.

"I've noticed," he said. "I've noticed you're too young for me."

"I'm not too young. Unless you feel too old," she'd retorted. "Well, if you're not interested, never mind."

She'd turned to walk away but then he'd grasped her arm. She'd stared at his hand and he'd dropped it. They both knew a man wasn't supposed to touch a *maedel*. It definitely wasn't a *gut* idea standing on the front porch of the house where church services had just been held and people were coming and going.

"Fine," he said. "We'll go to lunch."

"Never mind."

"One minute you want to go, the next you don't. Talk about contrary."

She smiled inwardly at the frustration she heard in his voice. "Not contrary. I'm just worth a nicer invitation."

"Emma, would you like to go to lunch?" he asked.

"If you're *schur* you can eat it with your teeth clenched like that," she told him with saccharine sweetness.

"I'll get the buggy."

Emma smiled at the memory. She'd never been so bold with a man, but she knew what she wanted and she'd wanted Eli to pay attention to her.

Eli and Gideon were *zwillingbopplin*, handsome twins who were any *maedel*'s dream. Tall, dark-haired, with dreamy deep-blue eyes. But they were different as night and day. Gideon was quiet and studious and had been interested in Hannah for years. Emma had no doubt that they'd end up married one day.

But Eli was the man she was interested in. *Schur*, she knew he loved to flirt and had taken many a *maedel* out for a ride in his buggy. Few could resist that mischievous glint in those blue eyes or that cocky grin of his. His charm was legend.

Well, they'd gone for that lunch and then they'd kept on seeing each other. Turned out that Eli liked that Emma wasn't a shy *maedel* who was willing to mold herself to a man to get married. They bonded over the knowledge that they were both feeling a little constricted by the rules of their community.

Or rather, the rules of their *dats*.

Eli's *dat* wasn't as strict as Emma's. Then again, who could be as strict as her *dat*? She'd been surprised he'd let her see Eli but suspected it was because Eli was a successful farmer and more mature than *buwe* her age.

"You're awfully quiet," Eli said now. "You *allrecht*?"

"I'm fine." She leaned back against the seat and enjoyed the gentle motion of the buggy rolling along the road. "I was just thinking."

"About what?"

"About when we first started seeing each other."

He shot her a grin. "You were different from the other *maedels*."

"I know."

"I liked that."

She couldn't help it. She smiled. "I know." She heard John stir in his sleep in the back seat and her smile faded. "We moved too fast, let our feelings take us to a place we shouldn't have gone."

"I'm not sorry."

"Nee?"

"Nee."

"Not even when I show up with the result of a night that shouldn't have happened?"

Eli pulled the buggy over to the side of the road and faced her. "*Nee*. Are you?"

"I can't be when I look at him," she admitted after a long moment. "But life feels pretty complicated right now."

She resisted when he tried to take her hand. "I didn't stop loving you, Emma. Did you stop loving me? Has your heart turned hard against me?"

"No, it hasn't turned hard," she said after a moment. "But it's not just me I have to think about now."

"We moved too quickly before. But I don't see how we can go slow this time."

"Maybe not. But it's hard for me. I'm afraid of being hurt again."

"You came back," he reminded her. "That tells me something." He rubbed the knuckles of her hand.

"I came back to make you take responsibility for John."

"If that was all you wanted you could have written me from Ohio."

He was right. She stared out at the darkened field.

"Maybe you're not ready to say you still love me," he said slowly. "But I think you want more, Emma. And I want more. Maybe we can start there."

A car drove past, too fast, and the wind shook the buggy.

"Reckless driver," he said. He pulled his hand back and got the buggy back onto the road.

"I'm going to work for Hannah," she told him.

"Really?"

"*Ya*. Just part-time. I don't know how long I can afford to stay at the motel."

"We'll work something out."

She saw him glance at John in the back seat.

"I guess we should get started back so you can put him to bed." He did a U-turn and headed back to town. "I'll come by and pick you both up for supper again tomorrow. This time we'll find someplace a little more private and talk some more."

"*Allrecht.*"

He parked at the motel and insisted on taking the sleeping John from the seat in the back and carrying him to her door. She unlocked the door, took John from him, and was surprised when he kissed her cheek and didn't press her for more.

"Sleep well."

"You too."

She watched him start for the buggy. "Eli?"

He turned. "*Ya?*"

"Where did you get the car seat?"

"Hannah's *schweschder* Linda loaned it to me."

"*Danki* for thinking of it." Some Amish didn't believe in them in their buggies. But she appreciated Eli thinking of John's safety.

"I care for John, Emma. Even if he's not *schur* he wants me for his *dat* yet."

She watched him walk back to the buggy and then went inside, locked the door, and lay John down in the crib beside the bed. Then she got ready for bed.

But as she lay there in the dark waiting for sleep to claim her, she found herself thinking about what he'd said tonight. Was he right that she hadn't come back just to make him take responsibility for John? Did she want more with Eli? And even if she did it wasn't going to be easy. They'd have to talk to the bishop, ask for forgiveness, be granted permission to marry outside the traditional marriage season, which took place after harvest.

And their community would know everything. She'd been turned away by her *eldres*. What would happen when other people in their community found out she was back with a *boppli*? John was little now, but as he got older she didn't want him treated differently. He was precious. She didn't want him to feel any shame.

She sighed. Life was indeed complicated, as she'd told Eli. Very, very complicated.

Well, she could have stayed in Ohio and not faced any of this. She could have continued to live the lie that she was a widow. Maybe at some point she'd have fallen in love with someone and had a *dat* for John and made a family with him.

But Eli was right. She'd come back here because she still loved him.

Would it be enough for what she'd face?

She tossed and turned for hours before she fell asleep.

Chapter Twelve

Hannah folded the wedding ring quilt, laid it into a box lined with tissue paper, and closed the top. She lovingly tied it with a silver ribbon.

"I'm so glad I stopped in," her customer said as she watched Emma tuck the box into a shopping bag. "I've been wanting something extra special as a wedding present for my niece and this is it."

"I'm so happy we had what you wanted." And she was going to make Sarah Byler very happy when she let her know that the quilt had sold. "I hope your niece has a wonderful wedding and many happy years with her husband."

The woman patted her hand. "Thank you. I'll be sure to mention your shop to my friends."

Hannah had just enough time to call Sarah and give her the *gut* news before several customers came in.

The morning flew by, and before she knew it Emma arrived with John for her afternoon shift.

"There's my favorite guy," Hannah cooed at John as she took him from his *mudder*'s arms so that Emma could put her purse in the back room.

"I thought Gideon was your favorite guy," Emma said, laughing as John reached eagerly for Hannah.

"Sssh, we won't tell him, will we, John?"

He chuckled and patted her cheeks as she carried him and followed Emma into the back room where she stashed her purse and slipped John's bottles into the refrigerator.

"I had a *gut* morning. I sold the wedding ring quilt. The woman who bought it said it's for her niece who's getting married."

"Oh, that's *wunderbaar*. It's a beautiful quilt."

"I don't know if you've heard that Sarah's *mann* is having chemo for the cancer."

"*Nee*, I hadn't heard. I'll say a prayer for them." She frowned. "Sarah's my *mudder*'s best friend."

Hannah touched her arm. "Emma, Sarah said she really needs the money so she's coming into town later today to pick up the check." She watched Emma's face for her reaction.

Emma squared her shoulders. "I knew when I came back that I'd see people from the community. I've been lucky not to run into anyone since I've been staying in town."

They walked back to the front of the shop. "Eli and I talked last night," Emma told her. "I told him I'd decided to stay for a while. That you'd hired me to help part-time. He wants me to give him a second chance, Hannah, and if I do, that means that we won't be able to hide that we have a relationship." She reached out to touch John's head. "That we have John. It's not going to be easy. But I'm not afraid of things not being easy."

She picked up John and hugged him. "That's what John taught me. He taught me not to be afraid. I was terrified when I found out I was pregnant, but there was no saying I wasn't going to have him. I didn't think I could go through childbirth." She laughed. "Well, you can't exactly escape it. That *boppli* has to come out. So, I got through it. And I'll get through this."

She shook her head and looked rueful. "Brave talk. Eli told me he wants a second chance and all I could think to say was I'm afraid of trusting my heart to him again."

John yawned and snuggled against her neck.

"Time for a nap," Emma said.

Hannah watched her tuck John into the crib, and then they used the time without customers to organize some shelves.

"I almost forgot," Emma said suddenly. "You went out with Gideon last night. How was it? Bet you didn't have a woman Gideon had dated show up at your table."

"What?" Hannah stared at her.

Emma filled her in on the previous night's drama, and it was Hannah's turn to shake her head.

"Well, as he said, I was gone and he didn't know if I

was ever coming back. And maybe I'd have dated too, if I hadn't been so busy taking care of John and living the lie that I was a widow."

She bent to retrieve a box on the bottom shelf. "What's this?"

Hannah glanced at it. "A quilt I started. I haven't had the time to work on it much."

Emma spread the quilt out on the cutting table. "I love it. I've never tried something this complicated before." She looked at Hannah. "The owner of a quilt shop ought to be seen working on her own quilt, don't you think?"

"There isn't much time when we're busy. And I need us to be busy to earn a living."

"Well, maybe now that I'm here to help you'll have the time to work on it during store hours. So, tell me about your supper with Gideon last night." She laughed. "Must have been nice. You're blushing."

"Eli's not the only one who can be charming," Hannah said after a long moment. "It was such an elegant restaurant. So romantic with linen tablecloths and candles on the table and music playing. And he brought me flowers. They were from his *mudder*'s garden, but they reminded me of how he'd picked Leah's roses for me years ago."

She broke off and stared off into the distance, remembering. Then she caught herself.

"Anyway, I didn't need such a fancy supper and for him to spend so much money. I enjoy being with him, even when we just have coffee in the morning before work. Gideon's quiet and he doesn't flirt like Eli, but he's got this way of just looking at me and listening as if I'm the most important person in the world to him. And Gideon's always had this ability to know what I'm thinking." She stopped and smiled "Did I ever tell you he suggested I open the shop?"

"*Nee.*"

"It was like this secret in my heart I was afraid to even dream about. I had never told anyone I wanted to have a shop, but one day I told him because I just knew he wouldn't think it was some wild, silly dream. So when the space came available to rent he was the one who pushed me to do it."

"You've always sewn the most beautiful quilts. And you're so *gut* with people. I'm not surprised you wanted to open a shop." She glanced at John, then at Hannah. "I don't know what I'd have done if I hadn't had your help since I came back."

Before Hannah could say anything, the shop door opened and Sarah walked in. She took one look at Emma and stopped. "Emma Graber!"

* * *

Gideon walked the fields of their farm with Eli after work on Monday.

It was just April but it was already getting warm with the sun beating down, making the scent of earth and growing corn plants strong and familiar. The deep green stalks waved in the breeze and looked healthy, promising a *gut* crop.

116

He'd missed this working in his shop.

"Looking *gut*," he said. "You've worked hard." He glanced at Eli when his *bruder* stayed silent. "What?"

"I guess I'm waiting for the criticism."

He frowned. "I'm not *Daed*."

"True." Eli sighed. He took off his straw hat, wiped his forehead with a bandanna, then put the hat on again. "Sorry."

"The two of you butted heads for *schur*." He chose his words carefully as they walked between the rows of corn, and Eli occasionally checked an ear for bugs or other problems. "I think he was so afraid you were going to walk away from this, from the land he worked so hard to hold. And the more he said the further the distance grew between the two of you."

"So it's my fault?"

Gideon shook his head. "That's not what I'm saying at all. What we try to hold on to too hard can slip from our grasp."

"I needed some time to know this way of life was for me. You've always been *schur* of it. But I haven't." He stopped and chuckled. "And *allrecht*, I enjoyed my *rumschpringe*."

"A lot."

Eli's grin was unrepentant. "A lot," he agreed. His grin faded. "It wasn't just that. *Daed* didn't want to listen to my ideas about what to plant. Everything had to be his way."

"And it was never that you wanted change just for the sake of change?"

"*Nee.*"

"*Nee?*"

Eli chuckled. "*Ya.* I remember *Mamm* saying one day, God willing, you'll have a *kind* just like you." He sobered. "What do you think she's going to say when I tell her about John?"

Gideon took out his own bandanna and wiped the perspiration from his face. "What do *you* think she'll say?" he asked, turning the question on his *bruder*.

"She'll expect me to marry Emma."

"And?"

"I'm working on it," Eli muttered. "Last night she told me that it was hard to trust me not to hurt her again."

Eli stopped and gazed at the farmhouse. "I don't have to wonder what *Daed* would have said. I can hear his words in my head every time I think of him. He'd have insisted I do the right thing the minute I found out. And if he'd been here, he'd have done everything in his power to make it happen even if I wanted to fight him on it and say I wasn't ready when she told me."

He kicked at a clod of dirt. "Emma says we need to talk things out, not act rashly. But who knows how much time we'll have before someone sees her in town? The waitress in the pizza restaurant remembered her, and we could tell she was curious about John but she was too polite to ask. But you know when someone from our community sees her word will get around fast. There'll be gossip about her having John outside marriage, and church members will shun her when they run into her."

"The Amish grapevine is faster than the internet. I'd be expecting a visit from the bishop."

Eli nodded grimly.

They walked into the barn and began feeding and watering the horses, working with an easy rhythm they'd developed from childhood.

When they finished they went inside the house and washed up. "It's your turn to cook supper, Eli."

"Nope," Eli told him as he poured himself a glass of water and chugged it down. "It's your turn. I cooked last time, remember? Chicken and dumplings?"

Gideon groaned. "That's right." He pressed a hand to his stomach as he remembered tough chicken swimming in a greasy gravy and gummy lumps Eli had called dumplings. "Fine. I'll make supper but you're washing the dishes. And you have to work on your cooking. A man should be able to cook a few things and not depend on his *mudder* or his *fraa*." He frowned. "Or his *bruder*."

"I'm going to go take a shower. Some of us don't get to sit in a shop and not sweat all day."

Gideon made a face. "Go right ahead, Stinky. But make it quick—otherwise I'll eat without you."

He went to the refrigerator and poked around. He'd put a frozen package of ground beef in the refrigerator to thaw before he left for work that morning. He browned the meat, started a pot of water boiling for spaghetti, and headed down to the basement. Shelves of vegetables and fruits canned by his *mudder* after the harvest lined the shelves. He found a large jar of spaghetti sauce made from tomatoes grown in his *mudder*'s kitchen garden and a jar of peaches, and carried them upstairs.

"Wow, smells amazing," Eli told him when he walked into the kitchen ten minutes later.

"*Danki*, dear, grab some bread and butter and let's eat."

Eli laughed. "Two old bachelors having supper," he said as they sat and began eating.

"Nothing like *Mamm*'s sauce." Gideon twirled spaghetti around his fork and closed his eyes as the taste of summer tomatoes filled his mouth.

"Is it as *gut* as the supper you and Hannah had at that fancy new restaurant the other night?"

"Better. Except for my supper companion."

"*Ya*, well, it's no fun looking at your ugly mug, either."

"You're looking in a mirror, pal," Gideon reminded him. They were as identical as *zwillingbopplin* could get.

Eli laughed. "Point taken." He buttered a slice of bread, bit in, and chewed. "I figured you took Hannah to such a fancy place to propose to her."

"*Nee*." Gideon couldn't help remembering watching the *Englisch* man seated near them proposing to the woman with him. He knew Hannah had seen them too, but hadn't said anything.

"What are you waiting for? Why didn't you ask her?"

"I have my reasons," he said shortly. He wasn't going to share with his *bruder* how he'd had everything planned but John's appearance had changed things. No way he wanted anything to stand in the way of Eli doing the right thing and marrying Emma.

"You're slower than molasses on a winter morning," Eli said, shaking his head. But he didn't press it.

Gideon finished his spaghetti and served himself a bowl of peaches. They were just the right finish to the big meal. He rose and put his dishes in the sink. "Dishes are yours. I'm going to get some work done."

"Fine. You play with your toys," Eli said, snickering as Gideon reached into a bottom cupboard and pulled out a box with pieces of wood and tools and set it on the table.

He gave him a mild look. "Pays my bills."

Eli sobered. "You know I'm just kidding. I'm glad you have work you like. You always enjoyed working with wood more than raising crops."

Gideon used a pencil to sketch on the wood before he began carving. "I like farming but I like my job better. Seems we both found what we like."

"And *maedels* to love."

He nodded. "*Ya*. Even better."

Eli turned, filled the sink with soapy water, and left him to work.

Chapter Thirteen

Things are really working out," Hannah told Gideon as they ate lunch at his shop. "Emma's come in three days this week and I've gotten so much accomplished having her help. Katie Ann was only able to come in one or two half days a week. I've already got my Christmas stock ordered, reorganized a few display tables, and we've done more sales because between the two of us we have more time to spend with customers."

She took a sip of her iced tea. "And she says she doesn't mind working Saturday afternoons. So I can finally schedule a quilting class for the *Englisch* customers who work during the week and can't take the weekday ones."

"Sounds like it's working out well."

She nodded. "I was worried when Sarah came in—

Sarah Byler. We knew it was just a matter of time before someone found out Emma was in town and had a *boppli*. I was really worried Emma might think about leaving. But she handled it well, said she'd been expecting she'd have to deal with our community at some point. But I don't think Sarah's said anything to anyone. No one's stopped by, and you know how fast the Amish grapevine works."

Then she frowned. "Then again, Sarah has a lot on her mind. She picked up her check for a quilt I sold for her. I told her I'd be happy to drop the check by her house but she wanted to get it into the bank right away. And she said she needed to pick up a prescription for her *mann*. He's got the cancer, you know."

"I know. Eli's been helping tend his fields along with some of the other men from the church. They'll harvest his crops when it's time."

"I'll be stopping by with some food my *mudder* and I are cooking for them this weekend." She brushed crumbs from her hands and drained the last of her iced tea. "Well, I should get back to the shop. It was nice of Emma to come in a little early so I could eat with you, but if it gets busy I don't want her to be overwhelmed her first week."

"Do you think Emma would be interested in working a few hours for me some afternoons when she isn't working for you? I could use the time to get some things done here. I need to do some planning myself."

"I can ask her for you, or you can call her on the shop phone."

"Ask her for me. If I call her I could catch her during a busy time."

"I'll do that."

He stood and leaned over the counter to kiss her. She felt a blush creeping up her cheeks. "I— what was that for?"

"Because I want you to think about me."

She pressed her hand against her lips. "I think about you often." She tried and failed to give him a stern look. Someone could have come into the shop and seen his PDA. It wasn't seemly, but she couldn't deny that she liked it. She gathered up her lunch tote and hurried to the door. "See you later."

* * *

Emma was indeed busy when she returned to the shop. Hannah didn't take the time to put her lunch tote in the back room but instead shoved it under the front counter and went straight to work cutting fabric for a customer waiting patiently.

"I'm so sorry you had to wait," she apologized to the woman.

"It's no problem. This young gentleman kept me company," the woman told her, smiling at John in his crib beside the table.

"We don't trust him with the scissors just yet," Emma joked as she walked over with a bolt of fabric.

"I think it's just so wonderful when you can bring your baby to work with you."

"We love it, don't we, John?" Emma asked him and he waved a rattle and grinned at her.

As soon as the shop cleared Hannah turned to Emma. "Gideon was wondering if you'd want to work for him for a few hours now and then. I'm *schur* he'd move the crib there for you so you could have John with you, or I could watch him for you."

"*Schur*. That would be fun and give me some more money for expenses."

"What was I thinking?" Hannah said. "I can advance you your first week's salary."

"There's no need for that. I'll be *allrecht* until you pay me."

Hannah shook her head. "I insist." She did the math on a piece of paper and withdrew the cash from the register. "Once you open a bank account I'll pay you by check."

Emma tucked the bills into her pocket. "I should see about doing that soon."

It started to rain a little while later, and tourists and locals hurried past with their umbrellas without coming inside. So the two of them spent the time cleaning and rearranging some shelves.

When it cleared Emma glanced at the time. "Would you mind if I took a quick break and walked down to talk to Gideon?"

"Not at all."

"John should sleep for a little while longer," she said after glancing over at him.

"It's no problem."

Hannah got out a bank deposit slip and began filling it out. She had just finished when everything happened all at once. Several customers walked in and John woke up squalling. Frowning—John never woke like that—Hannah reached for the bank deposit bag under the counter, couldn't find it, and quickly shoved the money from the register into her lunch tote before she hurried over to see to him.

"Let me know if you have any questions," she told her customers.

John held up his arms and cried piteously as she leaned over his crib. "There, there, *lieb*, I'm right here and your *mamm* will be right back." As she picked him up, she noticed that one of the customers was standing near the counter. It was the sole male—a teenaged boy—who'd come in with the group. But he didn't have anything in his hands, so he didn't appear to need help.

A woman walked up to her. "Miss, do you carry metallic thread?"

"No, sorry, we don't."

"You're sure?" The woman stepped closer, uncomfortably closer.

"Yes. Sorry." She stepped aside and glanced around to make sure no one else needed her.

Other women were browsing the aisles, but the teen was gone. She guessed he was like other males and didn't want to wait for his mother. But when she glanced at the door as Emma walked in she didn't see anyone sitting on the bench outside. That was where men usually parked themselves while the women shopped.

"There, see? *Mamm* is here just like I said she'd be." She looked at Emma. "He woke up crying. He never does that."

"He was a little fussy this morning. I thought he might be teething but when I rubbed my finger across his gums I didn't feel anything."

Emma held out her arms and John fell into them. She touched her lips to his forehead. "He's a bit warm. I hope he's not coming down with something. Since my shift is almost over, we're going to go on back to the motel unless you need anything else from me."

"That's fine. You let me know if John is sick and you need anything."

"I will. I don't have a cell phone but there's a phone in our room." Emma tucked him into his stroller.

"I have the number." She waved at John. "Bye-bye, sweetie. Hope to see you tomorrow."

When he gave her a wan smile she frowned, worried that he was indeed not feeling well. After a glance at the clock on the wall and a quick sweep of the shop to make sure she had no more customers, she walked over to the door, flipped the sign to **Closed**, and locked the door. As she turned, there was a rap on the door. She smiled when she saw it was Gideon and let him in.

"You're a little early."

"It was slow all afternoon because of the rain."

"Same here." She closed the door. "Then it got busy briefly. I'll get my things together. Emma just left. John was acting like he wasn't feeling well." She got her purse from the back room and then stepped behind the counter to get her bank deposit.

It wasn't there. She bent down and searched the shelves, remembering she'd shoved the deposit into her lunch tote when she couldn't find the bank deposit bag.

The tote was gone.

She straightened and stared at Gideon, stricken. "My money's gone!"

Gideon frowned at the panic in her voice. "It's not in your purse?"

She shook her head. "I was making out my bank deposit and John started crying just as four or five customers walked in. I got distracted and shoved the envelope with the money into my lunch tote under the counter instead of putting it back in the register."

Gideon walked around the counter. "Maybe it fell down, got shoved behind something." He knelt and searched the shelves himself, then stood. "It's not there. Let's walk around the store, make sure it isn't on the floor somewhere."

"Bank envelopes don't walk away on their own," she said, looking miserable.

But she walked with him anyway and looked on the floor and checked the back room. When they still didn't find the money, Gideon stepped forward and put his arms around her. "It's *allrecht*. Everything is going to be *allrecht*."

"But the money!" she said in a shocked whisper. "It's gone!"

Then, as if she realized what they were doing, she pulled back and stared at him.

"How much was it? You said you'd made out the deposit slip."

Hannah walked back to the counter and found the slip of paper she'd added up the cash and credit receipts on. She sighed as she handed it to him. "I suppose it could have been worse. It was a slow day. And I gave Emma an advance in cash."

"That was kind of you." Gideon frowned. "I wonder if Eli has given her any money for expenses."

There was a sharp rap on the door. Hannah was surprised to see Officer Tate, one of the local police officers, through the window. She opened the door. "Yes?"

The woman held up Hannah's lunch tote. "Lose something?"

"Where did you find it?" Hannah asked as she took it with shaking hands.

"In the parking lot. Your name was inside." Her eyes narrowed. "Something wrong?"

Hannah bit her lip, looked at Gideon, then back at the officer. "Yes but—" she broke off.

"Do we need to speak privately?" the officer asked, glancing at Gideon.

"No, Gideon didn't do anything, if that's what you mean," Hannah rushed to say. "We just discovered someone stole money from me today. I guess when they went behind the counter looking for a purse they took the lunch tote."

She looked inside it, then shook her head, and looked rueful. "Silly for me to think anything would be in it."

"I'd like to make out a report," Officer Tate said, as she held up a hand. "I know the Amish don't want to prosecute, but we need a record of any crimes happening in the area to try to prevent them from happening again."

Hannah nodded and held the door open for her to enter. "We only have a few minutes, though. Our ride will be here soon."

They sat at the quilting table and Hannah went over what she remembered, told the officer how much had been taken, and described the teenaged boy who'd come into the store with the women. The officer wrote down the description.

"I'm sorry I can't remember more about him."

"This is good. There are security cameras outside some of the stores. We can pull the video. Did the teen seem to be with one of the women?"

"I thought one of the women in the group that came in was his mother," Hannah said. "I mean, males rarely come into the shop, and this was the first teenager I think I've seen visit."

She closed her eyes for a moment then opened them. "I remember looking over and seeing him standing near the counter but he didn't have anything in his hands I needed to ring up. Normally I would have gone over and asked if he needed any help, but John woke up and he was crying."

"John?"

"My part-time worker's baby. He'd been taking a nap in the crib there."

"Did any of the women stand out to you?"

Gideon watched her frown then bite her lip. "It's probably nothing."

"Just tell me. You never know what's important."

"This one woman asked for metallic thread. I remember I was looking at the teenager and she seemed to walk into my field of vision. I tried to look over her shoulder. But she got closer, too close to me, and made me feel a little uncomfortable."

"Can you describe her?"

She shook her head. "Sorry."

Gideon got up and walked over to the shop window when he heard a horn honk. "Our ride is here."

"I just feel so stupid," Hannah said with a sigh as she rose.

"You're not stupid," Tate said. "Someone took advantage of a moment when you were distracted. I hope we can catch the thief so we can redirect him, get him on the right path."

She closed her notebook and stood. Reaching into her pocket, she withdrew a business card and handed it to Hannah. "Please call me if you remember anything else. I won't pressure you to prosecute if we find the person who did this. I've worked in this town for four years and I do understand you don't want to prosecute. But I'll be trying to find him to see if I can get your money back."

"Thank you." She followed the officer to the door and said her goodbyes. Gideon trailed after her and waited for her to lock up. Then they both walked over to the van and got in. Liz leaned over the seat and looked at them as they sat in the second row of seats. "You folks okay? I saw Officer Tate come out of the shop."

"Someone stole money from Hannah today," Gideon told her.

"They didn't hurt you, did they?" Liz demanded quickly.

Hannah shook her head. "I put my bank deposit envelope under the counter when some customers walked in, and when John woke up, he distracted me. I didn't lock up the deposit bag."

"Where is the little guy?" she asked as she turned, checked traffic, and pulled onto the road.

"He's with his mother. She's helping me part-time."

"Liz, I'm getting off at Hannah's house," Gideon told the driver.

"No problem." She turned her attention to traffic. Gideon took Hannah's hand and squeezed it. He frowned at how cold it felt. And he noticed that she was trembling, too. She held herself straight and tried to act like she was fine but clearly she wasn't.

She turned and smiled at him, then they looked ahead and saw one of their fellow passengers standing on the sidewalk waiting for the van. Liz pulled over and stopped so Martha could get in. She said a brief hello to everyone and took a seat.

And so it went, the stops for the Amish men and

women who relied on their driver to get them to and from their jobs. It was usually quieter on the way home. The passengers were tired after a long day of work, a day that had begun before dawn and wouldn't end for hours yet. There was supper to cook, chores to do, *familyes* to tend to.

When they finally arrived at Hannah's house and got out, Liz called "Take care" before she drove off.

Hannah turned to Gideon. "Staying for supper?" she asked him with a rueful smile.

He remembered the last time he'd asked Liz to let him off at Hannah's. That was when he hadn't wanted her to face her *mudder*'s questions after she took care of John. But no way would he have had her face an uncomfortable questioning about who John was and why Hannah was taking care of him alone.

"I just want to make *schur* you're *allrecht*," he told her. "I'm not inviting myself over for supper."

She smiled at him but it didn't quite meet her eyes. "I'm fine, really."

Mary stood watering the pots of flowers on the front porch. "*Gut-n-owed*, Gideon. Are you staying for supper?"

Gideon glanced at Hannah. "*Danki*, Mary. I didn't plan on inviting myself."

"Since when do you need an invitation?" she asked. "Come on, I'm about to put it on the table." She opened the front door and walked inside.

"You're going to tell them, aren't you?" Hannah asked him.

He took her hand. "*Nee*, you are. It'll make you feel better to have their love and support." He touched his forehead to hers and looked deep into her eyes. "You have mine. You'll get through this. It's a part of business."

She sighed. "*Danki*."

They climbed the steps to the porch. "You haven't had something like this happen."

"*Nee*, but I've had shoplifters. And the roof leaked last year and damaged part of my stock, remember? And—"

Chuckling, she held up her hand. "*Allrecht*, I get the point."

Relieved that he'd chased the sad look from her eyes, he gestured for her to precede him inside as he held the door open. "I wonder if your *mudder* made those *wunderbaar* biscuits of hers."

Chapter Fourteen

Emma paced the small motel room with John crying fitfully in her arms.

John almost never cried. He almost never turned down his favorite strained pears either. She finally dug into her diaper bag and found the baby thermometer. *Schur* enough, he had a fever.

He'd been sick only once since he was born and when that had happened, some baby Tylenol had brought the fever down quickly.

So she measured out the dosage and got him to take it, then gave him some juice. But the fever still wouldn't go down.

When she was back in Ohio she'd had her friend with her, and even though she'd never had a *kind*, Grace had been so *gut* about keeping her calm.

Emma felt so alone as she sat with John in the motel room and waited for the fever to break.

She sang to him but he fussed. She walked him and he fussed. She even turned on the small portable television to distract him, but it didn't soothe him. Finally she climbed into bed, settled him onto her chest, and piled pillows around them in case he rolled. Maybe he'd sleep this way.

When she woke a few hours later John's forehead felt cool. Relieved, she drifted back to sleep and slept until the alarm went off. She sat up slowly, not wanting to wake him. Tiptoeing to his crib, she laid him in it and went into the bathroom to shower. When she came out he was waking and acting fussy again. She checked his temperature. It was up again. She soothed him by talking to him as she dressed quickly.

Then she lifted him from his crib and gave him another dose of Tylenol, following it up with a small bottle of juice while his bottle warmed in a pan of hot water. He needed a diaper change, but she figured she'd do it after he ate because he'd be less fussy.

He seemed happier after he was fed and after a quick bath felt cooler when she dried him, dressed him, and put him down for his morning nap. She frowned as she sat on the bed and watched him sleep. As the youngest in her family she hadn't helped take care of her siblings. Maybe if she had she'd have felt more confident about her parenting skills.

She sighed and got up to fix herself a cup of coffee. She ate the second to last of the granola bars in the box and decided she'd make a trip to the grocery store soon. Then she made the bed—a habit too ingrained to allow her to leave it for the motel staff to do. After propping herself up with pillows she used the remote to watch the television with the sound turned low. It was an unaccustomed treat. She hadn't had a *rumschpringe* before she got baptized. Having a super-strict *dat* meant there had been no looking at the *Englisch* world to decide if she liked it or wanted to stay in her community and be baptized.

But today she was too distracted to enjoy the drama she knew was called a soap opera, although she didn't know why. She changed channels. The game show she watched for a few minutes didn't catch her attention. People were doing all manner of silly antics to win prizes. The noon news was depressing with its stories of so many bad things going on in the world.

When John woke he seemed better, so she fed him and dressed him for their afternoon. After strapping him in his stroller she set off for the quilt shop.

Hannah smiled when she walked in. "I wasn't *schur* you'd be in today. How is John?"

"We didn't have the best night but I'm hoping he just has a mild cold," she said. "I checked his gums again, but he doesn't seem to be teething." She frowned as John rubbed his ear. It was the second time he'd done it since they came.

"Hi John," Hannah said as she bent down to stroke his cheek. "Emma, he feels warm."

"Oh no. He was fine when we left the motel." She

pushed the stroller over to the quilting table so she could sit and dig out the thermometer. *Schur* enough, his fever was back. "I really wish I could ask my *mudder* for advice."

Then she bit her lip. "*Nee*, I can't do that," she said quickly when she saw the question in Hannah's eyes.

Hannah glanced at the clock on the wall. "Today's Friday. Rebecca takes a quilting class this afternoon. I'm *schur* she'd be glad to look at John when she comes."

"That would be *wunderbaar*." Emma sighed. "I was thinking that I'd feel a lot more confident as a *mudder* if I'd taken care of siblings, you know?"

"It can't be easy to be a first-time *mudder*."

Emma checked the clock and decided it was time for another dose of medicine. John took it but then fussed until she picked him up and walked him around the shop. She bounced him on one hip as she straightened some displays and felt guilty that she wasn't doing enough.

"Maybe I should go. Doesn't seem right for you to pay me when it's slow."

"We're fine. It may be another slow day because it's looking cloudy again."

The bell over the door tinkled as it opened and a police officer walked in. She held some papers in her hand and smiled at Hannah before her glance shifted over to Emma.

"Well, I don't believe we've met," she said. "I'm Officer Tate."

"Emma Graber. And this is my son, John." She jiggled him when he didn't respond with his usual smile. "He's not feeling well today."

"Sorry, John." She turned to Hannah. "I think you might like to hear my news." She handed Hannah the paper she carried. "This is the young man who took your money yesterday."

Emma gasped. "You were robbed?"

"It wasn't that dramatic," Hannah assured her quickly. "He took it from under the counter when I was distracted." She looked at the officer. "I hadn't had a chance to tell Emma yet. She just came in."

"The good news is that I located this young man," Tate said. "I've already paid him a visit and had a little chat with him. He was surprised I found him. But we buy the yearbooks of the local schools, so it was just a matter of looking through them. He was a bit...cocky about what he'd done. Seems to think you won't press charges."

"I won't."

"Well, I chatted with him in front of his mother. It's the law since he's a juvenile. She wasn't the woman you described, the one who asked you about thread and you felt might have been trying to distract you. So I suspect she's having a talk with her son now and I'm hoping he'll be returning the money. And staying out of trouble." She smiled.

"Well, that would be nice on both counts."

"You let me know if he shows up."

"I will. And thanks."

"My pleasure."

"I'm so sorry that happened," Emma said after the officer left.

Hannah nodded. "*Danki*," she said, then glanced at the door as it opened again. "Rebecca! I was hoping you'd be coming to class."

"I wouldn't miss it. Cassie Martinelli should be here soon, too."

"We're a little concerned about John," Hannah told her. "Could you take a look at him?"

"*Schur.*" She set her quilting tote down on the counter and looked at Emma. "What seems to be the problem?"

"He's acting fussy and running a bit of a fever," Emma told her. "He just started rubbing at one of his ears."

Rebecca glanced at Hannah. "Do you mind if we use the back room? It'll give us a little privacy."

"Go right ahead."

They walked to the back room, where Emma handed John to Rebecca and then dug into her diaper bag for her thermometer. "He had Tylenol about two hours ago."

Rebecca sat in a chair, put John on her lap, and took his temperature. "A hundred and one." She asked about his health history and immunizations as she undressed John and checked him for rashes and any injuries. "You haven't seen a doctor here since you arrived, have you?"

Emma shook her head. "I just decided to stay recently."

"I think it might be a *gut* idea to get him checked out. If it's an ear infection he'll need to get some medicine." She straightened John's shirt and stood. "I can take you to Dr. Smith's clinic. I have my buggy parked out back."

"But your class—"

"Emma! John's more important than a class."

"*Danki*." She took John back and they walked out into the shop. "Hannah, I'm sorry, but Rebecca thinks John may have an ear infection. She's going to drive us to the doctor."

"That's *gut*," Hannah said. "You let me know how it goes and if you need anything."

John blinked as a raindrop landed on his head when they walked out to the buggy. "This is the second time you've helped me with John," Emma told her.

"I'm so happy to do it. I worried a bit when you left to have John in Ohio." Rebecca climbed into the buggy. "Then I reminded myself of what *Mamm* used to say."

Emma looked at her curiously.

"She said worry is arrogant. God knows what He's doing." With that she called, "Giddyap," and the buggy began moving.

* * *

Eli paused to glance up at the sky. Storm clouds were gathering. It wouldn't be much longer before it began raining.

He began walking down the rows of corn, checking the occasional plant. He had just made it to the porch when the sky seemed to open up. The rain poured, drumming on the porch roof. He took off his hat and went inside. After he washed up he fixed himself a ham sandwich and a glass of cold tea.

His cell phone rang. "Gideon. What's up?"

"I thought you might like to know Emma's taking John to the doctor."

Eli sat down heavily. "What's the matter with him? Is it serious?"

"Hannah said she didn't know. Just thought I'd call you in case you wanted to go see for yourself. Rebecca was at the shop and she's taking them to the clinic." He paused. "And Eli? If you go, pay for the visit."

Eli stiffened. "I don't need to be reminded to do what's right. Thank you for telling me. I'll head over right away." He broke the connection, grabbed his hat, and rushed out the door. He was soaked by the time he hitched up the buggy, but he barely felt it as he climbed inside and began the trip to the clinic.

And as he drove there he thought about how he hadn't offered Emma any money for expenses since she'd come back to town. He just hadn't thought about it.

Well, he could fix that.

When he pulled up at the clinic, he saw Rebecca walking out. He jumped out of his buggy and rushed up to her. "How's John?"

She stared at him for a moment and he realized that Emma must not have told him who John's *dat* was.

"John's mine."

Rebecca nodded with comprehension. "I think it's an ear infection," she said. "Emma's in the waiting room."

"*Danki* for bringing them."

"You're *wilkuum*. I'd stay but I got a call from one of my *mudders*. She's in labor. I told Emma I'd arrange for someone to come get her when she's ready."

"I'll take them back to the motel."

She nodded. "*Gut.*" She said her goodbyes and rushed off.

He went inside and saw Emma holding John as she struggled to fill out some paperwork on a clipboard. She looked up, surprised, when he sat beside her.

"Gideon called me and told me you were here."

"Hannah must have called him. You didn't have to come."

That hurt. "Of course I had to come. Emma, he's my *sohn* and I love you both."

She glanced around to see if anyone was listening. That stabbed at him again. She seemed reassured when she realized the waiting room was empty but for them.

They needed their relationship to be made legal so she wouldn't feel she had to hide it. But this was no time to press the issue.

John looked miserable. Tears stained his cheeks and he kept tugging at one ear.

"Hey, little guy, you're not feeling *gut*?"

But instead of calming down John screwed up his face and cried harder. Frustrated, Eli took off his hat intending to put it on the seat beside him. The action caught John's attention and he stopped midcry. Acting on an impulse, Eli settled the hat on John's head. It slipped down of course and covered his eyes. He pushed it up and Eli cried, "Peekaboo!"

John chortled. Eli took advantage of his laughter to reach for him and settle him on his lap. They played with the hat while Emma quickly completed the paperwork and took it over to the receptionist.

When she returned and sat back down, she lifted her eyebrows as if asking if he wanted her to take John back.

He shook his head. "Please, let me hold him. I want him to learn to love me."

Emma nodded. "I think it's going to cost you a hat."

Eli glanced down at John who was smushing the straw hat to pieces. He laughed when John chomped on the brim and made a face. "It's worth it."

When the receptionist called Emma over to ask her a question about the paperwork, Eli looked at John. "I'll buy you your own straw hat when you're old enough. And a pony. Would you like a pony? Sssh, here comes your *mudder*. Don't tell her about the pony."

"What's going on?" Emma asked when she sat down.

"Just guy talk."

The door near them opened and a nurse stepped out. "Mrs. Graber? We can see John now."

Emma stood and reached for John. Eli kept him firmly in his arms and got up, walking toward the nurse so Emma had no choice but to follow.

He'd made his point about being included, but when the doctor came in and began asking questions as she examined John, Eli had to defer to Emma. He didn't know his *sohn*'s medical history. He'd missed his birth. His first cry. His first smile.

As he watched Emma answer the doctor's questions, he sensed her nervousness. He suddenly realized he hadn't been there for her at a time that must have been scary for a young woman.

The doctor used an instrument to peer into John's ears. John wasn't happy about it, but the woman had a way of teasing him and diverting his attention that allowed her to look into both of them.

"Definitely ear infection," the doctor said as she stepped back. "I'm surprised John's not crying more than he is."

"He's usually a happy baby." Emma dressed John while the doctor tapped at the keyboard of her laptop.

"I've sent a prescription for an antibiotic to the pharmacy you listed closest to your home. Bring John back in a week for a recheck, and don't hesitate to call us if he doesn't improve in a few days or you have any questions."

Eli paid the bill on the way out. He could tell Emma was surprised and felt a little annoyed. What, did she think he wouldn't do so?

"Rebecca said I should call her and she'd see that I got a ride back to the motel," Emma told him.

Now he really *was* annoyed. "Did you think I intended to just walk off?" he demanded.

She blinked. "I don't know what you intended."

"I'm taking you back to the motel. After we get John's prescription."

They rode to town in silence. John fell asleep just a block or two from the doctor's office. Eli glanced over at Emma and saw her eyes drifting shut.

When a car passed them and the wind shook the buggy, her head bobbed up. She yawned. "John and I didn't get much sleep last night."

He nodded with understanding as he parked his buggy by the pharmacy and went in with her. He pulled a shopping cart out for her to set John in his carrier inside, then grabbed a cart of his own. "Get whatever you need. Diapers, milk, baby food. Whatever."

"Did you win the lottery?" she teased.

"It's about time I paid for the things my *sohn* needs," he growled. "I'll go get his prescription." He walked away from her quickly, knowing he was letting what Gideon had said bother him.

He helped carry the bags into her motel room and then stood there awkwardly as she put John in the crib the motel had provided. John settled right down and went back to sleep. When Emma turned to him, Eli saw lavender shadows under her eyes. He didn't think he'd ever seen her look tired.

"If there isn't anything else I can do for you I'm going to head home."

She nodded. "*Danki* for everything."

"Don't want thanks," he said gruffly. He bent down and kissed her cheek. "Get some rest. I'll talk to you tomorrow."

He brooded all the way home, and after he unhitched the buggy and put his horse up he walked into the house. Gideon was already there, bending down to check on something in the oven. Normally he was happy to see Gideon making a meal so he didn't have to cook, but all he could do was remember Gideon's pointed suggestion that he pay for John's doctor visit.

"I went to the clinic and paid the bill then paid for John's prescription and a bunch of stuff he needed," he said as he opened the refrigerator and pulled out the pitcher of cold tea. "You happy?"

Gideon closed the oven door, straightened, and turned to look at him. "Came home with a chip on your shoulder, did you? Well, I'm happy to knock it off for you."

Eli set the pitcher down so hard tea slopped over the rim. "*Ya*, you and whose army?" he snarled as he started across the room.

"Well, I can see my *sohns* are getting along just like usual," Leah said as she strolled into the room.

Chapter Fifteen

Y ou didn't tell me she was here," Eli told Gideon.

"You didn't give me the chance."

Leah folded her arms across her chest. "Nice to see you, *Mamm*," she said drily.

"Nice to see you, *Mamm*," they repeated in unison.

She frowned. "Very funny. I was talking to you, Eli. Gideon said hello when he came home and found me here."

"It's *gut* to see you," Eli told her as he crossed the room to kiss his *mudder* on the cheek. He sniffed the air. "Is that your famous meatloaf I smell?"

"It might be," she said, pulling out a chair at the kitchen table and gesturing for him to sit. "But your charm isn't going to work right now. Sit."

Eli eyed her warily as he took a seat. He glanced accusingly at Gideon. "Did you tell her?"

"Don't go blaming your *bruder*," Leah said as she sat opposite him at the table. "One of my friends wrote me. Thought I should know about Emma and your *boppli*."

He remembered Emma telling him Sarah had visited the quilt shop. His *mudder* and Sarah had been friends for years. But he had no idea how she'd figured out John was his *sohn*.

"Busybody Sarah," he muttered. "Ow!" he cried when his *mudder* cuffed him upside his head.

"Don't you be talking that way!" she scolded. "She's a *gut* woman who felt I should know what's going on. How long were you going to hide him from me?"

"I didn't know about John until a little while ago." He saw the doubt in her eyes and turned to Gideon. "Tell her."

Gideon took a seat at the table "Emma did just come back to town. But..." He trailed off meaningfully.

"She did come to tell me when she first found out she was carrying," Eli admitted. "But she left town before I could do anything."

Leah leaned toward him, looking stern. "So now she's back." Before he could respond she asked, "And what do you intend to do now?"

"I'm trying to do it."

"Don't try. Do."

He got to his feet, paced the room. "I'll admit I wasn't prepared for the news when Emma told me. I didn't react the way she wanted. That she needed. But since she's come back she's not exactly wanting to jump into marriage, either."

"There's a *kind* involved now. He shouldn't have to wait around while his *eldres* decide if he should have a name and a place in our community."

"I'm working on her," he said as he took his seat. "I'm showing her I want to be John's *dat* and her *mann*. I just came from the doctor's office and got his medicine and—"

"He's sick?" Leah stood so quickly her chair fell backward. "What's wrong with him?"

Eli stood and righted the chair. He laid his hand on his *mudder*'s shoulder. "It's nothing major. Doctor thinks he has an ear infection. We got his prescription and some other things he needed and I took her back to the motel."

"Motel? Why isn't she staying with her *eldres*?"

"They wouldn't have anything to do with her."

Leah pondered that. "Her *dat* is stern. No question." The oven timer buzzed.

"I'll get it," Gideon said. He rose and turned off the timer, then pulled on oven mitts and took the roaster from the oven. After setting it on top of the stove and tossing the mitts on the counter, he got plates from a cupboard and set the table.

"I want to see him," Leah said suddenly. "When can I see him?"

"I'll call Emma in the morning and find out."

"He looks just like Eli," Gideon said as he retrieved silverware from a drawer and brought it to the table.

"If you're lucky he won't be as much of a challenge as you were," she told Eli with some asperity. "Still are," she muttered as she rose to walk to the stove.

Feeling chastened, Eli glanced at Gideon. To his credit, his *bruder* didn't say anything. Eli knew he'd been a bit of a trial growing up. Gideon had always been the *gut sohn* who behaved himself. Gideon had never skipped *schul*, talked back, or tried to fly off the roof of the house. Eli figured he was probably responsible for some of the gray hairs on her head.

Eli watched his *mudder* transfer the meatloaf and vegetables to a platter. He got up, and nudged her gently aside when she lifted the platter. "Let me carry this. Least I can do when you cooked after a long bus ride."

"*Danki.*" She followed him to the table and sat.

After they'd given thanks for the meal, he waited for her to serve herself, then helped himself to a large portion of meatloaf and roasted potatoes and carrots. "I really missed your cooking. Gideon made some of your recipes while you were gone, but it just didn't taste the same."

Gideon took the platter Eli handed him and frowned at him. "That's the thanks I get for cooking." He turned to his *mudder*. "He'd have lived on peanut butter sandwiches the whole time you were gone if I hadn't cooked."

"Enough," she said firmly. "Eli, I want to hear about John."

So he found himself telling her everything he knew

as they ate. It wasn't much and he felt guilty about that. "I'll call her after supper and see if John's feeling better. She's working part-time for Hannah at the quilt shop."

"Invite her to supper tomorrow."

"Allrecht."

"I made dessert," she told him. "My chocolate chess pie. You can have some after you make your phone call."

Eli made speedy work of his supper and headed out to the phone shanty. Now he had to hope that Emma would agree to come to supper tomorrow night. He sent up a prayer that she would. He hadn't brought Emma to the house much before she'd moved away, but she and his *mudder* had always gotten along.

But as he waited for her to pick up the phone he found himself holding his breath. So much depended on Emma seeing his *mudder* wanted her to be part of the *familye*.

* * *

"You're *schur* you didn't make her ask us to supper."

Eli turned to Emma. "How many times do I have to tell you? She was the one who invited you. I think she'd have insisted I bring you last night but I'd told her that you took John to the doctor."

She chewed on her thumbnail as she glanced into the back seat, where John was strapped into the car seat. He was sound asleep.

Eli reached over and took her hand. "Stop that. You have no need to be nervous. *Mamm*'s always liked you."

"She can't be happy about John."

"She's not happy with me for not doing what I should have earlier, but that doesn't mean she's upset about John. Or you. So relax."

"Easy for you to say," she muttered.

"What?"

"Nothing."

Emma rubbed at the stain on her skirt. She should have known better than to give John a dose of his medicine after she'd put on her only clean dress. He hadn't meant to bat it away just as she got it close to his mouth, but now she wore some of it that she hadn't been able to sponge off. She sighed.

"You look pretty today."

She gave him a disbelieving look. She'd glanced in the mirror just before she left the motel room. Did the man think she didn't know what she looked like after a sleepless night with a sick *boppli*? She had dark circles worthy of a raccoon under her eyes.

"What? I can't tell you that you look pretty?"

"I'm tired, Eli. John kept me up most of the night."

"I'm sorry." He glanced into the back seat, then back at her.

She shrugged. "He isn't sick often. Maybe he'll sleep tonight."

"Should we wake him up so he will?"

"*Nee*. Let him sleep."

She felt herself growing drowsy as the buggy rolled along. "I thought your *mudder* was going to stay at her *schweschder*'s another month."

"She was. A certain busybody apparently wrote her about John."

"Don't talk like that. It's not kind. I knew it was just a matter of time before someone said something to somebody. My *eldres* know I'm in town. I've wondered if the bishop is going to come talk to me."

"I heard he's down with the flu."

The farm came into view. Emma found her heart beating fast as she took in the sight of the sprawling white farmhouse and the fields with their carefully tended crops. She had been here with Eli a few times when they dated, and it had always felt like home. Still, she felt herself tensing as she thought about seeing Eli's *mudder* and introducing her to the *grosssohn* she didn't know she had until recently.

"Well, we're here," she heard Eli say as she just sat there, making absolutely no move to get out of the buggy.

John stirred, then woke. He let out an irritable cry.

"It's okay, sweetie. We're here to see your *grossmudder* and Gideon," she said as she got out and leaned in to get him out of his seat. She picked him up, touched her lips to his forehead, and let out a sigh of relief when it felt cool.

"No fever," she told Eli as she grabbed the diaper bag and looped it over her left arm.

"Gut."

Emma felt her spirits rise as she walked with John toward the kitchen door at the back of the house. John swiveled his head from left to right as he stared wide-eyed at his surroundings.

The kitchen door opened and Leah stepped out onto the porch. "Emma! *Wilkuum!*"

Emma climbed the steps and watched Leah's eyes widen as she caught sight of John.

Leah gasped and pressed a hand to her mouth. "Look at him! Oh you sweet *kind*!! You look just like Eli did when he was a *boppli*!"

John responded to the delight he heard in her voice and reached out his arms to her. Leah took him and pressed her cheek against his. Then she turned and walked into the house. "I got your *dat*'s highchair from the attic and cleaned it up for you to sit in," she told him. "But I just want to hold you for a while."

"Hi, Eli, how are you?" Eli asked sardonically. "'*Gut* to see you.'"

"Tell me about it," Gideon said from his seat at the kitchen table.

Leah laughed as she sat and settled John on her lap. "There's nothing more special than a *kinskind*." She slipped John's hooded sweater off and handed it to Eli. Then she looked at Emma. "Eli said John went to the doctor yesterday for an ear infection. I remember both my *sohns* getting them a few times. Miserable things."

"John's always a happy *boppli*." Emma set the diaper bag on a bench near the door and took off her jacket and bonnet. She was surprised when Eli took them from her and hung them on pegs over the bench. "That's why he cried so much yesterday. Then he began tugging at his ear."

"Dead giveaway," Leah said with a nod. "Have a seat. Supper's almost ready."

Emma pulled out a chair and sat, relieved at how welcoming Leah was being. While she'd always been pleasant to her when she'd been invited to supper in the past, Emma couldn't be blamed for being worried over Leah's reaction to suddenly being presented with a *grosssohn*. But she couldn't help feeling a little on edge wondering if Leah would ask if she and Eli intended to get married.

The oven timer went off, startling John. Leah made a game of it, laughing and bouncing John when his lips trembled. "Eli, turn that off, please. Well, John, looks like I have to let you go." She rose and put him in the highchair, nodding with satisfaction when he began banging the plastic spoon she gave him.

"Can I help with anything?" Emma asked, watching as Gideon filled glasses with iced tea and set them on the table.

"*Nee*, you just sit and get some rest," Leah said, grabbing oven mitts and pulling out a roasting pan from the oven. "Eli, get the butter from the fridge."

Emma's mouth watered as the scent of the golden brown chicken wafted toward her. Breakfast had been a quick bowl of cereal; lunch a quickly slapped-together sandwich of cold cuts and cheese she kept in the mini-fridge. She'd had Leah's baked chicken before and it was worth whatever discomfort she might experience having supper tonight. She was hungry for a good homemade meal.

Leah transferred the chicken to a platter and brought it to the table. She added a bowl of mashed potatoes and one of green beans. A basket of biscuits wrapped in a napkin to keep them warm completed the meal.

Gideon sat at the head of the table and said the blessing and then carved the chicken with obvious experience. Eli sat at one side of John and tried to engage him but John had his eyes on Emma's plate. She scooped a little mashed potato on a spoon and offered it to him and he eagerly took it and rolled it around in his mouth while he made the funny little noise he always did when he liked a food.

"I can get him a little plastic bowl," Leah said.

Emma shook her head. "He won't want much more. I fed him before we left."

John grinned with his mouth full. Emma knew she should tell him to close his mouth but he just made her laugh especially after worrying about him since he started acting sick.

Leah kept the conversation going through supper, asking Emma questions about John and her life in Ohio. Emma noticed that Gideon didn't say much. He got up before Eli did to clear the table—ever the responsible older *bruder*, she supposed—and after he ate dessert he excused himself to see to some paperwork.

Was he leaving so that Leah could ask Emma and

Eli what they planned to do? Emma wondered. She felt her stomach turn over.

As Gideon walked past John's highchair he made a funny face and John let out a high-pitched giggle and grinned.

Leah's fork clattered to her plate. "Oh my!" she exclaimed. "Look at him, Eli! He has that same dimple in his left cheek that your *dat* did! That you do!"

She burst into tears, startling everyone in the room.

Chapter Sixteen

Gideon descended the stairs and walked into the kitchen. He inhaled the scents of coffee and bacon and eggs. What a nice surprise to find that his *mudder* had already gotten up and fixed breakfast. But she was nowhere in sight.

Banging came from behind the door to the *dawdi haus*. He opened the door and found her pushing a sofa across the living room inside the small apartment.

"What are you doing?" he cried, moving quickly to help her. "You'll hurt yourself doing this."

They settled the sofa against one wall, and she stood back and surveyed it. "Looks better here. And it wasn't that heavy."

He looked at her. She wore her oldest dress and a kerchief covered her hair. Dust spotted her apron.

"What's going on? Why are you cleaning in here?"

"Isn't it obvious?" she asked, using a cloth to wipe down the coffee table in front of the sofa. "I'm going to be moving my things in here."

"Now?"

She nodded.

"There's no reason for you to leave your bedroom upstairs," he said, puzzled. "This is still your house. Eli and I told you that. *Daed* left us the farm but the house will always be yours to live in."

"That was two years ago, after your *dat* died," she reminded him as she looked around. "Things have changed."

"What's changed?"

She tossed the cloth down on the coffee table and started for the kitchen. "I think I'll take a break and have a cup of coffee before I do more work in here."

"*Mamm*, what's changed?"

She washed her hands and poured them both a cup of coffee. "Gideon, one or both of you will be getting married soon. It's time for me to move into the *dawdi haus*. *Eldres* always move into the *dawdi haus* at some point when the grown *kinner* marry and take over the farm. You know that."

"Is Eli marrying Emma? Did they tell you that last night?"

With a sigh she settled into a chair and took a sip of coffee. "I didn't ask them. When I first came home Eli told me he intends to marry Emma, but he said she needs some time to trust him. So I didn't say anything to her last night."

He took the covered plate sitting at the back of the stove and carried it to the table. When he lifted the cover he found bacon, two *dippy* eggs, and a couple of biscuits. "I *schur* have missed your cooking."

"*Danki*. And what about you?"

"What about me?" he asked as he took a bite of eggs.

"How are things with you and Hannah?"

"Fine."

"Fine? That doesn't sound *gut*."

He set his fork down. "John changed things."

"Go on."

"*Daed* left Eli and I the farm but we knew that whoever married first would live in the house," he said. "Obviously Eli will be marrying first, before Hannah and me." He frowned. "If Hannah and I even get married now."

"Explain. Has something happened between the two of you?"

Gideon shook his head. "I had it all planned out. I was going to marry Hannah and live in the farmhouse. But like I said, John changed everything. Now Eli and Emma will need the house. And so I don't have anything to offer Hannah."

"You have yourself."

He pushed aside his plate, his appetite gone. "I wanted us to have our own home. And it doesn't seem fair to stay here when Eli and Emma are newly married."

"Don't be ridiculous. Neither of them would hear of you not doing so," she said bluntly. "Now eat your breakfast and no more of such silly talk."

"It's not silly talk." He picked up his fork and resumed eating. "Do you think three women can live in one house and not have a problem with who runs it?"

"I do. Probably get along better than the two of you men who still seem to be butting heads. I heard the two of you when I came home, remember?"

He winced. "I just want Eli to do the right thing."

"I think he will. Gideon, there's always another alternative. You and Hannah could stay at her house with her *eldres*."

"I know. But I hope—" Gideon broke off as Eli walked in.

He watched his *bruder* take off his jacket and hat and go to the sink to wash his hands.

"Ned's leg looks fine this morning," he told Gideon as he dried his hands on a dish towel. He poured himself a mug of coffee.

"Gut."

Eli sat at the table. "What were the two of you talking about when I came in?"

"Nothing important," Gideon said quickly.

"What is it you hope?" Eli persisted.

"Your *bruder* said the two of you decided the first one that married would get the house. He seems to think if you and Emma get married you wouldn't be comfortable with him and Hannah living here after they married until they got their own house."

"That's crazy," Eli said immediately. "What makes you think Emma and I will get married before you and Hannah?"

Gideon just stared at him. "You *have* to marry Emma as soon as possible. You don't want people from the church talking about her, shunning her."

Looking frustrated, Eli shoved a hand through his hair. "I can't force her."

"Use that famous charm of yours," Gideon said as he rose and carried his empty plate to the sink.

"What about you?" Eli returned. "I swear, you move slower than molasses on a cold winter morning."

Gideon turned to his *bruder*. "John changes everything. Even in our community you know what people will say about him being born outside marriage. He deserves better. Emma deserves better. You need to marry her quickly and take responsibility for John."

He grabbed his jacket and hat. "I'm going to wait on the front porch for my ride." He kissed his *mudder*'s cheek and left the room.

Eli came out a few minutes later. "You forgot this." He set Gideon's lunch tote on the table between the two rocking chairs.

"*Danki.*" Gideon stared out at the field to the side of the house.

"A bit chilly out here."

"You don't need to keep me company," he said shortly.

"I know John changes everything. I'm working on Emma."

The van pulled up in front of the house. Gideon rose, grabbed his lunch tote, then turned to Eli. "Work faster."

* * *

Hannah could sense something was wrong with Gideon the moment she got into the van.

"Good morning," he said to her as he buckled his seat belt.

It was his usual friendly greeting, but she knew him. She could tell something was bothering him, but she didn't dare say anything.

Instead, she smiled and made small talk as they rode toward town. There would be plenty of time to ask how things had gone the night before when Liz and the passengers she was picking up weren't around.

She managed to contain her curiosity until the van dropped them off at Gideon's shop. She waited for him to unlock the door, and then followed him inside.

"So how did it go last night?"

"Hmm?" he asked as they moved to the back of the shop. He set his lunch tote in the refrigerator and moved to the sink to fill the percolator with water.

Hannah put her purse and lunch tote on the table and took a seat.

"Emma and John went to your house for supper last night, didn't they? Your *mudder* met John for the first time, right?"

"They did."

Was it her imagination that he seemed distracted? she wondered as she went behind him and turned the flame on under the percolator.

"What happened?" She touched his arm and made him look at her. "What did your *mudder* think of John?"

He smiled. "She loved him from the moment she saw him. But who doesn't?"

"That's *gut*. And?"

"And she fussed over him and we ate supper."

She put her hands on her hips. "Gideon! This is like pulling teeth! Tell me what happened."

The percolator began burbling as he frowned and looked thoughtful. "It went well. Emma seemed comfortable. *Mamm* didn't pressure her and Eli to get married, if that's what you're asking."

"*Nee*, I didn't expect that. But there was no awkwardness? It couldn't have been easy for your *mudder* to find out she had a *grosssohn* or for Emma to introduce him to her."

"You're right. But *Mamm* welcomed Emma just like she always has. And then she took one look at John and had to hold him. It was love at first sight." He leaned against the sink. "Who could resist John?"

The rich scent of coffee filled the small space. When the percolator stopped, he turned the flame off and poured two mugs.

She jumped, startled, when the shop phone rang. Gideon rushed to the front to answer it. Hannah picked up the two mugs and followed him.

It was easy to tell who he was talking to when she set his mug on the front shop counter. He said, "*Ya, Mamm*" repeatedly and rolled his eyes when he saw Hannah watching him.

Hannah pulled over a stool and sat, sipping her coffee.

"She's right here, *Mamm*. Maybe you'd like to talk to her yourself." He handed the phone to her and picked up his mug.

Wary, Hannah took the receiver from him. "*Guder mariye*, Leah."

"*Guder mariye*, Hannah. I just wanted to ask you if you could come to supper tonight."

"Tonight?"

"*Ya*. If you're not busy."

"*Nee*, I'm not busy."

"That's *wunderbaar*. It'll be nice to see you again. Have a *gut* day!"

Before she could return the sentiment the line went dead. Hannah handed Gideon the phone. "Why is she inviting me to supper?"

"I have no idea. What did she say?"

"That it would be nice to see me again."

He nodded. "I don't think it's anything more than that. She asked me about you last night. Said she'd missed you while she was gone."

"I missed her, too. I like your *mudder*. Always have."

Gideon stared into his coffee, then looked at her. "Hannah, do you think I'm slow?"

"Slow?" Puzzled, she stared at him.

"I don't mean like I'm dumb." He frowned. "Eli said I move slow as molasses on a cold winter morning."

"That's not true." She studied him, sensing that it wasn't a simple question. That his *bruder*'s words had hurt. "You're a planner. You think ahead. That's a *gut* thing, not a bad one."

He appeared to think it over, then leaned forward to take her hand. Just as he opened his mouth there was a sharp rap on the shop door.

"It's Officer Tate." Hannah jumped up and went to the door to open it. "Good morning."

"Good morning, Hannah, Gideon. I thought I might find you here, Hannah."

"Can I get you some coffee?" Gideon asked her.

"No, thanks, I've had two cups already this morning." She turned to Hannah. "I have some good news for you."

"You do?"

The officer nodded. "Are you opening your shop soon?"

"Yes. I was just having some coffee with Gideon but I can come now." She walked over to the counter and picked up her purse and lunch tote. "I'll see you later, Gideon."

They left the shop and Hannah started to ask what the good news was but then she looked ahead and saw the teenager who she'd suspected had stolen her bank deposit envelope. He sprawled on the bench in front of her shop with his legs stretched out casually. An older woman stood next to him, her arms crossed over her chest, frowning and saying something to him Hannah couldn't hear.

Hannah stopped and looked at Officer Tate, who grinned. "Someone has something he wants to tell you. I think you'll be happy to hear what he has to say."

Hannah began walking again, and as she drew closer she saw the teenager glance in her direction and look sulky.

"You remember what I said," his mother said sharply.

He straightened and the sulky expression vanished.

"Ms. Troyer, this is Jamie Mattson and his mother, Ms. Mattson."

"Nice to meet you," she said politely. "Please, come inside." Hannah unlocked the door, held it open, then turned on the lights. She walked over to the counter and set her things down.

"I'm sorry I took your money," Jamie said as he handed over an envelope.

Surprised, Hannah took it. "Thank you for returning it."

"You might want to count it to make sure it's all there," his mother said, giving him a stern look.

"There's no need for that," she assured the woman. "I'm sure it is." She looked at the boy. "Thank you for returning it, Jamie."

"I would suggest that he come in and help you with some chores around the store like sweeping, but I can't imagine that you would be able to trust him," Ms. Mattson said.

"It's enough that he returned it," Hannah told her quietly. "And he's said he's sorry."

"Jamie's assured me I won't be seeing him again," Officer Tate said. "So thanks again for your help, Ms. Mattson."

She nodded briefly, then took Jamie by the arm and they left the shop.

"I think Jamie's probably grounded until he's thirty," the officer told Hannah.

"I can't believe this," Hannah said. "Thank you for your help."

She grinned. "Happy it turned out well." She turned and glanced around the shop. "That cute baby not working today?"

"Later," Hannah told her with a smile.

"I might have to stop in then." She started for the door, then turned. "Just to establish good community relations with the juveniles."

Hannah laughed and watched the officer leave, then she walked into the back to put her lunch tote in the refrigerator and lock her purse and the bank envelope in a file cabinet. She found herself smiling. She hadn't had such a nice start to her day since the first day she'd opened her shop.

She couldn't wait to tell Gideon her good news.

Chapter Seventeen

Hannah, *wilkumm!*" Leah cried when Hannah and Gideon walked into the kitchen that evening.

The two women embraced and began chattering as Hannah handed her a small bag from her shop and took off her jacket and bonnet.

"For me?" Leah grinned.

"Just something I thought you'd enjoy."

"Hi, Gideon, how are you?" he asked, as Eli had done the night before when he'd been ignored in favor of John. " '*Gut* to see you.' "

Leah just laughed and invited Hannah to sit at the kitchen table. She took a seat beside her, began untying the fabric strip Hannah had bound the handles with, and reached inside. When she pulled out a plastic bag filled with squares of fabric printed with baby animals she stared at it for a long moment.

"So many women are buying these kits to make baby quilts for their *kinskinner* I thought you might like to make one for John."

Leah teared up. "Oh, Hannah, what a thoughtful gift! *Danki!*"

She pushed aside the plate in front of her and began laying some of the fabric squares on the table. "These are adorable." She pressed her fingers to her trembling lips. "It's just beginning to hit me that I have a *grosssohn*."

She looked up. "Gideon, isn't this sweet?"

Gideon bent down to kiss her cheek. "It is." He looked at Hannah. "Very sweet."

He took off his jacket and hat, hung them on pegs, and walked over to check out what was in the roasting pan at the back of the stove, although he had a pretty *gut* idea from the scents. He lifted the lid. Pot roast with potatoes and carrots. Mmm. His favorite. He put the lid back on then peeked in the oven. A pan of rolls were browning nicely.

His *mudder* was so busy chatting with Hannah she didn't even chide him for opening the oven the way she usually did when she was baking.

"*Mamm?* Hannah? Coffee?"

They both shook their heads and didn't skip a beat talking. He poured himself a cup of coffee and sat down at the table to drink it. After he'd finished he reached over and picked up the wooden spoon his *mudder* had given John to play with the night before and idly tapped it on the tray.

"Very funny, Gideon," his *mudder* said. "Hannah, I think Gideon is feeling neglected." She reached over and ruffled his hair.

Gideon ducked his head and winced. "*Mamm!*" When he glanced over at Hannah she was laughing.

The oven timer buzzed. Leah got up, turned it off, and used mitts to pull the pan of rolls out. She set them on top of the stove.

Hannah rose and busied herself getting the pitcher of iced tea from the refrigerator, moving about the kitchen with the ease of *familye*.

Gideon knew he should offer to do something, but he was enjoying the sight of Hannah in the room. She looked so right here...in the room he'd heard people call the heart of the home. Certainly this one had been for his *familye* all his life.

His glance slid to the *dawdi haus* and he remembered his conversation with his *mudder* that morning before work. She'd said she was moving in there because her *sohns* were marrying soon, and he'd been dubious that he and Hannah would be. If only he and Hannah hadn't been interrupted by the police officer...He wanted to talk to Hannah about their relationship.

"Gideon? Are you ready for supper or too busy daydreaming?" his *mudder* teased.

"Hmm?" He realized both women were both staring at him. "Where's Eli?"

"He went into town to eat with Emma and John." Leah tucked the quilt squares back into the bag. "I can't wait to get started on this."

She rose, set the bag on the nearby bench, and began putting the food on the table.

Gideon waited for his *mudder* to question Hannah about her relationship with him. But just like the previous night, Leah simply carried on a friendly conversation and seemed eager to catch up with her female guest.

So he enjoyed the meal and the time with the two women he loved and considered himself a lucky man indeed.

"You were kind of quiet tonight," Hannah said when he walked her home.

"Couldn't get a word in edgewise," he told her with a grin and dodged her elbow aiming for his ribs. "Seriously, I think *Mamm* enjoyed her time with her *schweschder* but she missed you."

"And you."

He shrugged. "Maybe. Her first day home I thought she would knock my head against Eli's. Said we were bickering."

"Were you?"

"*Ya.* It was his fault, of course."

"Of course," she said. Her eyes sparkled with mischief. "What were you telling him to do?"

She knew him too well, he thought. "I just want him to take responsibility for John."

"I know. I think he is."

"Not enough. Eli needs to think about Emma's reputation in our community. And John doesn't deserve to be labeled as a child born outside marriage."

"Now who's the slow *bruder*?"

"Why you—" he began. But she surprised him by taking off running. He had no trouble catching her. She was fast but he was faster. He caught up with her at the front of her house and lifted her in his arms and spun her around and around.

"Stop!" she cried, laughing. "You're making me dizzy!"

"I'll show you dizzy," he growled. He stopped and bent to kiss her.

He didn't know how long they might have stood there kissing, but the front door opened and light spilled out. Gideon groaned as the family dog bounded out barking.

"Sam! You hush!" she cried.

The dog quieted and rushed up to them.

"Hannah? Is that you?" her *dat* called.

"*Ya, Daed.* Gideon just walked me home."

"*Gut-n-owed*, Gideon!" the man called.

"*Gut-n-owed*, Lester!"

"Hannah, bring Sam in after he's done his business, *allrecht*?"

She winced. "*Schur, Daed.*"

Lester went back into the house and shut the door. Sam, a medium-sized dog of indeterminate breed, pushed his nose against Gideon's hand until he petted him, then he bounded off into the front yard.

"Well, there's a mood breaker," Hannah said. "I guess I'd better be going inside."

Gideon clasped her hands in his. "I wish you didn't have to go."

She smiled. "Me too. It was a nice evening. I'll see you in the morning like usual."

"*Ya*," he said. "Like usual." He kissed her quickly before she could move, then watched her walk away from him.

Tomorrow is another day, he told himself as he turned to walk home. *Maybe tomorrow you'll have that talk with Hannah and plan your future. Tomorrow.*

* * *

After she shared morning coffee each workday with Gideon, Hannah usually hurried to her own shop. But the next day she found herself walking slowly and enjoying looking in the windows of the shops between theirs.

The jewelry shop generally didn't interest her. After all, the Amish didn't wear jewelry. But this morning a ray of sunshine glanced off the display of engagement rings and caught her eye. She stopped to look at them sparkling in their little black velvet boxes.

Had it been her imagination that Gideon had seemed more romantic last night? Reluctant to leave her at her home after he kissed her and swung her in that dizzying embrace?

There was no doubt in her mind that their relationship had deepened this past year, especially after she opened her shop. And even if he proposed immediately they couldn't marry until harvest was over, and that was still months away.

This morning he'd started to say something but then they got interrupted by the mail carrier arriving early with a package. Then he'd gotten a phone call from an *Englisch* friend who maintained a website selling toys on the internet. He'd looked frustrated when she said she had to go open her shop but a customer knocked on his door at that moment, so he'd nodded and reluctantly said goodbye.

"Morning, Hannah!" Micah Green, the jewelry store owner, paused at her side, his keys in hand. "See anything you like?"

She laughed and shook her head. "The sun lit up your display just now. I couldn't help but stop and admire it."

"Got some nice engagement rings. They're still selling well even though most of the June brides have theirs already. How's business?"

"Good. Katie Ann's starting her own bakery, so I took on a new part-time helper. She'll be working a few hours for Gideon now and then as well."

"Sounds great." He glanced to his right. "Looks like you already have a customer waiting."

"I do," she said, experiencing a sinking feeling in her stomach when she saw the familiar figure standing by the door of her shop. Ruby was a nice woman, but she was the bishop's wife. Hannah had the feeling she was in for an uncomfortable conversation. "Have a good day, Micah."

"You too, Hannah."

She closed the distance and smiled as she unlocked her shop door. "*Guder mariye*, Ruby. How is Abram?"

"Much better. First time I've been to town since he fell ill with the flu." She walked inside and glanced pointedly at the portable crib by the quilting table. "Heard you had a new helper."

"*Ya*. Emma Graber." Hannah turned the sign on the door to say **Open** and walked over to put her things under the shop counter.

"We heard she was back in town."

Hannah met Ruby's gaze directly. "If you want to speak to Emma she'll be in this afternoon, after lunch."

"I won't be in town that long," Ruby told her as she wandered over to finger a fabric on a nearby display table. "I can't leave Abram alone that long until he's back on his feet."

"I'll tell her you stopped by."

Ruby nodded. "Please do. I'd love to talk to Emma."

She picked up a bolt of fabric and walked over to the cutting table. Hannah went over to join her. "I thought she'd be at her house. But her *mudder* said she wasn't."

Hannah smiled. "How many yards do you need?"

"Four." She pulled over a chair and settled herself into it as Hannah measured and cut the material. "Where is she staying?"

"I'd rather you ask Emma that." She folded what she'd cut, wrote out a slip, and pinned it to the fabric. "Do you need matching thread or anything else?"

"Thread."

They walked over to the display of thread, and after

great deliberation Ruby chose a spool that matched the fabric.

"It's *gut* that you are being a friend to Emma and her"—she paused delicately—"unforeseen blessing. But our faith says her *boppli* cannot enter into the congregation of the Lord."

Hannah knew well the verse she referred to and felt a spurt of anger. No *boppli* deserved to be considered less because his birth hadn't happened within marriage.

Ruby laid her hand on Hannah's. Her thin face creased in a friendly smile. "I don't mean to sound judgmental. But please get Emma to talk to Abram and me. We must help her and the *dat* marry within the church and abide by the *Ordnung*."

Long after Ruby took her purchases and left the shop, Hannah thought about what she'd said. While this bishop was less stern than some of his predecessors had been, she knew that Emma would be shunned if she didn't marry Eli. And if the church members found out who John's *dat* was, Eli would be shunned as well.

She sighed. Shunning wasn't meant to be a punishment but a way to lead those straying from the path back to their salvation.

Customers kept her busy for the next several hours. When she was finally able to sit down and work for a few minutes on the new wedding ring quilt she'd decided to make, her stomach growled. She retrieved her lunch tote from the refrigerator in the back room and sat at the shop counter to eat her sandwich.

Emma and John came in a short time later. John

looked happy and waved his arms as Emma wheeled him inside in his stroller.

"You're early."

"We thought you might like company for lunch." Emma pushed the stroller over behind the counter. John bounced and grinned when he saw Hannah. She put her sandwich down and picked him up.

"I'm so glad to see you!" she told John as she sat down on the stool and settled him on her lap.

"We didn't mean to interrupt you eating."

Hannah shrugged. "I can finish in a minute." She kissed John's cheek. "How is he feeling?"

"*Gut.* We both slept all night last night."

She didn't want to start off the afternoon with awkwardness but figured it was best to let Emma know about her morning visitor. So she told Emma about her conversation with Ruby.

"I wondered what took her so long to stop by," Emma said wryly. "I've kind of lived in a little bit of a bubble working here. I knew the bishop wouldn't come to a quilt shop." She sighed. "Well, Eli and I will have to talk about it."

"You shouldn't have to do it alone. Talk to Abram alone, I mean."

"*Nee,* I shouldn't."

Emma was helping several customers when the shop phone rang a while later. Hannah picked it up and was surprised to have Emma's *mudder* ask to speak to her.

"It can't be *Mamm,*" Emma whispered when Hannah told her who was on the line. "She wouldn't speak to me when I went by our house."

"It is." She pushed the receiver into Emma's hands.

"*Mamm?*" Emma said. Hannah saw her lose all the color in her face. "*Ya*, I'll be right there."

She hung up the phone and turned to Hannah. "My *dat*'s had a heart attack. My *mudder* wants me to come to the hospital."

"You must go. I'll watch John for you."

"How am I going to get there?" The normally calm Emma wrung her hands.

"I'll call Liz and see if she can drive you."

She watched Emma check John's diaper bag while she made the phone call. After she hung up, Emma showed her John's thermometer and medicine. "He hasn't had a fever since he went to the doctor, but just in case the dosage is circled on the bottle and I wrote down the directions—" she began.

Hannah patted her shoulder. "He'll be fine."

Minutes later Emma was gone. No sooner had she walked out when the shop door opened and it seemed like a bus had dropped off a large group of customers. John chose that moment to spit up the strained carrots Emma had fed him.

"Oh my," Hannah said as she surveyed him. What a day this was turning into. First the uncomfortable visit with Ruby, and now this.

Chapter Eighteen

Gideon figured he'd surprise Hannah with a box of pastries and iced coffees from the coffee shop.

She wouldn't be expecting him now. But Eli had come into town on errands and stopped by the toy shop, so Gideon had asked him to watch it so he could take an afternoon break.

"Maybe Emma can take a break here with me," Eli suggested with a sly smile.

"We'll see," Gideon said, wondering if Eli had an ulterior motive when he stopped by. "That's up to Hannah, not me."

When he walked into the quilt shop he stopped in his tracks and stared at all the women milling around.

"What's going on?" he asked a harried-looking Hannah as she rang up a sale, a fretful-looking John balanced on one hip.

"A quilt guild from another town," she told him, giving him a quick glance before smiling at her customer. "That'll be $55.94."

"Where's Emma?"

"*Familye* emergency," she said tersely.

"I'll be right back." He carried the bakery box and drink holder into the back room, set them down on the table, then returned to the front of the shop.

"Young man, do you know where the pinking shears are located?" a woman asked him.

"Right this way," he said, leading her to the selection.

"My, you're so helpful," she complimented him. "My husband doesn't even know what they are." She considered the choices. "I guess that's what comes from being married to the owner, eh?"

He smiled, unsure how to answer. She'd obviously come to the conclusion Hannah was his *fraa* after seeing her with John. He waited as she took her time choosing. He wouldn't have known what pinking shears were, but he'd helped Hannah set up her shop and she'd explained the reason for the strangely toothed scissors.

"Can I help you with anything else?" he asked politely while wishing he could hurry her along and get back to Hannah. She obviously needed help up front.

"Thimbles. I collect them."

"Hannah has a nice assortment over here," he said, guiding her to them. "Some are practical and some are meant to be decorative for collectors." *Mudder*'s Day was coming up. Maybe he should think about getting his *mudder* the one with the violets painted on it. His *mudder* loved violets.

"I love this one with daffodils. Perfect for my collection," she said and placed it in the basket on her arm. "This has been such a lovely stop on our tour."

"I'm glad you're enjoying it. Let me know if there's anything else I can help you with. I'll be at the front of the shop."

He hurried back there and took John as the boy reached out his arms to him.

Hannah looked relieved. She placed items in a shopping bag, tied a scrap of fabric around the handles, and beamed at her customer. The woman thanked her then stepped aside so another customer could be rung up.

"Holler if you need my help," he told Hannah before he walked away with John.

He was stopped often as he wandered the shop. Sometimes a customer had a question. Sometimes someone just wanted to interact with John.

It seemed John charmed the ladies like his *dat.*

"Gideon!"

He turned and saw Hannah waving at him. "Sounds like someone needs our help," he told John.

They returned to the shop counter. "I need to cut some fabric," Hannah said. "Could you handle the cash register for me?"

"*Schur.*"

"John can sit in his stroller if you need both hands."

He'd watched her handle things while holding John. What made her think he couldn't do the same?

"We'll be fine."

But it didn't take long for him to discover that doing cashier duty while holding John was easier said than done.

"She's just had more practice," he told John after he fumbled with the cash register. "Look, how about you take a seat in this handsome vehicle here for a few minutes and let me take care of business?"

John protested for a moment but when Gideon pushed the stroller out where he could see the ladies moving about and was able to get their attention again, he was all smiles.

Working the counter at the quilt shop wasn't much different from working the one at his toy shop, he mused. Well, his customers often played with the toys he created and sold. And most of the things sold here weren't already made. The ladies bought material and yarn and such and turned them into quilts and garments. But the things sold at both shops seemed to provide a lot of pleasure to their customers.

The women began filing out of the shop, and gradually it emptied.

"Wow, that was interesting," Hannah said as she walked over. "Well, for some of us."

She gestured at John. He'd fallen asleep in the stroller and his head was bent at an awkward angle.

"I'm going to put him in his crib so he'll be more comfortable." She lifted him carefully, and he didn't wake as she carried him over to the crib and laid him down in it.

"*Danki* for your help," she said when she returned. "But that wasn't fair of me to let you help while you had your shop closed."

"Eli stopped in, so I took advantage of him. I thought you might like a break. Be right back."

Gideon went to the back of the shop and got the pastries and drinks. "I'm afraid the iced coffee isn't anymore." He handed her one then opened the box of pastries.

She smiled as she chose a whoopie pie, took a sip of her drink, and sat down on a stool behind the counter. "Delicious. And it's so *gut* to get off my feet."

"So what's Emma's *familye* emergency?" he asked as he bit into a whoopie pie. "I thought her *familye* wasn't speaking to her."

"Emma's *mudder* called. Her *dat* had a heart attack. Emma went to the hospital."

"I'm sorry to hear that. I hope he's going to be *allrecht*." He finished the whoopie pie in two bites. "Well, I'd best get back to the shop and let Eli go on about his day."

"Maybe he could go by the hospital and see if Emma needs a ride back here."

"That's a very *gut* idea." He stood. "I'll see you later."

Hannah stood as well. "*Danki* again. I don't know what I'd have done without your help. You were so *gut* with the ladies."

He glanced over at John asleep in his crib. "John did a lot of charming the ladies. Runs in the *familye*," he said wryly.

"Tell Eli *danki* for me."

He sighed, wishing he could stay longer. Leaning down, he kissed her cheek. "See you later."

She nodded. "Later."

* * *

Shop traffic was light the rest of the afternoon. After Hannah walked around returning bolts of fabric to their assigned places on shelves and display tables and doing general straightening up she sat at the quilt table and worked on the wedding ring quilt.

When John slept an hour past his usual time she leaned over and touched his forehead. He felt warm. A few minutes later he woke and cried out irritably.

"I'm right here," she crooned. "Did you have a nice nap?"

He rubbed his eyes and frowned.

"Your *mudder* will be back soon." She dug into the diaper bag and took out the thermometer—one of those fancy ones that you touched to the forehead. She frowned. It read one hundred. She talked to him while she did a diaper change, cleaned her hands with sanitizer, then dug out a bottle of juice. John sat on her lap and drank it but he continued to be cranky.

So she carried him around the shop and talked to him and watched the door, hoping Emma would return soon. She remembered how Emma had told her she occasionally felt less than confident taking care of John.

The shop phone rang. "Maybe that's your *mamm* now."

It was, but the news wasn't *gut*. "My *dat*'s in surgery," Emma said, her voice filled with tears. "I want to stay with *Mamm* if I can. Can you watch John for a while longer so I can be with her?"

"*Schur.* Don't you worry about a thing." Hannah bit her lip and debated whether to tell Emma that John had woken up feeling warm. But she pressed her lips to his forehead the way she'd seen her *mudder* do and found it cool. No need to worry Emma, she decided.

So when it came time to close the shop she locked the door, turned the sign from **Open** to **Closed**, and put John in his stroller so she could make up her bank deposit.

After a few minutes, Gideon knocked on her door. She walked over to let him in.

"Emma's still at the hospital," she told him as she locked the door again after he'd entered. "Her *dat*'s in surgery and she wanted to stay with her *mudder*. I said I'd watch John."

"It's *gut* that she stays," he told her. "Maybe they can heal their relationship. Eli is there with them. All I had to do was tell him what happened and he said he was going to join Emma at the hospital."

Gideon had been the support she'd needed that afternoon. It was nice to hear that his *bruder* was with Emma.

They waited outside for their ride, since the days were getting a little warmer. John sat in his stroller and stared wide-eyed at the cars driving past on the road in front of him.

When Liz pulled up in front of the shop in her van, he waved his hands in excitement. Hannah picked him up out of the stroller and had trouble holding on to the wriggling little bundle.

"I think John remembers riding in the van with us," Gideon said.

"Well, look who's here!" Liz exclaimed as she leaned over the seat to greet them. "I put the child seat in right after you called me, Hannah."

"Thank you so much. John's been helping me since you took Emma to the hospital."

"How's her father doing?"

"Emma called and said he was going into surgery, but I haven't heard anything since."

Hannah climbed into the van, set her purse and diaper bag on the floor, and got John settled into the car seat in the middle. It wasn't easy buckling him in when he was so excited, but she finally managed and then fastened her own seat belt. Gideon folded the stroller and put it in the back of the van with their lunch totes. Then he got in and buckled his seat belt.

With her passengers safely secured, Liz checked for traffic and then pulled out onto the road. "I told Emma I'd pray for him. My Hank had a stent put in last September and he's good as new. They're doing wonders catching heart problems early and fixing them these days."

As they rode home Hannah couldn't help thinking

about her own *dat*. He hadn't met John yet. What would he say when she walked in with him?

She glanced at Gideon and it was as if he read her mind. "Liz, I'm getting out with Hannah at her house."

Liz nodded. "No problem."

Hannah and Gideon kept their conversation confined to small talk about their day until Liz let them out at their stop. Gideon got the stroller and their lunch totes out while Hannah took care of getting John from his seat.

She waited until the van was on its way down the road before she turned to Gideon. "Staying for supper?" she asked wryly.

"Last time I didn't want you facing your *mudder* by yourself," he said as they walked up to the house. "I'm *schur* your *dat* is going to have some questions about John. You shouldn't have to face him alone."

"*Daed*'s not going to give me a hard time. He's not like Emma's *dat*."

"Then maybe I'll get lucky and your *mudder* will have made biscuits."

"I knew you had an ulterior motive."

He chuckled as he parked the stroller on the front porch. He watched her pick John up, and he opened the door for her. He followed her inside and gathered his courage as they walked to the kitchen.

"*Gut-n-owed*, Gideon," Lester boomed as they walked into the kitchen. He looked at John. "Well, well, who's this?"

"This is John, my *bruder*'s *boppli*," Gideon said

before Hannah could. "Eli and Emma are at the hospital. Emma's *dat* had a heart attack today."

"I hope he's *allrecht*," Mary said.

Hannah nodded. "Emma's *mudder* wanted her there so I said I'd take care of John."

Lester raised an eyebrow as he took a seat at the head of the table. "Well, *gut-n-owed*, John. So nice of you to join us for supper."

"Hello, Gideon," Mary said as she carried a platter heaped with fried chicken to the table and then set it down. "Are you staying for supper?"

"*Ya*, please," he said looking at the dish.

Hannah saw him glance at the stove. She knew what he was looking for.

Mary held out her arms to take John. "Hi, sweet *kind*! We're having fried chicken. Do you like it as much as your *onkel* Gideon does??"

Hannah laughed. "John has some strained vegetables for supper. He didn't do too well with carrots earlier," she told her, remembering how John had spit them up earlier that day. "He's had an ear infection and was a little warm but I think he's *allrecht* now."

"Lester, why don't you go get the highchair for John?"

"Let me do that," Gideon said. "Hannah can show me where it is."

"Suits me. I'll just sit here and get acquainted with John," Lester said easily.

"It was nice of you to offer to help with the chair," Hannah said as they climbed the stairs to the second floor.

"I don't want your *dat* carrying it and tripping on the stairs."

"Good point. But don't say that in front of him."

He looked at her. "Do you think I'm stupid?"

Hannah laughed and shook her head. "*Nee.*" She opened the door to her *schweschder* Linda's old room. "It's right there—" she began and found herself swept into Gideon's arms.

He kissed her, then grinned as he stepped back.

"*Nee*, not stupid," she murmured. "Sneaky but not stupid."

Gideon picked up the highchair and headed for the stairs. "It'll be interesting to see what your *dat* has to say about John."

"I'm telling you, he isn't like Emma's *dat.*"

"We'll see."

When they returned to the kitchen Lester glanced at them. "Found it *allrecht*, did you?"

Hannah felt herself blushing.

"Where shall I set this?" Gideon asked Mary.

"Put it right there where Hannah sits," she said, gesturing at a chair.

He set it down then took the basket of biscuits she held. "Let me take that for you, Mary. It looks heavy." He grinned at Hannah. "Looks like this is my lucky night. I can't resist your biscuits, Mary."

"Seems that's not all you can't resist," Lester said.

Hannah felt her blush deepen as she saw his mouth twitch at the corners.

Chapter Nineteen

Emma sat in the hospital waiting room with her *mudder* and couldn't help thinking how strange it felt. She couldn't have been more surprised when her *mudder* called Hannah's shop and asked to speak to her.

It didn't make any sense to her that her *mudder* would want her at the hospital, not after her *eldres* turned her away when she first came back to town. Emma wondered if it was because, as she was the eldest *kind*, her *mudder* had always relied on her help. Deep in her heart Emma hoped her *mudder* was softening about John, although if her *dat* recovered and still didn't accept him that could change.

In any event it just wasn't in Emma to refuse her *mudder* when she sounded so terrified. Now as they sat in the hospital's surgical waiting room and waited to hear news she was glad she'd come. Her *dat* was a man of such strong will she couldn't envision him being felled by anything. Why, she couldn't remember him being sick a day in her life.

But here they were, watching the minutes tick by so slowly on the clock on the wall. A 100 percent blockage in one artery, the doctor had told her *mudder* as she sat with her. Surgery had to be performed immediately, and he was worried about her *dat*'s high blood pressure. The doctor had talked of something called a stent, and her *mudder* had just stared at him, looking bewildered. So Emma focused hard on the doctor's words, and she'd been the one to ask the questions. And after he'd rushed out of the room to do the surgery, she'd felt like they'd reversed the usual *eldre/kind* roles as she explained things to her *mudder*.

So she sat beside the woman she hadn't thought she'd ever speak to again and prayed with her while they waited. She fixed her cups of tea from the beverage station set up on a table on one side of the room and worried over how pale and thin and...*old* her *mudder* looked. There were so many gray hairs on her head, so many lines etched on her pale face. How was it possible that she had aged so much in the time that Emma had been in Ohio?

"*Mamm*, you need to eat something. You've been here all day."

Lillian shook her head. "I couldn't. Go get something if you want it."

"*Nee*, I'll wait. The doctor should be out soon."

She hoped.

Finally the doctor came in and sank into a chair in front of them. "Your husband came through the surgery just fine, Mrs. Graber. He's in recovery now. A nurse will come for you when you can see him."

"He's going to be all right?" she asked as if she couldn't believe what he was saying.

He nodded. "You got him here in time. If he does what we tell him he should be around for a good, long time."

"He's awfully stubborn."

The doctor chuckled and patted her hand. "I saw that. He tried to argue with me about having the angiogram. Said he was feeling better and he wanted to go home. I said he could do that. But I told him that generally the patients who did that came back later the same day and they were in worse shape. So he decided he'd stay for the test. When he heard the results—that an artery *was* a hundred percent blocked and he was lucky to be here, he apologized for giving me a hard time."

"I'd like to have seen that," Lillian blurted out. "The man's never apologized to me once in all the years we've been married."

Then she glanced at Emma and bit her lip. "I shouldn't have said that. It's wrong for a wife to speak ill about her husband."

"But it's true," Emma told her.

Lillian nodded and sighed.

"Well, hopefully he'll use that stubborn will to follow our instructions for cardiac recovery," the doctor said.

He looked at Emma. "After you both see him, I suggest you take your mother home and make her take care of herself. I expect that your father will be able to go home tomorrow or the next day, and she'll need every ounce of energy to see that he doesn't overdo it. You both have a good evening."

"Thank you, Doctor," they said in unison.

"You're very welcome." He rose and left the room.

Lillian stared at the empty doorway for a long moment and then burst into tears.

It was the first time that Emma had ever seen her *mudder* break down.

So she'd gathered her *mudder*'s frail body against her and let her cry. Finally, the storm passed. Emma reached for the box of tissues on the table beside her and handed it to her *mudder*. Then Emma used some tissues to dry her own tears.

"Your *dat* scared me to death collapsing like he did. He was in such pain and he had trouble breathing. I was so afraid to leave him. Your *bruder* Ike was still at the kitchen table. I sent him out to the phone shanty to call nine-one-one. He did and when he came back in he said the woman on the phone told him to tell me what to do, to keep your *dat* quiet, do CPR if he stopped breathing, and stay calm. And then Ike said he was going to go stand in the front of the house to flag down the ambulance when it came." She glanced at Emma. "Ike's a bright *bu*. I've been able to trust him to help with the *kinner* since you've been gone."

"He is." Emma blew her nose, rose to toss the used tissues in the wastepaper basket, then returned to her chair.

"I've sat in the emergency room waiting room with

one or another of my *kinner* so many times," Lillian said. "Never once had to come here for something for your *dat*."

"Ike was always breaking something."

"Where's your *boppli*?"

"Hannah's watching him for me. Listen, *Mamm*, really, you need to eat something."

Lillian shook her head. "I couldn't. The nurse should be here soon."

The room was so quiet Emma could hear the minutes ticking by on the wall clock.

"Why didn't you tell me?" Lillian asked suddenly.

"What?"

Lillian turned to her. "Why didn't you tell me that you were pregnant?"

Emma stared at her. She knew she should have expected the question but when it hadn't come in the first hour she'd been here and she'd seen how worried her *mudder* had been, she'd figured it wouldn't be asked.

"If I'd told you then you would have had to tell my *dat*, and *he* would have thrown me out of the house. You know he would. If he knew I was here right now he probably wouldn't be happy."

"But to just leave without telling anyone where you were going." She stared at her hands folded in her lap. "I was worried sick until I found the note you left."

"I'm sorry—" she began, when a deep voice interrupted her.

"It's not her fault."

* * *

Eli stepped into the room. "It's not Emma's fault. It was mine. I didn't support her."

He saw both women look up at him but he focused his attention on Emma. "I let you down when you needed me the most. I can't change what I did. But I want to make up for it."

"So, you're the *dat*," Lillian said.

"I am."

"What do you intend to do?" Lillian Graber's tone was tart, her eyes direct on him.

He met her gaze. "I've asked Emma to marry me but she's not *schur* she can trust me."

"Well, she'd have reason for that, wouldn't she?"

"True," he agreed, surprised at her bluntness. Lillian had always seemed like a quiet woman cowed by her *mann*. "But a man can change. *This* man can change."

"Now's not the time for this," Emma told him.

"*Nee*, you're right. How is Abraham?"

"The doctor just came in and told us *Daed* came through the surgery to insert a stent just fine. *Mamm*'s waiting for the nurse to take her to see him."

"That's *gut*. He's a strong man. I'm *schur* he'll be fine now." He took off his hat and sat in the chair that the doctor had vacated.

An awkward silence fell over the room.

"Is there anything I can get you?" Eli asked Lillian.

She shook her head and kept her eyes on the doorway.

"I tried to get *Mamm* to get something to eat but she wouldn't," Emma said.

"I can't eat. Not until I see Abraham."

Eli watched Emma rise and walk over to a table where there were pots of coffee and hot water. He joined her and poured himself a cup of coffee. "Are you *allrecht*?" he asked quietly.

She nodded. "I'm fine." She fixed a cup of tea and added creamer and two packets of sugar. Then she carried it to her mother and pressed it into her hands. "Drink this, *Mamm*."

"*Danki*." She sipped it, then winced. "How much sugar did you put in here?"

"Enough to keep you going until you eat."

Lillian shivered. "Why do they keep it so cold in hospitals?"

Emma started to take off her sweater but Eli shook his head. He set his coffee on a nearby table, rose, and took off the jacket he wore. He draped it over Lillian's shoulders.

She glanced up in surprise but didn't refuse the jacket. "*Danki*, Eli." She sipped her tea. "Is your *mudder* still visiting her *schweschder* in Ohio?" she asked politely.

"She's home now."

A nurse walked in and Lillian jumped to her feet, nearly spilling what was left of her tea.

"Mrs. Graber, you can see your husband for a few minutes now."

She set the cup of tea down on a table and turned to Emma. "Can my daughter come, too?"

"No, *Mamm*. It's best if I don't see him now," Emma said quietly. "I don't want him to get upset in his condition."

Lillian studied her for a long moment and then she nodded. "You might be right." She handed Eli his jacket and left the room with the nurse.

"I was surprised when Gideon told me your *mudder* called Hannah's shop and asked you to come here."

"*You* were surprised? Imagine how I felt." She rose to pace the room. "I almost didn't come. I mean, when I went to see her and my *dat* he told her to shut the door and she did."

"But you couldn't not come when she called. Your heart is too big."

She sighed. "It's not our way." She sank down in her chair. "She was so scared. When I saw that, when she thanked me for coming, I couldn't be mad."

"What happens now?"

"What do you mean?"

"Will you go stay with them?"

She shook her head. "You must be joking. My *dat* won't allow that."

Eli didn't know what to say. She looked up every time someone walked past the room but no one else came in. He reached out and took her hands. They were ice-cold. So he got up and put his jacket around her shoulders, then went to the table with the hot drinks and made her a fresh cup of tea.

"Here," he said and put the cup in her hands.

She looked up at him, surprised.

"Your hands are like ice. If you don't want to drink it, at least hold the cup and get warmed up."

She sipped at the tea. "Shouldn't be much longer.

Doctor said *Mamm* could only see him for a few minutes in the recovery room."

He shrugged. "I'm not going anywhere."

"*Danki* for coming."

"You should have called me."

She shrugged. "I'm used to doing things on my own."

He put his hand on her arm. "Emma, let me in. Let me take care of you and John."

Lillian appeared in the doorway. Emma stood and Eli's hand fell away.

"Your *dat* woke up for a few minutes," Lillian said. "Complained about being here. Wanted to know when he could go home. Then he fell back asleep. Nurse said he'll sleep until morning and I should go home now."

She pressed her fingers to her trembling lips. "He's hooked up to all these machines."

Emma hurried to her side and slipped her arm around her *mudder*'s waist. "*Mamm*, the doctor said he did well and can go home tomorrow or the next day."

Eli stood. "I'll take you home. You need to get some rest. Both of you."

Lillian nodded. "*Danki*, Eli."

The three of them left the waiting room and made their way out of the hospital and to the parking lot where Eli's buggy was parked.

Emma insisted her *mudder* sit in the front seat and she got into the back. An awkward silence fell again as they rode to Lillian's house. When they got there Lillian and Emma got out.

"Lillian, I'll be happy to take you to get Abraham

from the hospital when he's ready. If you think it won't upset him. I mean, that Emma and I..." He trailed off, not knowing how to phrase it.

"*Danki*, Eli. I appreciate it. I'll think about it and let you know."

Emma walked her *mudder* to the door and stood there talking to her for a few moments, then she returned to the buggy and got into the front seat.

"You *allrecht*?" he asked her when she remained silent as he turned down the road to Hannah's house. "Emma?"

When she said nothing, he turned to look at her and realized she was just sitting there, her hands twisted together in her lap, trembling.

He pulled over onto the shoulder of the road and pulled her into his arms.

"I thought he was going to die," she sobbed. "I tried so hard to comfort *Mamm* and tell her *Daed* was going to be fine. But I thought he was going to die and I'd never have forgiven myself because we had this...this hardness between us."

"You can cry now," he said as he patted her back. "You don't have to hold it all in anymore, my brave girl."

She took a shuddering breath and drew back. Eli pulled a bandanna from his pocket and dried her tears with it.

"This is my fault," she said quietly. "It wouldn't have happened if I hadn't come back. If I hadn't stopped by the house with John."

"What kind of nonsense is this?" he demanded.

"There's no way it's your fault! Don't you dare blame yourself for that."

Emma sank back against her seat looking so sad and defeated, it made him feel guilty for sounding harsh. "I'm sorry. Let me take you someplace and get you something to eat. I bet you haven't eaten all day."

She shook her head. "I want John. Can we go get John?"

Chapter Twenty

That's some appetite," Hannah's *dat* said.

Hannah watched Gideon freeze as he reached for his third biscuit. He glanced guiltily at the man, then saw Lester grinning at John.

Hannah smiled as she fed John a spoonful of applesauce. "Look who's talking. *Daed*, how many pieces of fried chicken have you eaten?"

Lester chuckled. "Who's counting?" he asked as he added another chicken leg to his plate. "Your *mamm* makes the best."

"And the best biscuits," Gideon said as he buttered one. He glanced at Hannah and grinned as he bit into it.

There was a knock on the door.

"*Kumm!*" Lester bellowed.

"Lester!" Mary admonished, getting up to answer

it. "Why, Emma, since when do you knock when you come here?"

Emma stepped inside. "Good evening, everyone. I came to pick up John."

Mary hugged her. "How is your *dat*?"

"He came through the surgery well. The doctor said he may get to go home tomorrow."

"I'm glad to hear it."

John banged his hands on the tray of the highchair. Emma moved swiftly to his side and bent to kiss his cheek. "Have you been a *gut boppli*?"

"He's always *gut*," Hannah assured her. "He ate a lot for supper."

"Where's Eli?"

She turned to Gideon. "Waiting for me in the buggy."

"Have you eaten?" Mary asked.

Emma shook her head. "I didn't want to leave *Mamm* and she wouldn't go to the cafeteria to get anything with me."

"Then sit and eat. We've got plenty."

Hannah smiled as Mary didn't take no for an answer, gently pushing Emma into a chair, getting her a plate and silverware, and fussing over her. She'd told her *mudder* that Emma was staying in a motel room and that she was worried about how Emma was managing.

Then Mary went to the door, opened it, and stepped outside to holler Eli's name. A few moments later he stepped inside the room. Mary made him sit, and handed him a plate and silverware before she sat to finish her own meal.

Hannah watched Eli give her *dat* a wary look as he accepted the platter of fried chicken he handed him. Eli didn't look entirely *schur* of his welcome from the man of the house as he was passed the big bowl of mashed potatoes.

Eli didn't know that it wasn't her *dat*'s way to make a guest at his table uncomfortable. Now if Eli didn't do the right thing by Emma and John he'd speak up later, but not when he was sharing a meal in his house.

Emma looked too pale and her eyes were red from crying. She'd chosen a wing and barely nibbled at it and the small portions of mashed potatoes and gravy and green beans. Hannah met her *mudder*'s gaze and knew that leftovers would be sent home with Emma to eat later when she felt more like it.

"Uh-oh," Gideon said. Hannah glanced at him. He jerked his head at John, who'd used her lack of attention to push his hands into his dish of applesauce and smear it all over his face and hair.

"John! What have you done!" she cried, but she couldn't help laughing when he just giggled at her and finger-painted the applesauce all over the tray of the highchair.

"Time to get you cleaned up," she announced and rose to pick him up.

"I can do it," Emma began, but Mary touched her hand.

"Eat, *kind*, you look like a breeze would knock you over right now," Mary said quietly.

John gurgled happily as Hannah carried him past

Gideon, who moved out of the reach of his sticky hands. When John wriggled and wanted his *mudder*, Hannah bent to let him give Emma a kiss.

But as Hannah walked past Eli and he looked up to smile at his *sohn* she noticed that John sobered and drew closer to her. She felt sad as she saw the look of disappointment on Eli's face, which he hid quickly by staring down at his plate. John was still showing he liked Gideon more. Well, she had to hope that would change as he got to know his *dat* better.

Hannah carried John upstairs and undressed him. She put him in a tub of warm water and bathed him, washing the applesauce out of his hair. He splashed gleefully and whimpered a little when she lifted him out, but he was easily distracted by a plush toy when she lay him on the bed to dry him. She glanced down at her dress. There were damp splotches all down the front of it.

"I think I got as wet as you did, John." She chuckled as she dried him off and dressed him in a warm sleeper and a sweater. "You are such a wiggle worm!"

"He can't stay still for a moment," Emma said as she walked into the room. "He's always been that way."

Hannah handed John to her. "All ready for you."

"*Danki* for everything today. I don't know what I'd have done if you hadn't watched him."

"It was my pleasure. I hope you can get some rest tonight."

They walked downstairs, and Hannah held John again for a few precious moments so Emma could don her jacket and bonnet. Then John got wrapped in a warm blanket and Emma carried him out to the buggy, where Eli waited. Hannah couldn't help feeling disappointed that Gideon had left without saying goodbye.

Hannah gently nudged her *mudder* aside at the sink. "Go fix yourself a cup of coffee and sit down. You went to a lot of trouble feeding all of us."

"You've had a longer day than me working at the shop and taking care of John," Mary said, but she moved aside and poured herself a cup of coffee.

"I'm not tired. John brightens the day."

"Hannah, I noticed that John...likes Gideon more than Eli."

She nodded and sighed. "I think it's just because Gideon spent more time with him when they first arrived here."

"Gideon seems to act easier around him," Mary said slowly, as if she was choosing her words carefully. "I don't mean to criticize Eli, but he's awkward with John and so John responds better to Gideon..." She trailed off.

"I think John will accept him more after Eli spends more time with him." But she'd noticed as well how John had shied away from Eli as she carried him past his *dat*.

She plunged her hands into the dishwater and was surprised when Gideon came through the kitchen door. "I thought you'd gone."

He shook his head. "I went out to help your *dat* in the barn. I figured Eli and Emma needed to talk. I can walk home. If I can wash my hands I'll dry."

"*Allrecht*." She moved over a little so he could use the left sink and watched him scrub and then rinse his hands. How strong and capable those hands were, she couldn't help thinking. Yet they could help take care of John with ease, and create such marvelous toys for *kinner*.

Gideon picked up a dish towel and waited for her to hand him a plate to dry. One eyebrow went up when she continued to stare at his hands. "Hannah?"

She recovered and handed him a plate. A glance at her *mudder* a few feet away had her blushing. Mary winked at her then took her coffee and left the room, leaving the two of them alone.

Gideon watched Mary leave, then he turned to her. "I stayed because I wanted to talk to you," he said.

Hannah glanced at him and saw his expression was serious. "Is something wrong?"

"I saw Ruby walk past my shop today," he said. "I wondered if she stopped by your shop to talk to you and Emma today."

She nodded and sighed.

"Tell me what she said."

Chapter Twenty-One

Emma leaned back against the buggy seat as Eli drove them home from supper at Hannah's house.

"Long day."

She looked over and watched Eli hold the reins easily in one hand. "I'll say. *Danki* for coming to the hospital. I know it wasn't easy facing my *mudder*."

"It had to be harder for you."

"I thought it would be," she said thoughtfully as she looked down at her hands folded in her lap. "But she was so upset. And I wonder if she was a little afraid of calling a friend. She hasn't had a lot of time outside of home to really make them. My *bruders* and *schweschders* keep her busy and my *dat* is . . . well, hardly welcoming."

"The women of the church would have come," he

told her. "They will come to help her with whatever she needs when they hear what's happened to your *dat*. I imagine Mary will start making calls first thing in the morning."

Emma looked at the tote bag sitting on the seat between them. "It was kind of her to send home leftovers from supper."

"You don't eat enough to feed a bird. You've lost weight."

She shrugged. "New *mudders* do sometimes. A *boppli* keeps us busy."

When he said nothing for several long minutes she glanced over and saw him frown. "What?"

He shook his head. "It's nothing."

"If it's really nothing then tell me."

"John likes Gideon more than me."

It sounded so silly. Kind of like when you told your *bruder* or *schweschder*, "*Mamm* likes you best." She almost laughed. But she could see it really bothered him.

"Why do you say that?"

"Didn't you see him shy away from me when Hannah walked past me?"

"That doesn't mean he likes Gideon more. Sometimes *bopplin* have moods and they aren't exactly friendly. It doesn't mean anything."

"This wasn't the first time I felt he didn't want to be with me."

"I know. But he doesn't know you as well as Gideon. Give him time."

They passed her house and she stared at the darkened windows. She hoped that meant that her *mudder* had gone to bed and was sleeping. The tears began again.

"Emma?"

She shook her head and turned away from him. "I shouldn't have come back. This wouldn't have happened if I hadn't come back."

"We talked about this earlier, Emma. You can't blame yourself."

She used her hands to wipe away her tears. "I'm just so tired." She stared out the window.

"Try to go to bed when you get to the motel."

She glanced into the back seat. "I intend to. But that'll depend on John," she said ruefully.

"He's not sleeping through the night?"

"He usually does but with him sleeping right now . . . I don't know if he'll cooperate with me wanting to go to bed early."

"I wish there was something I could do."

She turned back to look at him. "You did. I appreciated you coming to the hospital today."

He surprised her when he reached for her hand and kissed it. "I intend on being there for you from now on, Emma." He pulled to the right and let a car pass the buggy. "Do you need anything? Diapers for John? Anything? I can run in a store while you wait in the buggy."

"*Nee*, *danki*, we're fine."

He pulled into the motel parking lot and stopped. Almost immediately she heard John stir in his seat in the back.

"Hey, John, we're home," Emma told him as she got out then unbuckled his seat. "Home sweet home."

Eli followed her with the stroller filled with her purse, diaper bag, and the tote filled with supper leftovers and pushed it inside the room.

"Well, I'll see you tomorrow," he told her as he leaned down to kiss her.

John pushed his hands against Eli's chest and Emma chuckled. "Doesn't want to share his *mudder*," she told Eli.

"Well, get used to it," Eli told him. "I'm sticking around." He kissed Emma again and this time John didn't push him away. "Tomorrow."

"Eli?"

"Hmm?" He lingered close, his gaze on her lips.

"Don't expect my *mudder* to call you to pick her and my *dat* up at the hospital when he's discharged. I'm not *schur* it would be *gut* for him to know you're John's *dat* right now."

"You're probably right." He shrugged. "It's fine. If she wants my help I'll be there. It's up to her. Night."

Emma watched him walk to his buggy then turned and closed the door. "Well, John, how do you feel about going to bed early?"

He chuckled and patted her cheeks.

"Somebody is wide awake," she said and sighed. "I have a feeling it's going to be a long night."

She set him in his crib and gave him some toys to play with. Then she began the task of getting ready to go to bed. The leftovers went into the mini-fridge in the room. She packed the diaper bag with supplies for the next day. Then she took off her *kapp*, brushed out her hair, and changed into a flannel nightgown. She hung up her dress in the tiny closet and sighed over how few clothes she had and how worn they looked.

John banged his toy against the bars of the crib. Emma felt a pang of guilt watching him play in the small portable crib the motel had provided. She wanted to put him down to practice his crawling around some, but she just couldn't make herself do it. The carpeting looked clean, but it was so old and worn. She sighed. Well, this was temporary, she told herself.

"Night-night time," she said as she laid him down and covered him with his blanket. "Time to go to sleep. We're going to Hannah's tomorrow to make up time I missed today being with your *grossmudder* at the hospital. We want to be rested."

He popped up immediately and grinned at her.

She settled him down and tucked him in again and turned to climb into her bed. It felt *gut* to rest her weary body. The quilt that served as a spread was thin and faded, but it comforted her, reminding her of the one that had topped her bed as she grew up.

Home, she thought. Soon she hoped she and John would have a home of their own, not this small, temporary space in town. She leaned over to turn off the bedside lamp and saw John was staring at her as he lay in his crib sucking his thumb. "Night, Johnny," she whispered, and promptly fell asleep.

* * *

"Waiting up for me, *Mamm*?" Eli asked sarcastically as he walked into the kitchen and shed his hat and jacket.

Gideon looked up from carving a toy as he sat at the table. "Very funny." He set the wood and his carving knife down. "We need to talk." He glanced at the doorway to the living room to make *schur* their *mudder* wasn't around.

"I don't need another lecture," Eli said tiredly as he touched the side of the percolator, found it still warm, and poured himself a cup of coffee.

"The bishop's wife paid Hannah a visit at the shop today," Gideon told him quietly. "Hannah said she was obviously hoping to find Emma there."

Eli muttered something under his breath and shook his head. He pulled out a chair and sat at the table. He ran a hand through his hair. "It's not fair to give Emma a hard time. Why didn't Ruby come talk to me? Why hasn't Abram?"

"They don't know you're the *dat*."

He sighed. "True. I'll go talk to Abram."

"He's sick with the flu."

"So Ruby's the messenger?"

Gideon stared at him. "Does it matter who is talking to Emma?"

"*Nee*." He sighed. "I'll call Abram tomorrow, explain the situation. If he's too ill to see me I'll talk to Ruby."

"That would be a *gut* step," Gideon said carefully.

"But it's just the first step. I know." He stared into his

coffee. "I didn't need this tonight. How do you think I felt seeing John want you and not me? And he didn't do it just once. When I went to kiss Emma good night he pushed me away."

"So you'll have to win your *sohn* over, not just his *mudder*. You can do it. You've always had more charm than I have."

Eli snorted out a laugh. "True."

"John just spent more time with me at first. You can fix that now."

He nodded. "Emma said he doesn't know me as well as you. She told me to give him time."

Gideon yawned and decided it was time to call it a night. He packed up his tools and the toy and set them aside. "See you in the morning."

"*Ya*." Eli finished his coffee, washed the mug, and headed up to bed.

But sleep didn't come quickly. He tossed and turned, unable to stop thinking about the day. Life had suddenly become so complicated. He had always gone through life pretty much taking things easy, unlike his more serious *bruder*. Now it felt like it had backfired on him.

Disgusted with himself, he punched his pillow into a more comfortable shape and willed himself to sleep.

* * *

Dawn came too early.

He dressed and went downstairs. His *mudder* was already at the stove cooking breakfast.

"Morning." He knew his greeting came out grumpier than it should when she frowned.

"Something wrong?" she asked.

"Sorry, didn't get much sleep." He gulped coffee and burned his tongue. "Going to do chores."

"I'm making pancakes. That should cheer you up."

He nodded. "*Danki.*"

He headed out the door and took care of the horses, then stood looking out at the fields as dawn broke. It's a new day, he thought. And here he was doing work he loved.

His mood brightened as he walked his fields and remembered all the times his *dat* had taken him and Gideon out to show them how to plant seeds in the rich soil and nurture the plants that sprung up from them. He'd learned so much about farming and weather. The value of hard work. And how to trust that God would always provide in *gut* times and bad.

He wanted to teach his *sohn* those things and have more *kinner* with Emma, enjoy the kind of *familye* life on this farm that they'd held for generations.

Last night he'd been upset that John hadn't been friendly to him. Emma and Gideon had both said that he just needed to spend more time with his *sohn*. So today he'd find a way. Make that step toward righting things between him and Emma.

As he walked back to the house he remembered how Emma had told John they were home when they got to the motel. He'd make her see that he loved her. That she could depend on him. That he'd provide a home for her and their *sohn*. The home they deserved.

He couldn't wait to see them again.

But first he had to make the call to the bishop. His *mudder* knew about John, but he decided he wanted some privacy and veered off to use the phone shanty instead of making the call on his cell in the house.

Ruby answered and didn't seem surprised by his call. She told him she'd noticed the two of them going off together after church a few times before Emma left the community. She said Abram was napping but that he had already talked to Elmer and the lay minister would marry the couple.

"Talk to Elmer and set it up quickly," she told him firmly.

"I will. Tell Abram *danki* and I hope he feels better soon."

Relieved, he went inside the house to shower and put on clothes for a visit to town. When he went to hitch Ned to the buggy he saw that Emma had accidentally left John's blanket in the back seat. As he climbed into the buggy he wondered how he was going to persuade Emma to marry him—let alone quickly, as Ruby wanted him to. And how he would get John to respond to him the way he did with Gideon, to want to come to him.

He was on his way into town when he heard the wail of a siren behind him. After he guided the buggy to the right to allow it to pass he watched it turn down the road in front of him. He frowned, thinking of the *familyes* he knew who lived down that way. So he said a quick prayer as he checked traffic and eased back onto the road to town.

When he got into Paradise he stopped in at Gideon's first. His *bruder* made wooden toys, but he also stocked soft-cloth toys made by a number of talented Amish women in their community. Maybe he could find something for John.

"Well, what brings you into town?" Gideon asked when he walked in.

"Thought I'd throw some business your way," he said, looking at the display window.

"You want to buy a toy?"

"Got a *sohn* now, don't I?"

Gideon nodded slowly. "That you do. You know where the toys are for *kinner* under two. I'm going to take a quick break while you're here."

"That's fine."

Eli browsed the baby and toddler section and found just what he wanted. What could be better than a collection of little stuffed farm animals? He carried them up to the front and tucked them into a small shopping bag, then counted out the cash he owed Gideon.

His *bruder* walked over, carrying a mug of coffee. "Find what you wanted?"

"Waneta's stuffed farm animals. Here's the money."

"You don't have to pay for them."

"*Ya*, I do." He picked up the bag and rounded the counter. "See you later."

"*Danki* for the break."

"You're *wilkumm*. See you later."

Eli was halfway to Hannah's when he realized he was passing a florist shop. It wasn't just John he hoped to win over...so he went inside and had a harder time choosing flowers for Emma than he did toys for John.

A display of arrangements obviously made for new mothers caught his eye. He felt a stab of guilt as he looked at the china baby bootie filled with silk roses. Gifts to a new Amish *mudder* were more practical than flowers...meals so she wouldn't have to cook, help with housework, or the *kinner*.

He hadn't been present to give Emma anything at all when she delivered John. Nothing. Not even emotional support. All she'd had was her friend in Ohio.

"Can I help you?" A smiling *Englisch* woman appeared at his side. "You're Eli, right? Gideon's twin?"

"Yes. People don't always get us straight."

"I see him more often than most since we have shops close to each other. He's the more serious of you two, carries himself a little differently."

He could sense her curiosity about the flowers but didn't ask any questions. Most of the time the local *Englisch* allowed them privacy.

"I'll take this," he told her handing her the bootie.

"It's lovely, isn't it? My assistant does these. And such a practical gift, too. Silk flowers will last forever."

They should at that price, he thought. But Emma deserved them and more. He watched the woman tuck the arrangement into a shopping bag. Then, armed with his gifts, he headed down to the quilt shop.

He'd timed it just right. Emma sat on the bench in front of the shop with John in his stroller.

"What's all that?" she asked when she saw the bags.

"I got you both something." He sat and put the bag with the flower arrangement in her lap. Then he pulled out a stuffed cow and handed it to John. "Moo cow," he told him.

John's eyes lit up and he grabbed it and immediately stuffed it into his mouth.

"He thinks he's supposed to eat everything."

"I thought he should get to know farm animals," he told her. "He's a farmer's *sohn*. There's a chicken and a horse and a pig and a lamb."

"You bought him toys."

"So he'll get used to them. One day he'll take care of the real ones on the farm, right?"

He watched emotions chase across her face. "I—" she broke off as if she didn't know what to say. She glanced down at the bag in her lap.

"I got you something, too. Not farm animals."

She lifted out the arrangement and her eyes went wide. "Oh, how pretty." She stroked the silk petals.

"I wasn't there when John was born. You didn't have my support. You didn't have your *familye*. Flowers won't make up for that, but I wanted you to have them." He took a deep breath. "I want you to marry me, Emma, and let's make a *familye* together, the three of us."

Tears began sliding down her cheeks.

"Don't make us wait any longer, Emma. Let's get married. Soon."

She nodded. "*Ya*," she said slowly. "I'll marry you."

Chapter Twenty-Two

Gideon walked into the kitchen when he got home from work and was startled to see his *mudder* sitting at the table crying.

He dumped his hat and lunch tote on the bench by the door and rushed over to her. "What's the matter? Is it Emma's *dat*?"

She shook her head. "Abram died."

Gideon sank down into the chair beside her. "I thought he was getting better."

"Ruby said he laid down for a nap and passed in his sleep." She pulled a tissue from her pocket. "I just heard."

"He was only what, sixty?"

Leah nodded, then rose to fill the teakettle with water and set it on the stove. After she adjusted the gas flame she sat again. "We never know when God will call us home."

She'd know that better than most, he thought. Her *mann*—his and Eli's *dat*—had only been fifty-five when he'd died.

Gideon noticed that there was no sign of supper cooking. "Why don't I fix supper for us tonight?"

"I think I'll let you. Want some tea?"

"Nee, danki."

When the teakettle whistled she turned the gas flame off beneath it, poured a mug of hot water, and brought it to the table. "I was planning on making spaghetti and meatballs."

"One of my specialties," he said with a grin.

His *bruder* liked to tease him that he made it often, but it was a favorite meal of theirs. He got a skillet out, poured a little oil into it, and heated it. Then he got the ingredients out for meatballs and began making them.

"Eli came into town to take Emma and John out to supper." He remembered why his *bruder* had visited his shop and what he'd seen afterward and decided to share it with his *mudder*. "He bought John some stuffed animals. He seemed...kind of anxious about something."

He put meatballs in the skillet and turned to her. *"Mamm*, I walked out to sweep the sidewalk in front of the shop after he left and saw him coming out of the florist."

She came to attention and met his gaze. "The florist? He bought flowers? Do you think..."

"That he's going to ask Emma to marry him again?" He shook the pan as the meatballs began to sizzle. "I hope so."

"And what about you?"

"What about me?" He filled a pot with water and set it on a burner to boil.

"Have you given some more thought to asking Hannah to marry you?"

He'd thought of little else since they'd talked. He rummaged in the cupboard and found a box of spaghetti but no jars of sauce. "Gotta go down to the basement and get some spaghetti sauce."

"How convenient," she said drily.

Gideon went down the stairs and found a jar of sauce. He thought about dawdling in hopes his *mudder* would be gone from the room and he wouldn't have to answer her question, but he'd left food cooking on the stove. When he returned to the kitchen his *mudder* was adding the spaghetti to the boiling water.

He opened the jar and poured the sauce into a pan to heat, then he used a slotted spoon to scoop up the cooked meatballs, and set them on a paper towel covered plate to drain. His *mudder* was better at slicing bread than he was, so he put the loaf on a cutting board in front of her when she sat down at the table to finish her tea. When he saw she was watching him instead of slicing the bread he busied himself getting a dish of butter from the refrigerator and pouring glasses of iced tea.

"Well?"

Were all *mudders* relentless? He sighed inwardly. His *schur* was. "Well what?" he stalled as he added the meatballs to the sauce.

"Are you going to ask Hannah to marry you?"

"I need to think about how to ask her. It's important to do it right." He remembered the man in the restaurant that night and how he'd made his proposal look romantic by getting down on one knee. Gideon didn't think he had that in him, but he wanted the moment he asked Hannah to be memorable.

"*Gut.*" She got plates from the cupboard and began setting the table. "I remember when your *dat* asked me to marry him."

"*Ya?*" He leaned against the counter and looked at her.

She gazed off into the distance and smiled. "He didn't have much money back then. So one day after church he brought me back here to the farm and had this basket of food he'd packed—just sandwiches and such. We walked down to the little pond at the back of the property, had a picnic and talked about our hopes and dreams, and suddenly he was asking me to marry him."

"You never told me that story."

She chuckled "Boys don't like to hear romantic stories about their *eldres.*"

Gideon tested a strand of spaghetti and found that it was done. He drained it, poured it into a big bowl, and set it on the table with a bowl of the warmed sauce with meatballs.

"I guess not."

"Well, sounds like your *bruder* went to some effort to make his proposal romantic," Leah mused as she twined spaghetti around her fork. "Toys for John—"

"That's romantic?"

"In its own way. I'm *schur* Emma appreciated him doing something for their *boppli*. He needs to prove he loves John. Going to the doctor the day John had the ear infection went a long way to making her see he wants to be his *dat* and a *mann* to her." She buttered a slice of bread and added it to her plate. "Flowers were a nice touch. Wonder what kind he bought her."

"I couldn't see. He was carrying them in a bag."

"Well, it sounds like he had a plan. Let's hope it works."

"It probably did. Eli's always been the one with charm."

"You have your own charm," she told him. "It's quieter and more thoughtful. But it's there."

"You're just saying that because you're my *mudder*."

She shook her head "Hannah finds you charming, I'm *schur*."

He shrugged. "I don't know about that." But she did look at him in a way no other *maedel* had done.

"Have you given Hannah flowers lately? Done anything thoughtful?"

"*Ya*. Of course." But it had been a while. And it wouldn't do to tell her he'd taken them from her garden.

Eli had had a plan. Well, Gideon was no dummy. He'd think of a plan too, and while he didn't think he had the charm his *mudder* thought he did, he'd do his best asking Hannah to marry him. He still didn't think he had much to offer her, but as his *mudder* had reminded him, they didn't know how much time we had on this earth.

He looked at his *mudder* and saw she'd stopped eating and was staring off into the distance. "What?"

"I'm just wondering if I planted enough celery in the kitchen garden."

* * *

On Saturday, Hannah stood outside the bishop's barn watching the long line of buggies arriving for the funeral service for Abram.

So many of Abram's fellow Amish would be attending that it was necessary to have the service inside the barn rather than his home. Hannah and other women from the church had visited Ruby and supplied emotional support and food. And everyone—women as well as men—had pitched in and done the daily chores since he died.

Gideon, Eli, and the other men had helped to unload the benches from the wagon and set them up in the barn. Then they'd gone home, cleaned up and changed, and returned.

Now Gideon was helping people park their buggies, and occasionally their gazes met. Eli seemed more solemn than usual, but that was to be expected when the leader of their faith was soon to be taken to his final resting place.

People filed into the barn and took seats. Hannah joined them and felt a stab of sympathy for Ruby as she entered leaning heavily on the arm of her oldest *sohn*. Hannah knew Ruby had taken her *mann*'s death hard because she'd believed him to be recovering from the flu.

The service began with a prayer as it would end with one. Elmer gave the sermon and the assemblage sang the hymns "Walking with God" and "Take My Hand and Lead Me, Father" in German. Elmer didn't speak of Abram's character and faith; those were well-known and there was no need to speak of them. Instead this was the last service for a man who had ended his life's journey. It was God's will, the beginning of a new life. But there would be no speaking of where that began, for it wasn't for those left behind to say. There was simply hope.

When the service was over, the assemblage followed the horse-drawn hearse in their buggies. The plain pine coffin was lowered into a hand-dug grave, and hearts lifted with a final prayer as they stood in the field of simple stone markers. The clouds that had gathered during the day suddenly parted and a shaft of sunlight poured down as church members drifted back to their buggies.

Hannah thought it felt like a benediction as they walked away from the dead.

There was food back at the farmhouse afterward. So much food. Big casseroles and funeral sandwiches, a favorite that often appeared each time someone in the community passed. Hannah noticed that Gideon took two of the small rolls filled with ham and melted cheese and lavished with a warm buttery sauce. She took just one and a small slice of chocolate cake. There was always a big selection of desserts at an Amish gathering.

"Can I give you a ride home?" Gideon asked quietly as he put a slice of custard pie on his plate.

She nodded. She'd come with her *mudder* but it was a simple thing to look over at her as she stood talking with a friend and send a silent message that she'd go with Gideon.

"I should see if I'm needed to help with the dishes first," she told Gideon.

"*Allrecht.* I'll wait for you."

But if he had a reason for asking to take her home he didn't immediately reveal it. Instead they rode in silence and the only sound was the clip-clop of the horse's hooves.

"It turned into a beautiful day," she said, breaking the silence.

"It did. Weather's nice this time of year. Spring's too short. Before we know it summer heat will be here."

He paused, looked at her, then returned his gaze to the road ahead. "Eli proposed to Emma."

She nodded. "I know."

"I'm happy she accepted."

"Me too."

"I thought maybe we could go for a picnic lunch after church this Sunday."

"*Schur.* That would be nice. What shall I bring?"

He shook his head. "I'll bring the food."

"You?"

He spared her a glance. "*Allrecht*, so it won't be fried chicken like you and your *mudder* make. But you won't go *hungerich.*"

"I'm *schur* I won't," she said with a smile. "I'd love to go for a picnic."

She blinked in surprise when she realized he was pulling up in front of her house.

"Well, *danki* for the ride. See you tomorrow morning."

"Hannah." He touched her arm as she started to get out of the buggy and she turned back curiously. He leaned down and kissed her thoroughly. "Tomorrow."

Bemused, she got out and walked up the steps. She turned and touched her lips as she watched the buggy rolling on down the road. "Well, Gideon, that was some kiss."

* * *

Finally, Sunday had arrived. Gideon loved working in his shop, but six days was a long week. The alternate Sundays when he attended church were welcome breaks, renewing him spiritually and physically.

And today he'd be spending the afternoon with Hannah.

"So where are we going?" she asked him as she climbed into his buggy after church.

"You'll see."

"Ah, Mr. Mystery," she teased, smiling.

He glanced over as he guided the buggy to their destination. She leaned back and relaxed, enjoying the warm breeze coming in the window.

"I love this time of year, when it's getting warmer and everything's growing," she told him.

When he pulled up in front of his house she turned to him. "We're having a picnic at your house?"

"On the property. *Kumm.*" He retrieved the picnic basket from the back seat, handed her a quilt, then took her hand and began leading her down a path behind the barn.

"The pond," she murmured when it came into view. "I remember coming back here with you and Eli and friends when we were *kinner*." She sighed happily. "I have some *gut* memories of this place."

He set the basket down, took the quilt from her, and spread it on the long grass beside the water. "Since the shops have been getting busier we haven't been able to have lunch together often."

She nodded. "It feels *gut* to relax," she said as she kicked off her shoes and wiggled her toes.

He found himself staring at her toes. She had really cute toes. Determinedly he forced himself to look away. He'd brought her here to talk to her today.

"The shop's getting busier," she told him, obviously unaware of his temporary lapse of attention. "I'm glad Emma came back and that she's working part-time for me." She frowned. "I hope she keeps working for me after she and Eli marry."

Gideon stopped in the act of opening the wicker picnic basket. "Why wouldn't she?"

"She might decide to stay home and help Eli with the farm. And I'm *schur* she and Eli will want to have more *kinner*." She leaned over and opened the lid. "What are you going to feed me?"

He handed her a ham and cheese sandwich and took one for himself.

"Anyway, I'm so happy for Emma," she said as she unwrapped her sandwich. "She and John will have a home. A nice big one. Some couples start out having to live with the *braut*'s *eldres* and have just one bedroom to themselves. Even when everyone gets along it's not always easy for two generations to share a house."

"My *mudder* will still be living in the house," he pointed out, feeling a little alarm bell go off.

She nodded. "But in the *dawdi haus*. That's separate enough. And she and Emma get along well."

His *mudder* had thought they all could share the farmhouse. It sounded like Hannah had reservations about doing that.

He stared out at the pond. He needed to think more about this before he said anything to her about a future together.

Then he realized she was still talking.

"A friend is living with her *mann*'s *eldres* while they save for a place of their own and she's feeling a lack of privacy," she told him.

"Who?"

"I don't want to say. It was a private conversation."

Gideon liked Hannah's *familye* but his original plans hadn't included living with them. Until Emma had come back, he'd planned on marrying Hannah and them living here in the farmhouse...How did he feel about living with Hannah in her bedroom at her house with her *eldres* a few rooms away? Would he feel the same lack of privacy Hannah's friend felt?

"You're not eating," Hannah said.

"Just thinking about something," he told her and bit into the sandwich.

She popped the last bite of her sandwich in her mouth and looked in the basket. "You brought cookies!" She pulled out the bag and helped herself to one. "Mmm. *Gut.*"

"*Mamm* made them." He stared at her when she chuckled. "What's so funny?"

"Silly. I didn't think you made them."

"I can cook!"

"Baking's different than cooking. Have you ever baked?"

"Eli and I made cookies with her when we were *kinner.*"

"Not the same." She finished the cookie, plucked another from the plastic container, then returned it to the picnic basket. After poking around she pulled out a thermos of iced tea and poured them both a cup.

They sat sipping their tea as they watched a duck bob on the surface of the pond.

"So I got the impression you wanted to talk to me about something," she said at last, turning to look at him.

Gideon considered what to say. They'd known each other all their lives. It hadn't been a sudden thing to ask her out that evening months ago. Dating wasn't casual and certainly marriage wasn't here. Divorce was *verboten*. So a man had to be certain a relationship could work for a very long time.

He felt their attraction had deepened into love on both sides. He wanted to tell her that and more, but he felt so confused about what to say or do since Emma had come back to town with John. He always had been one to plan things out, be sure of what he should do. But he'd always assumed he and his *fraa* would have the farmhouse.

Now that he had to figure out where he and Hannah would live...should he still tell her he loved her and wanted to marry her and then ask her how she felt about finding a place of their own? He'd brought her here to talk, but now he had his doubts about the timing. He sighed inwardly. Maybe his *bruder* was right. Maybe he *was* as slow as molasses on a winter morning.

But it was important to say the right thing, be certain he knew where they were headed in their future. Wasn't it? Wouldn't Hannah want to know he could provide a home for her?

"Gideon?"

"Hmm? *Nee*, I just wanted us to have some time together without anyone else around," he said, and felt sorry he wasn't telling the truth. "We haven't had much time to talk lately. And when we do get to talk it's often been about Emma and Eli and John."

"True." She sighed. "I'm so glad things seem to be working out for them."

How he wanted things to work out for *them*.

"Something's wrong with you," she said.

"What?" He hoped he hadn't drifted off and missed her saying something.

"You seem distracted."

"It's your toes," he said. "You have cute toes."

She swatted his arm with her hand. "You've seen my toes a million times, as much as I go barefoot in the summer around the house. Seriously, I have never seen you not eat a cookie or something sweet when we have a meal."

"You don't know how many I ate when I packed our lunch."

"That's true." She looked out at the pond. "I wonder if the water's too cold to dabble my toes in it." She got up, lifted her skirts, and waded in it. "Not too bad."

"Careful. Remember it gets pretty deep in places."

"*Ya*. But you'd jump in and save me, wouldn't you?"

"*Schur.* But let's not do that today."

She stepped out and sat on the quilt again. "Won't be long until summer. Then being in the water will feel a lot better."

Summer wasn't that far off. He'd need to figure out what to do soon. Like his *mudder* had pointed out, Hannah probably didn't want to wait another year to get married.

"This has been nice," she said as she put the thermos and their empty cups in the basket.

"We'll do it again soon."

"Next time I'll make the food."

"Maybe some of your fried chicken?"

"*Schur.*" She smiled at him. "I know how you like it. But you still like my *mudder*'s biscuits better than mine."

He searched for the right words.

"Oh, don't bother to try to find something to say," she told him. "I know how you feel about them."

"What? You want me to lie?"

"*Nee*," she said. "I like hers better than mine, too. But remember, she's had a lot more years to practice than I have."

A rumble of thunder had them both looking up. They'd been so absorbed in talking they hadn't noticed that clouds were gathering overhead.

They stood and gathered up the quilt, folding it quickly, then Hannah grabbed her shoes and they hurried back up the path to the house. They'd no sooner reached the buggy and climbed inside than rain began to fall. It fell steadily as they drove to her house. When they got there he pulled out an umbrella and walked her up to her porch.

Then he stole a kiss before he ran back to his buggy. When he got inside he glanced back and saw her *mudder* come to the door to open it.

He waved to her and remembered Hannah mentioning her *mudder*'s biscuits. If indeed he and Hannah married and they had to live with her *eldres* he'd be eating more of Mary's cooking—especially her biscuits.

Maybe there were compensations to living for a time in their house. He chuckled and shook his head as he drove home. Surely he wasn't that shallow.

But oh, Mary's biscuits were as light as a cloud.

Chapter Twenty-Three

"Maybe I should have called first," Emma said as she and Eli climbed the steps to her house. *Not my house*, she corrected herself.

"Your *mamm* hasn't returned your calls."

Emma sighed. "She's probably just been busy taking care of my *dat* since he came home from the hospital."

He just looked at her.

"Maybe we should have brought John along. No one can resist John."

"They're going to be happy that we're getting married. And remember no one can resist me."

She gave him a disbelieving look.

Eli grinned at her. "*Allrecht*, so your *dat* wasn't particularly friendly to me when he saw me at church back when I was seeing you. But your *dat* is one of the sterner *eldres* in the community. And he never chased me off when I came to pick you up to go out."

"He would have if he'd had any idea what you had in mind when we went out."

"That could be said of most young men of my age." He grinned at her.

"You know you had a reputation for enjoying your *rumschpringe* a little too much."

He took her hand and kissed it. "Those days are long over."

"I know." She took a deep breath. "Let's get it over with."

"Emma, we're sharing *gut* news with them, not going to a funeral."

"You're *schur* Elmer's going to marry us?"

"Of course. I talked to him after the funeral and he said he and the bishop had a conversation the day before he died. The church wants us to be married. You know that."

They walked down the drive then climbed up the back porch steps. Emma bit her lip as she knocked on the kitchen door.

Her *mudder* opened the door and her eyes went wide when she saw Emma and Eli. "You shouldn't have come." She cast a nervous glance over her shoulder.

"*Mamm*, we have *gut* news—"

"Who is it, Lillian?"

"It's Emma and Eli."

"Shut the door, Lillian." His voice was stern and brusque.

Eli reached out a hand and held the door open. "Abraham, sir, we've come to tell you we're getting married."

Abraham stepped forward. He was a tall, imposing man who'd always seemed to tower over her and her *mudder*. His face, always thin under his long beard, looked gaunt. But his bushy eyebrows drew together in a frown, and anger twisted his mouth.

"And you think this makes everything *allrecht*?" he boomed.

"I don't want you to be angry with Emma," Eli said calmly. "It's my fault what happened. I should have been better to her from the moment she came to me. She's been through so much because I wasn't there for her, and she was afraid to tell you she was in trouble."

"We won't speak of it," Abraham thundered and his face grew red.

Eli drew himself up. "I want to make things right. I want to marry Emma, be a *gut dat* to John, and Emma wants you to be there, both of you, when we get married."

"Abraham, please calm down," Lillian said putting a hand on his arm.

Emma watched her *dat* walk to the door looking so shaky she feared they had upset him too much. She tugged at Eli's arm. "Eli, please. Let's go."

They stood there, two stubborn men she loved. "Eli, please."

Eli turned to Lillian. "Don't you want to see your *grosssohn*?" he asked, appealing to her.

Before she could answer Abraham wrenched the door from Lillian and slammed it shut. The noise made Emma jump.

"I told you it was a bad idea," Emma said, fighting back tears.

"Emma, let me try to talk to him some more."

She shook her head. "It won't do any *gut*. His mind is made up. And he scared me getting so red in the face. He shouldn't get upset like that when he had the heart attack not long ago."

Turning, she rushed down the stairs knowing it was the last time she'd come here. If her *eldres* were determined to shun her there was nothing she could do.

Her tears fell as they climbed into the buggy and began the drive back to his house. Eli kept telling her everything was going to work out *allrecht*, but she just tuned him out. She used her hands to wipe away her tears.

Eli touched her arm. "Emma, I'm sorry."

She took a breath and it hitched in her chest. "I just want to get John and go back to the motel," she said, not looking at him. "Can we do that?"

"*Schur*. Once you've calmed down."

"Now, Eli. I want to go now." She pulled away from him. Once they arrived at his house, she hurried up the steps of the back porch. She opened the door without knocking and went into the kitchen.

"That didn't take long," Gideon began and then he saw Emma's face. "Oh, *nee*, it didn't go well?"

"It didn't go at all. My *dat* slammed the door in our face just like he did when I went to see them when

I first came back. I told Eli it wouldn't work but he wouldn't listen."

"I'm so sorry."

"I need to get John." She reached for a paper napkin kept in a wicker basket on the table, wiped her cheeks, and blew her nose.

"Sit and calm down. You don't want John to see you upset. Then he'll get upset."

Emma took a shuddering breath and sank into a chair at the table. "*Danki*. But I can't stay long. I just want to go back to the motel and think about what to do."

Gideon went upstairs calling for his *mudder*.

She came out of her room. "What is going on? Why are you yelling for me?"

"Emma's downstairs. Her *eldres* upset her. Can you talk to her?"

"*Schur.*"

He followed her down the stairs as she rushed to Emma. "What's wrong, *kind*?" she asked as she took a seat beside Emma.

"We can't get married!" Emma sobbed. "Eli and I can't get married."

Glad to have his *mudder* deal with Emma's tears— he'd never felt comfortable with a woman's tears—he beat a hasty retreat to his room.

* * *

Eli stepped into the kitchen and found Emma sobbing in his *mudder*'s arms.

240

For a moment—just for a moment—he wanted to turn on his heel and rush out to the safety of the barn. He didn't do well with women in tears. Did any man? Then he caught the look in his *mudder*'s eyes and moved forward.

"Emma, you're going to make yourself sick if you keep crying," he told her, patting her shoulder.

"He's right," Leah said. "Here, *lieb*, dry your eyes and let me make you a cup of tea. The water's still hot from when I boiled it a little while ago."

She poured a mug of hot water, set it before Emma, and pushed the little bowl of tea bags close.

Emma opened a tea bag and dunked it into the hot water. Her breath hitched as she added sugar and then took a sip.

"How can we get married?" she asked. "They won't talk to me. So they're *schur* not going to let us get married in their house."

"Then you'll get married here," Leah said.

Eli stared at her. "We will?"

"*Schur*. You don't have to have the wedding at the *braut*'s house. You can have it at the *breidicham*'s. So, when shall we have the ceremony?"

"The sooner the better," Eli said emphatically. "Elmer said he could marry us next week if we want."

Emma gave him a watery smile. "Eli, even though we'd only have a few people it's a lot of work for your *mudder* and on short notice."

"I don't mind." Leah got two pads of paper and pencils from a drawer, placed one set at Emma's elbow, and then sat back down at the table. "Start a list of the friends you want to invite."

Then she began a list of her own. Emma saw she was writing down the food they'd serve. It was almost always the same: baked chicken, *roasht*, mashed potatoes and gravy, vegetables. A small wedding cake, of course.

"The celery may not be ready yet," Leah mused, chewing on the end of her pencil and staring off into the distance.

"I'll just leave the two of you alone." Eli began backing away, but his *mudder* stopped him from leaving again with that look she was so *gut* at. She rose and got another pad of paper and a pencil. Eli wondered how many supplies she kept in that drawer. "Start a list of what you're supposed to take care of. This isn't all the job of the women, you know."

He was saved from the task of wedding planning when he heard John crying in the living room. "I'll go see what he needs."

John was sitting up in the portable playpen his *mudder* had mysteriously come up with since John had first visited the house. He didn't think it was one she'd used for him and Gideon because it looked too modern.

"Hey big guy. Want to get up?" he asked and held out his arms. John lifted his own and Eli scooped him up and was surprised when his *sohn* wrapped his arms around his neck. His heart full, he walked back to the kitchen with him.

Emma smiled when she saw them then she glanced

at the clock. "I'll have to work on this list some more later. John and I really should get going. We were up early and I have to work tomorrow."

"That's fine. We'll get it done. I'm *schur* Hannah will help and Gideon, too." Leah gave her an encouraging smile.

Emma sat there feeling overwhelmed by Leah's generosity. "I don't know how to thank you."

"You're going to be my *dochder*."

"*Schwardochder*."

"*Dochder*," Leah repeated firmly.

That set off the tears again. Emma remembered a time when she'd been upset at finding herself pregnant and she'd told Rebecca she didn't think Leah liked her. Must have been pregnancy hormones, she told herself. Leah had been nothing but warm and welcoming since she'd returned.

They embraced and when they separated she saw that Leah had tears in her eyes as well.

"Come to supper tomorrow and we'll talk some more," Leah invited. "Ask Hannah to come as well."

"I will." She was sorry to leave the warmth and welcome of this home and go to the motel.

"It won't be much longer," Eli said quietly as they walked out to the buggy. It was as if he could read her mind. "We'll get married next week, and soon you and John will have a home here."

"It doesn't seem real somehow." She watched as Eli settled John into his seat then climbed in front.

"*Mamm*'s already been cleaning and moving her things into the *dawdi haus*."

243

"She has?"

Eli nodded. "I'm sorry about the way things went with your *eldres*, but I promise you are *wilkuum* in my family."

She leaned back in her seat and found she couldn't stop yawning. It had been a long, emotional day. So she shouldn't have been surprised to jerk awake when the buggy stopped.

"Sorry."

He chuckled. "You conked out before John did." He got out and helped her with John and their things. "Shall I pick you up at the shop tomorrow or here?"

"Actually I could call Liz tomorrow and ask if I can get a ride with Hannah and Gideon. Save you a trip into town."

"Sounds *gut*."

She walked into the room and lay a dozing John down in the portable crib. With luck he'd sleep until morning. Then she turned and went back to Eli. He reached for her hand.

"Emma, I'm sorry for the way we're getting married."

"You mean at your *mudder*'s house?"

"Our house," he said firmly. "It'll be small because of circumstances. I hope you're not disappointed."

She shook her head. "I'm not. Honestly, I'm not. It means a lot to me that your *mudder* would do this for us."

He touched her cheek. "I'm glad you feel that way. Get some rest. We'll talk more tomorrow." He leaned down and kissed her and then walked back to his buggy.

Emma stood there for a moment watching as it rolled on out of the parking lot and down the road. Then she shut the door and locked it.

She hadn't been truthful, but what point was there in saying anything? Every *maedel* dreamed of her wedding day. Amish weddings were so rich with tradition and friends and family and the entire church community spent the day celebrating with food and games and socializing.

Hers and Eli's would be small, with just Hannah and Gideon as *newehockers* and the only *familye* other than Gideon would be Leah. Rebecca and Katie Ann would come. And Elmer's *fraa*, of course.

She walked over to sit on the bed and gazed at John. He'd be there, of course.

She'd wanted to marry Eli before John had ever become part of her life. Never could she have dreamed that she could love anyone more than Eli. Now she knew she loved this *kind* more than him, more than life itself.

She'd enjoy whatever the day of her wedding brought. Soon she and Eli and John would be a *familye* and that was all that mattered.

* * *

Eli climbed into his buggy and let Ned take them home.

He went over what had happened when he'd gone with Emma to her *eldres* and tried to talk to them. How he wished he could have saved her from the pain of her *dat* rejecting her. She'd been a *gut dochder* to them, and his reckless night with Emma had cost her so much more than she should have paid for it.

Well, it was their loss if they chose to continue to turn from her. Their faith was supposed to be about forgiveness, not judgment.

He'd make it up to her somehow. Give her and John all the love he could give. Provide a safe, happy home for them.

One day they'd have more *kinner*, God willing. And those *kinner* and Gideon's would carry on the farm that had been in the *familye* for generations.

Familye. If they never healed the rift with Emma's it would pain her not to see her *eldres* and her *bruders* and *schweschders*. He regretted that so much.

Well, if they didn't want to host the wedding, see their *dochder* get married, be a part of their *grosssohn*'s life, he and his *familye* would be there for them. Be their *familye*.

The moon was out and lit the way home. Cars whizzed along on both sides of the road, some passing too close and causing the buggy to sway in the rush of wind it created. Eli was glad he didn't have Emma and John with him. Cars and buggies didn't mix well on the road, especially at night when the buggies were harder to see.

He pulled into his drive and parked near the barn. Ned was eager to get into his stall, have a drink of cool water, and settle in for the night. Eli grinned and patted his side. "See you in the morning."

Gideon and their *mudder* were still up when he went

inside the house. Leah was working on the list she'd begun before he took Emma home.

Eli hoped he could go to bed without having to start the one she'd wanted him to do earlier.

Gideon looked up from carving a toy at the kitchen table as Eli walked in and hung up his hat. "I'm sorry Emma's *eldres* behaved the way they did."

He nodded at his twin. "It hurt Emma. But *Mamm* saved the day. So, are you going to be my *bescht* man?"

Gideon grinned. "*Schur.* Just as you'll be mine when I get married."

"Right." Eli rubbed his hand over his face and sighed. "I told Emma I was sorry that it wouldn't be the wedding she'd hoped for. She said it didn't matter and seemed to mean it."

"We'll make it special," Leah told him. "It'll be small, but remember He will be here."

Eli looked at her. " 'He'?"

"The Lord your God is in your midst."

He nodded. "You're right."

"I'll pitch in for some of the expenses. The food," Gideon said.

Surprised at the offer, Eli shook his head. "*Danki,* but you don't have to do that."

"I want to."

"Let your *bruder* do it," Leah said. She stood. "Well, I'm heading for bed. See you both in the morning."

Eli kissed her cheek. "*Danki* for being so kind to Emma tonight. It meant a lot to her."

"You know I've always liked Emma. Now I love her," she said simply.

She started for the stairs then turned. "I think I'll go see Emma's *eldres* tomorrow, talk to them."

"Do you think they'll listen to you?"

"I don't know. But it's worth a try."

"Danki, Mamm."

Eli got a glass, filled it with water, and leaned against the counter while he drank it.

"Did you talk to Emma about *Mamm*'s idea? For us to make this place a home for all of us?"

He shook his head. "It was too much to do on top of the upset with Emma's *eldres*. We'll talk about it later. I'm *schur* it won't be a problem. She and Hannah are *gut* friends." He set the glass in the sink. "Well, I'm heading to bed."

"Me too." Gideon put the toy and his tools in the box and stored it in a cupboard behind him.

They climbed the stairs together and then went on to their bedrooms. They'd shared a bedroom for many years even though there was room for them to have their own. Sometimes they'd fought over something and driven their *mudder* crazy and she'd make them go to separate rooms. But one of them always sneaked back and they made up and talked half the night.

It wasn't until they were in their late teens that they had finally decided to have their own rooms. But they'd never stopped being as close as *zwillingbopplin* could be. As he got ready for bed, he thought about what it was going to be like being with Emma and John and not being around Gideon so much.

Things were definitely going to be different.

Chapter Twenty-Four

Hannah watched Emma walk into the shop pushing John's stroller and looking happier than she had ever seen her.

She knew why Emma was happy, but it didn't seem fair to tell her Gideon had shared what had happened.

"It's not my day to work but I just had to come by and tell you. Eli and I set the date!" Emma blurted out breathlessly.

John bounced in his stroller as he listened to his *mudder*'s happy tone.

"You know I said yes but I didn't know how things would work out—until they did!"

"I'm so glad," Hannah said, chuckling at John's behavior.

Emma lifted John from his stroller and danced with

him around the room. John shrieked with laughter and patted his *mudder*'s cheeks.

"Come sit down before you make John dizzy and tell me all about it." She held out her arms for John and Emma handed him over and sat beside her at the quilting table.

"It didn't look *gut*," Emma began and her expression sobered. "We went to see to my *eldres* and things didn't go well. They refused to talk to us and my *dat* shut the door in our faces."

She took a deep breath. "Eli and I went to get John, and his *mudder* saw I'd been crying. She made me sit down and tell her what happened. And Hannah, she said we could have the wedding at her house."

"That's *wunderbaar*!"

Emma nodded and smiled. "So will you be my *maed vun ehr*?"

"I would love to. But Emma, do you think you should ask the friend who invited you to live with her in Ohio?"

"Oh. I hadn't thought of that. I guess I should call her and ask."

"I would be happy to help you with anything you need to do for the wedding."

"*Danki*. Let's look at fabric. I think I know what I want."

They walked over to the display table where Hannah stocked some finer material that Amish brides often used for their wedding dresses. Blue was the most popular, so there were plenty of bolts ranging from the palest to the deepest shades.

"What do you think of this one?" Emma asked, holding material the soft blue of violas up to her face.

"I love it."

"This is the one I want. And this white for the apron."

"This one is popular, too," Hannah told her. "I'm told it resists stains well. Naomi Rose told me someone got bumped at her wedding and spilled a glass of punch on her, and the liquid just rolled right off."

Emma considered it. "I'll be holding John some of the day. You know how *bopplin* are." She took the bolt of white fabric Hannah suggested and carried both to the cutting table.

"You need a pattern," Hannah reminded her.

"It's been so long since I sewed myself a dress." Emma pondered the selection of patterns for modest Amish dresses. She chose one and carried it to the cutting table, measured out what she needed, and cut the lengths recommended on the pattern envelope. Then she returned the bolts, chose spools of thread and a package of straight pins, and walked over to the register.

Hannah joined her but shook her head when Emma started writing up her purchase. "I want your dress to be my gift to you."

"*Danki*," Emma said, tearing up. "It means a lot that you and Gideon have been such *gut* friends since I came back."

They returned to the quilting table and sat. Hannah pulled out the box of quilt pieces she was working on. She smiled as she listened to John's soft snore as he drifted off on his morning nap and smiled in his sleep. She glanced at the front window as a soft rain began to fall.

"Doesn't look like many people are out today. I didn't think rain was predicted." She sighed and threaded a needle. "So you never told me how Eli convinced you to say yes."

"He bought toys for John," Emma said, shaking her head and giving her a baffled smile. She pulled a stuffed horse and cow from the storage bin at the back of John's stroller. "I know it's silly, but my heart melted when he gave the toys to John and said he thought John should get to know farm animals, that he's a farmer's *sohn*. That John would need to learn how to take care of the real ones on the farm as he grew up."

Emma looked up as a car horn sounded outside, then looked back at Hannah. "He brought me this little ceramic baby bootie filled with silk roses. Said he wasn't there when John was born, that I hadn't had his support or my *familye*'s. That he wanted us to make a *familye* together, the three of us."

She sobered. "*Familye*. Gideon and Leah have made John and me feel part of their *familye* since I came back. I think it will be *wunderbaar* getting married at their house."

"It will be."

"Leah invited me to supper tonight to plan the wedding. Said I should ask you and Gideon to come."

"I'd love to and I'm *schur* Gideon will, too. After all, he lives there," she reminded Emma with a grin.

Hannah didn't have plans with Gideon for the

evening so he'd be eating at his house anyway, but it was nice for Emma to invite him to work on wedding plans with her and Eli.

"I need to call Liz and ask if I can get a ride to the house, too," Emma said.

"Her number's in the address book under the counter."

Emma got up and walked over to make the calls. When she returned to the quilting table and sat down, she watched Hannah stitch for a few minutes. "First thing Gideon asked was if you were coming. He sounded happy that you were."

"That's nice to hear."

"I think we have *gut* men in these *bruders*," Emma blurted out.

"We do."

Emma glanced over at Hannah's project. "Working on a wedding ring quilt, hmm?"

"They're popular sellers. Sarah won't have much time to work on another while her *mann* is sick, so I thought I'd sew one."

Emma just looked at her and smiled. Hannah rolled her eyes.

"You know, you could get started on your dress today," she said. "You could cut out the pieces and use one of the sewing machines in the sewing room."

"You don't mind?"

"Not at all."

"You *schur* you don't mind me laying out the material on the cutting table? I can move it quickly when customers come in."

"No problem." Hannah glanced at the window. The day was just turning gloomier.

She watched Emma spread the blue fabric out on the table, pull the tissue pattern out, and pin the pieces on it. After she finished cutting the dress, she did the same on the apron material. When she was done with her task, Emma glanced at the clock, then at the shop door.

"Where is everybody? A little rain shouldn't keep customers away."

Hannah smiled. "Not everybody's in your happy mood and can ignore it."

"People in love just want everybody else to be happy. You're next."

"Next?"

"Gideon is going to ask you to marry him. I just know it. All you have to do is look at him when the two of you are together and you can see he loves you. And I can see how much you love him, too."

Hannah blushed. "Well, there's plenty of time for him to ask. We have months until harvest season."

Then she wished she hadn't spoken. Only weddings with situations like Emma and Eli's "unforeseen blessing" took place at times other than after harvest.

"It's *allrecht*," Emma said. "I'm fine with getting married now. I really am. I know Eli loves me. He's not just marrying me because we have John."

"And everyone who sees the two of you can see you love each other."

Emma's grin was as bright as a sunbeam. "*Ya*, they can."

* * *

Gideon grinned as he hung up the shop phone.

While it felt a little strange to have his future *schwei* ask him to supper in his own home, it was nice to hear she wanted his help in planning the wedding. And even nicer to hear that Hannah would be there, too.

He sat down on the stool behind the shop counter, struck by the thought that very soon Emma and John would be moving into the house. His *mudder* was already moving her things into the *dawdi haus* off the kitchen. But he would be using his bedroom until he married and moved out.

That didn't feel comfortable. He remembered that when they had the picnic by the pond Hannah had mentioned how happy she was Emma and John would have a home. It hadn't even occurred to him then that newlyweds might want some privacy.

Allrecht, so he could move to the downstairs front bedroom so they had the entire second floor of the house to themselves. And he'd be there for only a few months until after the harvest when he and Hannah could be married.

But during that conversation by the pond he'd also realized his *mudder*'s idea that the *bruders* and their *fraas* could share the farmhouse wasn't going to work.

He got out his business ledger and looked at his finances, then his personal checkbook and what he had in checking and savings. Land was now so expensive in Lancaster County as the *Englisch* community expanded and farm land became scarcer and more expensive. He gazed off into the distance. But he didn't need a farm—didn't want the work and responsibility of one. Eli was the farmer in the *familye* and Gideon a full-time shopkeeper who helped his *bruder* on a very part-time basis.

Making toys and selling them in his own shop. This was Gideon's lifework.

Still, property in the Amish community seldom came up for sale. The Amish grapevine worked well. If on a rare occasion the owner of an Amish farm died and left no heirs word quickly spread. Soon a church member bought it and it stayed in the Amish community.

Gideon looked up Elmer's number and called him, hoping he knew of a house for sale. He didn't but promised to keep an eye out and let Gideon know. He didn't ask questions, but Gideon suspected Elmer knew why he was asking:

He drummed his fingers on the counter and concentrated. There had to be a solution.

Then he got an idea. He'd used a Realtor to help him buy the shop years ago. She'd since retired, but he remembered that before she did she'd called him to let him know the agency's secretary who had helped with the paperwork had recently earned her real estate license. He looked in the little file he kept under the counter and found her card. Cassie Martinelli.

The weather was keeping customers away from the shop today. He wondered if it was also preventing Realtors from taking buyers around to look at homes. It only took a quick call to find out Cassie was available.

"I'm Gideon Troyer. Your agency helped me with the purchase of my shop. I'm looking for a house," he began.

"I remember helping with that paperwork before I got my license. I can hop on over and we can put our heads together," she responded cheerfully.

"Oh, I was just going to ask you a few questions," he said. "I doubt you'll want to come out in the rain."

"I could use a break from the office. Shall I stop and get us some coffee?"

"I'll put on a fresh pot."

"Sounds good. I'll be there in a few minutes."

Gideon got up, started a fresh pot of coffee and, remembering how his *mudder* always made guests feel welcome, put the cookies he'd brought for his lunch on a plate. He had the coffee and cookies on the shop counter when Cassie swept into the shop clad in a raincoat as red as her curly hair less than ten minutes later.

"What a day," she said as she put her umbrella in the stand beside the door and hung her raincoat on the coat rack. "I'm glad you called. I was just sitting at my desk dealing with some paperwork."

She sat on a stool at the counter, sipped the mug of coffee he brought her, and sampled one of the cookies he'd brought for his lunch.

"So, you're looking for a house," she said, dusting cookie crumbs from her fingers and getting an iPad from the pocket in her jacket. "None available in your community?"

He shook his head. "I'm hoping you know of one near it."

"I'll look. What kind of budget do you have in mind?"

"I don't know. I have no idea how much a house should cost. I never thought I'd have to buy one. My twin brother and I inherited our farm, but he's getting married next week and he'll be living in the house."

"I see."

He didn't like talking about personal financial stuff but he could see he was going to have to do so in order to get the help he needed. "I've been going over my finances," he told her, gesturing at his ledger and banking file. "I just bought this place a few years ago, so I don't have a lot saved."

"Well, I remember helping Rhonda with the paperwork for that purchase and she taught me some great creative ways to finance with the local banks. Let's talk about your wish list and perhaps your future wife's."

He liked her optimism. "I haven't talked with her about it," he said slowly.

"I understand. I'll keep this confidential, of course."

"Thanks. I don't want a farm. Just a nice house. I'd think at least three bedrooms," he said. "We can always add on more later. The Amish do that when they have more children. And the house should have a nice backyard for them to play in."

"And a wonderful kitchen. It's the heart of the home for every family, Amish or *Englisch*," she suggested.

"That's what my mother always says," he told her.

"I think all mothers do." She made notes in her iPad.

Then she looked up at him. "And a room for sewing and quilting," she said with a twinkle in her eye.

He felt a flush stealing up his neck. She was subtle, but they both knew who she meant. He'd seen Cassie at Hannah's quilting classes.

They talked a few minutes more, and then several people walked into the shop and he had to help them. After he rang up their purchases and they left, he turned back to Cassie. "Shall I get you more coffee?"

"No, thanks. I've got what I need. I'll go back to the office and do some research, look through the multiple listings."

"Thanks for coming. I appreciate it."

"My pleasure. I hope I can find you the home of your dreams." She looked out the window. "Well, how about that. The rain's stopped and there's a rainbow. You have a good day!"

She opened the door and paused to let another woman step inside.

"Cassie! Hello!"

Gideon froze at the sound of Emma's voice. He was hoping to keep his house hunting a secret for now.

"Emma. Nice to see you."

"You too."

After closing the door, Emma walked over to the shop counter. "You know Cassie?"

He nodded. "She helped with the sale of the shop."

"I see."

Gideon watched her glance at the two mugs on the counter.

"She stopped by to see how things were going." He hated not being honest with her, but he didn't want to share why he was talking to Cassie. "I wasn't expecting to see you before supper tonight."

"John and I are at Hannah's today. Things are slow, and you'd asked if I'd like some hours here, so I thought I'd see if you wanted me to give you some extra time today. Maybe you'd like to have lunch with Hannah then, I don't know, work on your toys or whatever you need me to do."

"Great. Do I need to get John's crib?"

She shook her head. "He's taking a nap so he can stay at Hannah's." She grinned. "He'll be your chaperone."

"Funny." He gathered up the mugs and headed to the back room to get his lunch tote. "Back in a half hour."

"Take an hour," she said with a grin. "We won't tell the boss."

"Very funny. See you." He opened the shop door, and when he stepped outside he saw that there was indeed a rainbow.

An unexpected lunch with Hannah and a rainbow. It was indeed turning out to be a *gut* day.

Chapter Twenty-Five

Emma watched Eli lean in the front window of the van and pay Liz for her ride.

It made her feel *gut* that he did so without her saying anything.

Gideon got John's stroller from the back of the van and then walked off with Hannah. Emma settled John in the stroller, and the minute Eli joined her she grabbed his arm.

"We need to talk," she whispered as she watched Hannah and Gideon stroll up to the house.

"Hello to you, too," Eli said with a grin. He leaned down to chuck John under the chin which made him giggle.

"Something's going on," she said. She smiled and

waved her hand as Hannah turned and looked back at them. "We'll be right there!" she called.

She turned to Eli. "Gideon was talking to Cassie today."

"Cassie who?"

"Cassie Martinelli."

"I don't know who that is."

"She's a Realtor. Eli, why was Gideon talking to a Realtor today?"

"I have no idea."

"I thought you two talked about everything."

Eli grinned and leaned down to kiss her. "Not everything."

She punched his arm. "Be serious. Why was he talking to a Realtor?"

"Emma, I don't know. If you were so curious, why didn't you ask him?"

"I didn't feel that I could."

He shrugged and began pushing John's stroller up the walk.

"Eli! This is important. Do you think he's going to buy a house?"

"I don't know."

Emma grabbed his sleeve and made him stop. "Eli, he shouldn't feel like he has to move out of his own home."

Leah opened the front door and looked out. "What's taking so long?" she called. "John, you get your *eldres* in here. Supper's ready!"

"You heard the boss," Eli told Emma. "We'll talk later."

Frustrated, she lifted John from the stroller and

262

followed him. Eli parked the stroller on the porch and they walked into the house.

"Something smells *wunderbaar*," he said as they entered the kitchen.

Leah held out her arms for John. "Everything's on the table and your *bruder*'s ready to start without you."

"It would serve him right," Gideon said. "Remember the time he told you I was eating supper at Hannah's and ate my share? I was just late and came home to find I had no supper."

"How long ago was that?" Hannah asked him.

"Last week."

Eli thumped the back of his head before he took his seat. "We were ten."

Hannah laughed. "Leah, sometimes I wonder how you survived these two."

Leah kissed John's cheek before tucking him into the highchair by the table. "Sometimes I do, too. With any luck John will be the same kind of *bu* his *dat* was."

"Wow, that's mean, *Mamm*," Eli said as Gideon chuckled.

She laughed. "*Ya*."

Emma noticed that Gideon said the blessing over the meal without Leah asking him. And it wasn't because he was eager to start eating as he'd been teased. He was his usual calm and deliberate self and made *schur* he offered Hannah the food being passed around before he served himself.

It took Emma a few minutes for her to realize that every time their eyes met he quickly looked away.

Something was definitely going on.

She filled her plate and ate hungrily. The day had been long and she enjoyed Leah's cooking—and the fact that Leah insisted on sitting next to John's highchair and feeding him. Emma didn't often get to eat a meal in a leisurely fashion. Her heart warmed as she watched how clearly Leah enjoyed her *grosssohn*. She felt a pang thinking about her *eldres* and how they were refusing to acknowledge him.

Some emotion must have shown on her face because Leah looked at her and gave her a gentle smile of understanding.

Dessert—a rhubarb pie—and coffee followed the meal. Then Leah was directing the men to clear the table. She set out pads of paper and pencils, and everyone got down to the business of planning the wedding.

The guest list was short. Emma remembered how Hannah had suggested Emma invite Grace, her Ohio friend. She borrowed Eli's cell phone and made the call to her asking if she'd come. Unfortunately, her friend couldn't attend because she was caring for her *mudder*, who was ill.

"I'm so happy for you," Grace said and Emma heard the tears in her voice. "Kiss John for me and let's hope I can come see you and meet Eli one day when my *mudder* is better."

After she said goodbye Emma turned to Hannah. "So I hope you'll be my *maed vun ehr*?"

"Of course," Hannah told her with a warm smile.

264

Leah announced she and Eli were going into town the next day to shop for the food. She asked Emma if she wanted to add anything to the traditional wedding feast of baked chicken, *roasht*, mashed potatoes and gravy, rolls, and desserts.

Emma shook her head. "Are you *schur* it won't be too much for you to cook all that?"

"*Nee.* I asked Ruby to help. I figure it'll be *gut* for her to have something to do to take her mind off Abram. You know how she loves being a part of celebrations."

Emma thought it was nice of Leah to term this quickly-put-together wedding a celebration, and she appreciated the way Leah was making her feel. It didn't quite take away the sting of not having her *eldres* attend, but Eli's *familye* was her *familye* now, and that was what was most important.

Leah turned her attention to Eli and Gideon. They were told to make a note on their pads to get the benches used for church service for the day of the wedding. And clean up the yard.

Then Leah cleaned up John's face with a wet washcloth, lifted him from his highchair, and handed him to Eli.

"*Kumm*," she said to Emma and Hannah. "I want you to see what I've done to the *dawdi haus.*"

They walked into the addition off the kitchen where the *eldres* moved when they turned over the work of the farm and gave the house to the next generation to raise their *kinner*.

Leah had chosen a sunny yellow paint for the walls. "Eli's done most of the work painting." She glanced around the smaller kitchen and dining area before leading them into the bedroom where Eli and Gideon had already moved her bed. A Sunshine and Shadow quilt covered the bed, and a vase filled with daffodils sat on the bedside table.

Emma bit her lip. "You're *schur* you don't want to keep your room upstairs? I mean, you shared it with David for so many years before he passed. I don't want you to feel pushed out."

"It's time for a change," Leah told her. "It's time to move on to the next chapter."

Her own *eldres* would do that one day, Emma mused as she stood at the back door and looked out on the small porch, where Leah had set two rocking chairs around a small table and grouped pots of spring flowers.

How gracious this woman was being about giving up her home to Emma and John.

Leah took her hand and squeezed it. "We're all going to be happy here."

But Gideon, Emma couldn't help thinking. Was Gideon going to feel comfortable?

She glanced at Hannah but couldn't read anything in her expression. And she didn't think she should ask her if she knew Gideon had been talking to Cassie that afternoon.

It was all so confusing. She needed to talk to Eli.

* * *

A little while later, Gideon and Hannah offered to do the dishes so Eli could drive Emma and John home.

"So did you get to talk to Gideon and find out why he was talking to Cassie this afternoon?" she asked the minute they were in the buggy.

He glanced back at the house as he called "Giddyap!" to Ned. "I did. But I can't tell you unless you can keep a secret."

"Of course I can keep a secret!" she huffed when he gave her a skeptical look.

"He's looking for a place for Hannah and himself."

"Then he's going to ask her to marry him! I knew it!" She sat back and grinned.

"Don't you dare tell her."

"I won't!"

"I want to help him somehow."

"What, be there when he asks her to marry him?" she teased.

"*Nee*, silly." He reached for her hand and kissed her knuckles. "After *Daed* left us the farm Gideon and I made this pact. The first one to marry would live in the farmhouse. I always thought it would be him." He turned to look at her. "Until you and John."

Emma burst into tears.

"Emma! What's this about?"

"Everyone's giving up so much for us. Gideon shouldn't have to leave his home. He's lived in it all his life."

"*Familyes* do this," he told her. "When it comes time for your *dat* to stop farming, one of your *bruders* will take over and your *eldres* will move into the *dawdi haus* at your old home. Your other *bruder*s and *schweschder*s will find places of their own."

He watched her dig a tissue from her apron and wipe her tears. "I know. I'm just feeling a little emotional with us getting married next week. Your *mudder* showed me how she was fixing up the *dawdi haus* and she was so gracious about it."

"She loves you and wants you to be happy." He hesitated. "She had this idea that maybe all of us could live in the house. You, me, John, Gideon, and Hannah. We could build on as our *familyes* grew."

"Really?"

"*Ya.*" He gave her a cautious look. "What would you think of that?"

"I love your *mudder* and Hannah is my best friend. I think it could work. Don't you?"

Eli hesitated. "Could three women share a home?"

"I don't think I like the question," she responded testily.

"Ouch." He searched for the right words. "Wouldn't a woman want her own kitchen?"

"Your *mudder* would have her own in her *dawdi haus*. That just leaves Hannah and me sharing a kitchen. She's been the best friend I've had here."

He nodded.

"And as you say, we could add on to the house."

They rode along in silence for a few minutes.

"I don't like the idea of him and Hannah not having what we do," she told him and he heard the sadness in her voice. "It doesn't feel right."

"I think Gideon wants them to have their own home, so he's looking into making that happen." He frowned. "But I don't know how he can afford it."

Eli pulled over to the right of the road to let a car pass. Then, after checking for traffic, he pulled back onto the road. "He likes Hannah's *eldres* but I think he wants them to go straight to their own place. Not live with them while they save up."

He glanced at the fields they passed as they rode toward town. "It doesn't seem fair to me that he's having to find a home. I just moved right into farming for my job, but he had to buy his shop. And now he has the additional expense of a home."

She squeezed his hand. "Maybe there's some way we can help."

"How?"

She shook her head. "I don't know. We'll have to think about it. Pray about it. Everything's working out for us. It has to for Gideon and Hannah."

He grinned at her. "Has to, huh?"

She nodded vigorously. "*Ya.* It just has to."

She glanced into the back seat and saw that John had nodded off with one of his stuffed toys clutched in his hand. "God has a plan for all of us. Every single one of us."

Eli couldn't argue with that. He'd thought he knew what he wanted, and then he found what happened was so much better.

As usual John didn't wake when Eli lifted him from his seat. He just snuggled closer into Eli's arms and made a funny little sound of contentment as Eli carried him into the motel room and lay him gently in his crib.

After the rest of his things were moved from buggy to room—who knew one little *boppli* needed so much?—Eli said goodbye and started out the door.

"I don't get a goodbye kiss?" Emma asked with a laugh.

He turned back. "Sorry, I've just got a lot on my mind." He swept her into his arms and gave her a long, romantic kiss.

"Wow," she said when he released her. "Wow."

Chuckling, he sauntered on out to the buggy. But all the way home he thought about what Emma had said. While he and Gideon often still drove their *mudder* crazy with their bickering, they loved each other. There had to be some way he could help him find a home.

He turned into his drive and parked near the barn. But he didn't get out right away. Instead he looked out at the fields...and upon row upon row upon row of corn stalks tall as a man. They seemed to go on forever.

An idea came to him out of the blue. It was so wild and crazy he glanced up to see if tonight was a full moon and he'd gone *ab im Kopp*.

He jumped out of the buggy, startling Ned, and unhitched the buggy. "It's *allrecht*, Ned. Didn't mean to scare you."

He led the horse into his stall, made *schur* he had water, then he hurried into the house. The kitchen was empty, which suited him fine. He pulled a pad of paper and a pencil from the kitchen drawer and sat down at the table with his cell phone.

First thing in the morning he had some phone calls to make.

Chapter Twenty-Six

Gideon hung up his cell phone and leaned back in his chair at the kitchen table. The call hadn't been *gut* news. After an intense day of searching Cassie had called to say she hadn't come up with any suitable properties to show him in his price range.

She'd asked him if he thought he could increase his budget. He'd promised to look into it, but after doing some figuring out on some paper he'd had to call her back and say that wasn't possible.

"So where does that leave me?" he'd asked Cassie.

"I'll keep looking," she promised. "Don't get discouraged."

But it was hard not to let it bother him. He glanced down at the notes he'd made on a pad of paper and sighed.

His *mudder* walked into the room. "I thought you were going to fry some chicken for your picnic with Hannah."

"I am."

"Then you'd better get started. It doesn't just take a few minutes."

Gideon glanced at the clock on the wall. Time had gotten away from him. "Wasn't watching the clock." He shoved the pad of paper and pencil in the drawer behind him and rose.

"What's wrong?" she asked as she turned the gas flame up under the teakettle. "You seem a bit down."

He shrugged. "Just doing some thinking."

He stood and went to the refrigerator for the bowl of chicken he had soaking in buttermilk, then gathered the other ingredients and lined them up on the kitchen counter near the stove.

"Stop me if I'm doing anything wrong," he said as he beat an egg in a small bowl and put flour in another.

"You'll do fine." When the water was hot she made a cup of tea then she sat at the table to drink it.

"You've forgotten how bad my first attempt was. It was nice and golden brown on the outside and raw in the middle."

"You just got impatient the first time you fried it and didn't let it fry long enough. It wasn't a loss. We just put it in the oven and let it finish cooking."

Gideon frowned as he set a cast-iron skillet on the stove and turned the flame up under it. "Eli says I'm as slow as molasses on a winter morning."

"You're patient and steady. Those are *gut* qualities."

He added shortening to the skillet and waited until it was hot. Then he dipped pieces of chicken in the beaten egg, rolled them in flour, and placed them in the skillet. Once they were all arranged to his satisfaction he went to the sink and washed his hands. Soon the kitchen filled with the delicious scent of frying chicken. He watched it carefully, turned it as needed, and didn't rush the process.

And as he cooked he worked out in his head what he would say to Hannah as they ate the chicken by the pond.

Today was the day he needed to talk to her. He didn't know yet how he could propose as he wanted to when he had no idea what their living arrangements would be. He needed to do some serious thinking. Fast.

* * *

An hour later, Hannah climbed into Gideon's buggy and smiled at him. "So, where are we going?"

"It's such a pretty day I thought we'd go for a picnic. Maybe a nice drive afterward."

She remembered the last time they'd gone for a picnic after church. "Sounds *wunderbaar*."

Hannah glanced into the back seat and saw the wicker picnic basket. "I thought I was supposed to bring the food next time we went for a picnic."

"I know you've been busy, so I brought our lunch. Where would you like to eat?"

"The pond," she said instantly. "It was so nice to sit by it last time."

They chatted as they rode to the farm, and after he parked by the barn they got out and walked hand in hand down the path to the pond.

Gideon spread an old quilt on the grassy slope by the water and they sat down. She gazed out at the glassy surface that reflected the blue of the sky above.

"Such a pretty spot," she said as she watched a gentle breeze stir wildflowers on the edge of the pond.

Gideon lifted the lid of the basket and she sniffed. "Something smells delicious." She watched him take out paper plates and several plastic containers. He opened one and held it out to her.

She stared in disbelief at the contents "Fried chicken? You made fried chicken?"

"*Mamm* helped me. We had plenty of time for a chicken-frying lesson, since it wasn't a church Sunday."

She chose a chicken wing and bit in. "Mmm, it's delicious."

He picked up a leg and admired the crispy golden brown skin before he took a bite. "*Ya*, it's pretty *gut* if I do say so myself."

"I wish mine had turned out so well the first time I fried it," she told him. "It was nice and brown like this on the outside but raw inside."

Gideon peered closely at the leg. "That happened when I fried chicken the first time, too. We baked it 'til it was done that time. Today I tried not to be impatient and take it out of the skillet too soon. *Mamm* showed me how to fry it at the right temperature then check it for doneness."

He set the leg down on a paper plate and put a spoonful of potato salad on her plate, then on his.

"I'm impressed," she said after she sampled a bite.

"I think every man should have to try frying chicken," he told her. "Then we might appreciate it more when someone makes it for us."

Hannah chuckled. "It's not easy."

She'd made fried chicken for several of their picnics in the past and was glad he now knew how much work it involved. She took another wing—her favorite piece—and looked at him.

"Maybe you should try making biscuits next," she told him. "Then you'd see why my *mudder*'s are better than mine. Like I've said, she's been making them for a lot more years than me."

"Ouch."

"Seriously, I do appreciate your going to so much trouble." She finished her chicken and refused another piece, but indulged in a little more potato salad.

He opened a container of cookies, and her eyes widened when she saw they were chocolate chip with pecans.

"My favorite. You baked my favorite cookies." She bit into one. "Mmm. Perfect."

"Again, *Mamm* helped me," he admitted. "She called your *mudder* for the recipe."

He poured her a cup of lemonade and handed it to her.

"You went to so much trouble." She swallowed the last bite of her cookie and washed it down with the tart, sweet lemonade.

Then she looked at him and felt the warmth of his gaze. A little shiver ran down her spine in spite of the warmth of the day.

"I wanted things to be special," he told her as he took her hand. "I brought you here because I wanted to explain something," he said at last. "When my *dat* died he left the farm to Eli and me."

"I know."

He shook his head and looked at her. "Let me finish. Eli and I talked about what would happen when one of us married. We decided that whoever married first would live in the farmhouse. I had everything all planned out," he told her. "I was going to ask you to marry me. And we'd get married after the harvest."

Her heart fell. All she could hear was the word "was." She forced herself to continue listening to him.

"But I didn't propose in time. Along came John, and then everything changed."

She couldn't understand how John changed things. Gideon must have noticed her confusion. "Eli is getting married first. He and Emma and John will be living here."

She nodded. "That's as it should be."

"Don't you understand?" he asked, looking exasperated. "Now I have nothing to offer you."

"Let me see if I understand," she said, feeling an unaccustomed temper rising to the surface. "You think

I don't want to marry a man if he doesn't come with property attached?"

"A man wants to feel he's providing a home," he told her stiffly.

"So, you brought me here today to tell me why you aren't going to ask me to marry you?" she retorted. "To let me down easy if I'd been expecting something from you after all the time we've spent together?"

She jumped to her feet and he stood as she did.

"Hannah, calm down, let me finish."

"Oh, you're finished! I don't want to hear any more!" she cried and pushed him aside.

Then she watched in horror as he lost his balance and tumbled into the pond.

Appalled at losing her temper, she stared at him sitting in waist-high water looking stunned. She started to offer him a hand to help him out but before she could he stood and climbed out.

"Hannah, let me explain!"

Shaking her head, she turned and rushed back up the path to the house.

Eli came out of the barn as she reached it. "Hannah! What are you doing here?"

"Pushing your hardheaded *bruder* into the pond."

"What?" He stared at her in shock.

She ignored him and continued on down the driveway. Maybe by the time she walked home she'd have cooled off. But she didn't think so.

* * *

Gideon stomped toward the house, dripping wet and carrying the picnic basket and quilt.

"What happened?" Eli asked as he hurried toward him.

Gideon just muttered under his breath and headed toward the house. Eli grabbed at his arm but he shook him off. Just as Gideon reached to open the kitchen door Eli grabbed him again.

"I don't think you should take this into the house," Eli said with a smirk as he plucked a lily pad from Gideon's shoulder and tossed it down on the porch.

Gideon glared at him then went inside, set the picnic basket on the table, and headed up the stairs to the bathroom. His boots squished with every step.

"Are you going to tell me what happened?" Eli asked.

"I fell in the pond. *Allrecht?*" Gideon began pulling off his sodden clothes and dumping them into the sink.

Eli reached over and plucked a water weed from his *bruder*'s head. "That's not what Hannah said. She told me she pushed you in."

"What else did she say?" Gideon knocked the damp plant from his hand.

"That was all." He picked up the plant and tossed it into the wastepaper basket.

Gideon climbed into the tub, yanked the shower curtain closed, and turned on the water.

"Are you going to talk to me?"

"*Nee.*" He heard the toilet flush and the shower turned cold.

Gideon yelped, yanked open the shower curtain, and

stuck his dripping head out. He glared at Eli. "What did you do that for?"

"Talk to me."

"Fine. When I get out."

Gideon showered, washed his hair thoroughly, and got out to dry himself off. He took his time dressing in clean clothes, stood before the mirror over his dresser, and dragged a comb through his damp hair. Furrows showed in it like rows in a sowed field.

He didn't want to go downstairs and talk to Eli, but if he didn't his *bruder* would just come back upstairs and harass him.

When he returned to the kitchen he found that Eli had put a pot of coffee on and was sitting at the table.

He sank into a chair and grunted thanks when Eli set a mug of coffee in front of him.

"How was the water?"

"You want to know how the shower was?" Gideon gave him a disgusted look.

"The pond. It's usually still a little cool this time of year."

"You been skinny-dipping lately?"

"Nope." He sat down with his own mug of coffee. "Tell me what you did to make Hannah push you into the pond."

"She didn't exactly push me into the pond," Gideon began. Then he shrugged and slumped down in his chair. "What makes you think it's my fault?"

"I know both of you. Hannah's too mild mannered to fight with you."

"Shows how much you know." He stared down into his coffee. "I was trying to tell her it might be difficult to get married after harvest."

"Why would you tell her such a thing?"

Gideon looked at him, hesitated, then blurted out, "Because you're getting married."

It took a moment for Eli to catch on. "Ah. The house."

"*Ya*. The house."

Eli frowned.

"We agreed that the first to marry would move into the house. You'll be the first to marry."

Eli looked at him. "It sounded *gut* when we talked about it. I always thought you'd be the first to marry." He shrugged. "I didn't have any interest in getting married for years."

"I have no problem with you moving in here with Emma and John." Gideon leaned back in his chair. "It just means putting things off a bit with Hannah until I save enough for a place of our own."

"Many couples start off living with the bride's *eldres*. You get along just fine with them."

"I just want us to start off with our own place."

"That's not only stubborn, it's stupid."

"Gee, thanks for calling me stupid, Stupid," Gideon snapped.

"Well, at the least it's pride. And you know what they say about it."

He did indeed. *Der Hochmut kummt vor dem Fall.* Pride comes before the fall. Gideon frowned. Was he being prideful?

The kitchen door opened. Leah walked in and shut the door. "Are you two at it again? I could hear you coming up the porch steps." She held out a limp, wet lily pad. "I found this on the back porch. Someone been taking a dip in the pond?"

Then she spied the picnic basket. "How was your picnic?" Her gaze went to Gideon's damp hair.

"It apparently didn't go the way he wanted," Eli told her.

For that he got another glare. "I can speak for myself," said Gideon.

Eli waved his hand. "Then do."

Leah set her purse and bonnet down on the bench by the door, then helped herself to a cup of coffee before taking a seat at the table.

"I didn't handle things well," Gideon told them. "I was trying to explain to Hannah why we might have to wait to get married. Before I could get out what I wanted to say she got up and started to storm off. I tried to stop her and landed in the pond."

Leah sighed. "I know you want your own place. But you're not thinking about what Hannah wants. Maybe she doesn't want to be a *maedel* for another year. Maybe she'd rather be married to you and live with her *eldres* or here and save for your future together. Did you think to ask her?"

"*Nee.*" Gideon's shoulders sagged even more.

"Give her some time to cool off then go talk to her," Eli suggested.

"This time ask her what she wants," Leah said. "Then listen."

"I talked to Emma about it," Eli spoke up.

Gideon looked at him. "You did?"

"*Ya.* I told her what you and I had discussed after *Daed* died. She was worried when she saw Cassie at your shop. She didn't think it was right that you and Hannah would have to buy one."

"You think she wouldn't mind if we stayed here while we saved up?"

"I know she wouldn't. Like I said, we talked about it."

"It could be for a while. Or forever," Leah said. "We have plenty of room to add on to the house," she told them. "Maybe the four of you should talk."

Eli nodded and looked at Gideon. "But maybe not near the pond again."

"Very funny."

He got up, patted Gideon's shoulder, then lifted the lid of the wicker picnic basket to peek inside. "What did you pack to eat?" Then he yelped when Gideon slammed the wicker lid down on his hand. "*Mamm!*"

"What was I thinking?" she asked as she stood. "The two of you would drive Hannah and Emma crazy in no time."

She walked into the *dawdi haus* and shut the door with a snap.

Chapter Twenty-Seven

Emma stretched as she lay in bed and smiled. Who wouldn't be in a *wunderbaar* mood? She and Eli were getting married today.

She'd been right to come back here with John. It hadn't been easy saving for months or riding for hours in a bus with an infant. Or having her heart broken when her *eldres* had refused to talk to her the day she'd gone to her old house after arriving in Paradise. Thank goodness she'd saved enough for a motel room and Hannah had offered her a part-time job.

After her *dat* had his heart attack and her *mudder* had called her and asked her to come to the hospital, she'd hoped her *dat* would soften. She knew he was safely home now and that he was *allrecht*. He'd looked a little pale and shaky when she and Eli had gone to invite them to the wedding but he'd *schur* had the energy to shout at them and slam the door in their faces. Well, she'd continue to hope that her *dat* would forgive her and she and Eli would be invited to their house one day soon. And that she'd be asked to bring John.

Emma sighed. She was resigned to the fact that her *eldres* wouldn't be at the wedding, though that hurt her heart so. But Eli's *mudder* and *bruder* had been so *gut* to her. They already felt like *familye*. And Hannah had become such a *gut* friend.

She felt blessed indeed.

Turning her head on the pillow, Emma saw that her sweet *boppli* smiled as he slept. What did *bopplin* dream of? she wondered. Toys like the stuffed farm animals that his *dat* had brought him that he snuggled with now? Yummy things to eat like pears and bananas and jars of blueberry buckle pudding? Or being held by someone they loved and who loved them? Did they dream of the *Dat* who'd sent them to earth?

John opened his eyes, yawned, and blinked sleepily. He smiled when he saw her.

"*Guder mariye*," she crooned. When he got older she'd teach him *Englisch* and he'd learn German as well so that he would be able to read the Bible and sing the old hymns in church services.

John was one bright *bu*, and she knew he'd learn all of the languages well.

He studied the stuffed pig near his face so intensely that his eyes almost crossed and carried on a conversation only he understood as she rose to dress and make their breakfast.

"We need to get ready quickly," she told John as she rose. "Hannah will be here soon to pick us up."

She almost made the bed but then remembered that this was the last time she and John would share the motel room, so these linens would be stripped and the bed remade with fresh sheets for the next occupant. Looking around it, she knew she wouldn't miss this room but she felt grateful that it had been a safe, comfortable place for them since they'd returned to Lancaster County.

After pulling on one of her everyday dresses she brushed her hair and pinned it back, then fastened on her *kapp*. She walked over to the little refreshment area and pulled John's bottle from the mini-fridge, set it in a pan, and ran hot water in it. She left it to warm while she fixed him a bowl of rice cereal and mashed-up banana.

She lifted John from his crib and gave him a big smacking kiss that made him giggle. Then she set him in his stroller and dodged his waving hands as she fed it to him. She didn't want to start the day giving him a bath. Or having to change her everyday dress. The one she had on was the best of the three she had. She'd change into her wedding dress and apron when she got to Eli's house. Leah had it hidden in her closet for her.

After she cleaned John up Emma laid him in his crib to drink his bottle while she ate a quick bowl of corn-flakes and made a cup of tea. Then she washed up the dishes and set them to drain. She couldn't make up the bed, but she wasn't leaving dirty dishes for someone else to wash.

A knock sounded on the door a few minutes later. Emma opened it to find Hannah on the doorstep.

"*Guder mariye!*" Hannah cried. She threw her arms around Emma and hugged her. "Are you ready to get married?"

"I am." She gestured at the suitcase and small bag by the door. "We're all packed up. I paid my bill last night so we could be ready to leave when you got here."

"You're always so organized."

Hannah had no sooner stepped inside the room and shut the door when there was another knock. She opened it, and a middle-aged *Englisch* woman beamed at her.

"Is Emma here? Oh, there you are," she said as Emma stepped forward. She handed Emma a little gift bag. "Just a little something for you. Congratulations on your wedding."

Emma blinked back tears. June Wilson owned the motel with her husband and had been so friendly and helpful that Emma had shared her news when she'd paid her bill.

"June, this is very nice but you didn't have to give me anything." She reached into the bag and found two linen dish towels decorated with wildflowers. "What beautiful embroidery," she said, tracing her finger over the delicate work.

June beamed. "I enjoy doing it when things are slow. And I have something for that sweet little boy of yours." She pulled a stuffed teddy bear from the voluminous smock she wore over her clothes. "Can I give it to him?"

John had sat up in the crib at the sound of female voices and he squealed when he saw June walking toward him with the bear.

"Oh, I'm going to miss this little guy so much," she said as she leaned over the crib and gave the bear to John. "You have to promise to come visit me some time."

"Of course. And you can come see us at Hannah's shop."

"That I'll do." She smiled at Emma. "You have a wonderful wedding. I'm so happy for you." She paused by the door and looked at the luggage. "Oh, I'll send the husband over to help you put your things in the buggy." She was off to summon him before Emma could tell her they didn't need help.

"Well, let's get going," Hannah told her. "We don't want to be late."

She grasped the handle of Emma's suitcase and lifted the small bag Emma used for John, but when she opened the door there was Mac, June's husband, ready to take them from her.

Emma grabbed her purse and diaper bag then picked John up. "Say goodbye to the room, John. We're going to our new home."

The ride in Hannah's buggy seemed to take a long time, but Emma knew that it was just because she was impatient now that her wedding day was finally here.

When the farmhouse finally came into view she was overcome by emotion. This would be her home now.

Hers and Eli's and John's. Her heart beat so fast she thought it would leap from her chest.

Leah was waiting for her and eagerly took John from her arms to entertain him. They quickly engaged in a discussion about John's new bear as she carried him off to another room.

Gideon helped bring Emma's things inside and carried them up to the master bedroom. "I'll go tell Eli you lost your mind and showed up," he joked.

He gave Hannah a look of regret before leaving to keep Eli company until the ceremony.

Emma gave Hannah an uncertain look. "Hannah—"

"Time to get dressed," Hannah told her briskly and took her own dress from the closet. "We don't want to be late."

She wanted to protest but Hannah shook her head so she subsided.

Hannah changed into the dusky rose dress she'd sewn to wear to the wedding and then helped Emma change into her wedding dress and apron. Emma pinned on a fresh *kapp* and as she did her gaze met Hannah's in the mirror over the dresser.

"You look beautiful. Wait until Eli sees you."

Emma smiled tremulously as she smoothed her hands over her apron. "*Danki.*" She sighed. "Oh, Hannah, I wish you and Gideon hadn't fought."

"So Eli told you."

"Of course he did. I wish you'd talked to me about it."

"We're not going to talk about that today of all days," Hannah said firmly.

"But—"

"*Nee.*" Hannah opened the door. "Ready to get married?"

Emma smiled and nodded. "I'm ready."

She turned and smiled when she saw Leah carry John into the room. He wore a new blue shirt and dark broadcloth pants. "Where did that outfit come from?"

"I made it for him," Leah told her. "Doesn't the blue shirt just bring out the color of his eyes? And it's his first pair of big *bu* pants."

Emma had loved Eli for a long time and had always wanted to marry him. Over the past weeks she'd come to love his *bruder* and *mudder* and see how much they loved her and John.

And if she hadn't known already, she saw it today in the way Leah beamed at John, then at her.

"Oh, Emma, you look so lovely. Blue is your color." She took a deep breath. "Now, Eli's beside himself waiting for you. Go!"

Emma's heart swelled with love as she fairly flew down the stairs to join hands with Eli in marriage.

* * *

Eli took Emma's hand as she reached the bottom of the stairs and stood there for a long moment taking in how pretty she looked. She . . . glowed.

"You're beautiful," he told her and she gave him a big smile.

"How handsome you look," she said. He wore a dark broadcloth suit and a white shirt.

"*Mamm* made me a new suit." He grinned. "I didn't want John to outshine me today."

"I have two handsome men," she said, beaming with happiness.

They walked together to Elmer. He was standing near the fireplace in the living room, which had been scrubbed and had a big bouquet of flowers from Leah's garden set inside it. More flowers sat atop it in a vase. Benches had been placed in front of the fireplace. Emma figured Eli and Gideon had set them there under their *mudder*'s stern supervision.

Now the benches were filled with their few friends; Ruby, the late bishop's *fraa*; and Elmer's *fraa* as well, women on one side and men on the other.

Emma's steps faltered when she saw her *mudder* sitting next to Leah and Ruby. Then Eli watched her gaze fly to the other side of the fireplace where she saw her *dat* sitting with the men.

"Eli?" she whispered, shocked, as her gaze whipped to his.

He placed his other hand on their joined ones and squeezed it in reassurance. She blinked back tears but resumed walking when he smiled at her. He knew his *mudder* had said she wanted to speak to Lillian but Ruby could have done so as well, knowing Ruby. The late bishop's wife had been determined to see Eli marry and could well have spoken to Lillian and Abraham. Eli wasn't *schur* which of the two strong-willed women had been responsible for persuading Abraham and Lillian to attend, but he was grateful for Emma's sake. He was just as surprised as Emma when they walked in the door just a short time ago and been shocked speechless, but his *mudder* had smoothly welcomed them and had Gideon take them to their seats in the living room.

He'd debated telling Emma that her *eldres* were here when she came down the stairs, but decided he would let her be surprised.

Her hand trembled in his and tears continued to slide down her cheeks as they approached the lay minister.

Elmer welcomed them with a solemn smile and expressed his pleasure in joining them in matrimony. John chose that moment to utter a cry of delight as he sat on Leah's lap, and Elmer nodded and grinned. "*Ya*, John, we are so glad to see Emma and Eli here to become one before God."

Eli listened to Elmer speak about the sanctity of marriage as he always did when he officiated at a wedding and found himself wondering why he had let Emma almost slip from his fingers.

Now as he gazed at her listening to Elmer with such absorption he hoped he had many, many years to make it up to her, to show her how much he loved her and John.

There were songs and prayers and the timeless vows: "Do you promise…this if he/she should be afflicted with bodily weakness, sickness or some other circumstance that you will care for him/her as is fitting for a Christian *mann/fraa*?

"Do you solemnly promise to one another that you will love and bear and be patient with each other and shall not separate from each other until dear God shall part you from each other through death?"

And finally they were *mann* and *fraa*. They walked back down the aisle between the rows of seats, collecting their *sohn* on their way.

Gideon was the first to rush forward and grasp his hand and then give him an emotional hug. Eli watched Hannah do the same with Emma and then take John so that they could accept the congratulations of their friends and *familye*.

Leah hugged her, and Eli saw Emma's surprise when Lillian stepped forward to do the same. Abraham shook his hand briefly, but Eli noticed that the man couldn't quite meet his gaze as he gruffly mumbled good wishes.

It was more than he expected, Eli thought, and while Abraham didn't embrace Emma she smiled and seemed content. He watched Lillian's eyes dart toward John, but she seemed hesitant and didn't ask to hold him.

But John took matters into his own hands, bouncing in Hannah's arms and reaching for Lillian. She quickly took him and held him tightly as tears slipped down her cheeks and Abraham stood there awkwardly patting her on the back.

Eli saw emotion sweep over Emma's face before she turned and ran from the room. He went after her and found her standing on the back porch weeping as if her heart would break.

He wrapped his arms around her. "Don't cry, *lieb*. Be happy."

"I am. I just want them to love John."

"I know. They will, Emma. They will."

"I wish they'd brought my *bruders* and *schweschders*. I've missed them so much."

"It'll take time, Emma. Your *dat* will come around. Be happy he and your *mudder* came today."

He pressed a handkerchief his *mudder* had given him earlier into her hands. She wiped her cheeks with it and gave him a watery smile.

"*Kumm*, let's go inside and be with our *familye* and friends," he said. He held out his hand.

She took it, and together they walked back inside. The men had set up two tables to form a V, and now his *mudder* and Hannah and the other women were setting bowls and platters of food out onto them as the men arranged chairs for seating. Everyone was talking, and the mood was happy and bright.

Eli and Emma took their seats at the *eck*, the corner of the table. He was starved. His *mudder* had been busy cooking the wedding lunch and told him to fix a bowl of cereal for breakfast. But he hadn't thought it would sit well with the frogs jumping around in his stomach. Gideon had teased him, waved his bowl of cereal under Eli's nose, and laughed at him when he groaned.

He restrained himself—barely—from pushing his *bruder*'s face into the bowl.

Now he indulged in a heaping pile of baked chicken, *roasht*, mashed potatoes and gravy, and vegetables. Creamed celery, a staple of Lancaster County weddings, wasn't a favorite of his, but he knew his *mudder* had hovered over the early stalks she'd grown in her kitchen garden. So he made *schur* he put some on his plate and winked at her when she glanced over to see if he was eating it.

Emma had served herself a plate with less food but was eating with some appetite. He wondered if she'd had frogs jumping in her stomach that morning as he had. He'd ask her later when they were alone.

John sat in a highchair between Leah and Lillian, and they took turns feeding him. John loved to eat as much as he loved attention, so he was a happy *boppli*.

As Eli buttered a roll he noticed that Gideon seemed quieter than usual and kept sneaking furtive looks at Hannah as he pushed food around on his plate. Hannah didn't look much happier when she thought no one was looking at her and pushed food around on her plate as well.

The four of them had been very busy planning the wedding for days. Emma had noticed Gideon and Hannah were super polite, but Hannah studiously avoided any attempt by Gideon to talk to her.

Eli sighed. Well, hopefully the two would resolve their differences. In the meantime, Gideon would be staying at the house. Eli hoped one day his *bruder* and Hannah would make up and they'd all share the farmhouse.

"Everything is so delicious," he heard Emma tell his *mudder* when she stopped by the table to pour them coffee. "*Danki* for going to so much trouble for us today."

"It's my pleasure."

"*Ya, danki, Mamm,*" he said. "Everything is *wunderbaar.*"

Leah filled their cups and went to do the same for their guests.

"Leah?"

She turned back and looked at Emma. "*Ya?*"

"*Danki* for getting my *eldres* to come today. It meant so much to have them here."

Leah smiled. "Why do you think it was me that convinced them?"

"They wouldn't have come if you hadn't done it."

She chuckled and shook her head. "Ruby and Elmer helped."

"Then I'll be *schur* to thank them as well." She looked over and saw her *dat* lose his stern expression as John tugged on his beard when Abraham leaned down to say something to him.

"I didn't think I could be this happy," Emma leaned over to murmur in Eli's ear.

"Me either," he admitted. And meant it.

Rebecca stopped by their table to say she wished she could stay longer but she had to go deliver a *boppli.* "I'll be back for cake if it doesn't take long. Otherwise Samuel promised to save me a slice."

"I like your *mann,*" Emma told her. "He seems nice."

"He is. And wait until you meet our *dochder.*"

"*Dochder?*"

Rebecca laughed. "I didn't have a *boppli* while you were gone. She was Samuel's, and now that we're married she's mine, too. See you later!" She rushed off.

"Cake," Eli said, looking at it. "When do we get to cut the cake?"

Emma laughed. "After everyone has eaten. They didn't bolt down their food like you."

When they finally got up to do the job, Emma teared up again as she gazed at the two-tiered cake Ruby had baked and decorated with a few fresh flowers. Eli made a point of thanking the *wittfraa* for making it. She had such a light hand with cakes, and it had saved him and his *mudder* the expense of getting one from a bakery.

After the cake was cut and eaten, Eli knew it was rude, but he began to wish his friends would hurry up and leave so that he could be alone with his new *fraa* and climb the steps to their bedroom.

Chapter Twenty-Eight

Hannah was thrilled that Emma and Eli had a small, wonderfully loving wedding, but she couldn't help feeling relieved that the reception didn't extend to a second meal and activities like so many Amish weddings.

She didn't think she could have pretended nothing was wrong for much longer. Her face ached from smiling and her head throbbed. She hadn't been able to eat much, so her stomach was beginning to feel empty. But she couldn't very well fix herself a plate now that the food had been put away and dishes were being washed.

So she carried dirty dishes into the kitchen and tried to avoid Gideon, who was carrying church benches out to the wagon.

It appeared that was fine with Gideon. He was

avoiding being close to her as well. And that wasn't easy. As *newehockers* their duties included helping clean up after the reception and restoring order to the house.

Leah had taken on the burden of cooking much of the food and babysitting John while Emma and Hannah dressed, so Hannah had tried to persuade her to rest after guests left.

"I'm not tired," Leah said.

"John is," Hannah told her. "Maybe you could take him upstairs and get him to take a nap."

"Well, I guess I could lie down for a little while so he takes a nap." Leah carried him off to the *dawdi haus* and shut the door behind them.

Eli and Emma had been shooed off, told they were not allowed to help with the cleaning up, and so they'd gone for a long walk, just the two of them. Hannah wondered if they would take a walk down to the pond...

She hoped if they went down to the pond they wouldn't end up having a disagreement and have Eli landing in the pond like his *bruder*.

A pang of guilt hit her as she remembered accidentally knocking Gideon into the pond. She felt herself blush as she carried dishes to the kitchen.

Gideon walked past her with the folding table and the moment their gazes met he looked away. Hannah handed the dirty dishes to Ruby, who was standing at the sink, and hurried back for more before he returned.

"Well, this is the last of them," she said when she returned with more dishes.

"Everything *allrecht*?" Ruby asked as she put them in the soapy dishwater.

"*Ya*, why?"

Ruby glanced at Gideon as he hurried back to get the other table. Then she looked directly at Hannah. "Just feels a little chilly in here."

Some people saw just too much.

"Shall I fetch your shawl?" Hannah enquired politely.

"*Nee*. Don't think that would help," Ruby said giving her a bland look as she rinsed a dish and passed it to Hannah.

Ruby had always been an inquisitive woman. Well, downright nosy, Hannah thought, and then chided herself for her uncharitable thought.

Once the dishes and cups were dried and put away Hannah went into the living room. The tables and benches were all gone, so she got the broom from the kitchen storage closet and swept up.

That task completed, she looked around for something else to do and found nothing. Just then Gideon came in, and they stood awkwardly in the middle of the room.

"Looks like everything's done," he said.

She nodded.

"Nice wedding."

"*Ya*. It was." *Wow, that's all you can think to say?* she asked herself.

"Guess I'll change and go out to the barn and see what needs doing. Give Eli a break for the rest of the day."

They both knew it was early for evening chores.

He walked toward the downstairs bedroom, and she realized that he'd probably moved his things from his upstairs bedroom to give Eli and Emma privacy.

He'd always been a nice guy, she mused. Just so...stubborn.

Well, she'd done her duty and now she could go home, and check in with her *schweschder* Linda, who'd agreed to work at the quilt shop that day for her. She said goodbye to Ruby and walked out to the barn for her buggy.

That meant she had to walk inside the building to get Daisy and see Gideon one more time.

She entered the barn to find that Daisy and Gideon had their heads together. Hannah sighed. Her horse was a shameless flirt and loved Gideon. He always spoiled her with a piece of apple or a carrot when he saw her, and so he was a favorite of hers.

"Traitor," she muttered under her breath.

Gideon turned when he heard her walking inside.

"I'm leaving now."

"Sorry, Daisy," Gideon said as he gave her nose a last caress with his broad hand. "Been nice talking to you, sweet girl."

Hannah shivered in spite of herself, watching him touch her horse with such love and care. She would *not* think about how it felt to have his hands touch her cheek, or his arms wrapped around her waist.

He opened the stall door and began leading the adoring Daisy to the buggy outside. "I'll hitch her up."

"I can do it."

He ignored her and did the chore himself, and gave Daisy a last pat. Then he turned to her. "Hannah—"

"I have to go. I have to call Linda and check with her," she said and quickly climbed into the buggy. "*Danki* for helping with Daisy." She avoided looking at him and guided the buggy down the drive and after checking traffic, onto the road.

She wouldn't look back. She wouldn't.

But as she started home she realized she was too restless, too unsettled, to go straight there. So she took a leisurely ride and enjoyed the first unstructured time to herself she'd had in a long time.

The day was sunny, warm but not too warm, and she enjoyed the breeze that floated into the buggy.

Farmers worked their fields. When it came time for harvest she'd spend time helping her *mudder* clean and can fruit and vegetables. There'd be no time for a ride like this, so she was determined to enjoy it.

Thoughts of what happened after the harvest intruded unpleasantly. There would be weddings. So many weddings. And she would be attending them as she had today and not planning one for herself as she'd hoped.

She'd sat and listened to the vows Emma and Eli had spoken today, knew them by heart from attending so many weddings that they were burned onto her memory.

She'd wanted to say them to Gideon.

Now she sat here feeling like always a *maed vun ehr* not a *braut*.

She burst into tears.

* * *

Gideon walked back into the barn and leaned on Ned's stall. "She's still mad at me."

Ned snorted and nodded his head.

"*Ya*, women," he agreed. "She wouldn't look at me all day."

He went about the work of feeding and watering the horses and then, with nothing else to do, walked out of the barn and shut the door.

Some evenings he sat in the kitchen and worked on carving a toy or in the living room reading *The Budget* newspaper or a book. But he wanted Eli and Emma to feel like this was their house now, so he poured himself a cup of coffee and went to his new bedroom.

He sat on the bed and glanced around the small space. He supposed he could make it feel more like his own by taking his books and other things from the boxes he'd packed them in to carry down here.

But not tonight. He was tired from all the work of the wedding and he felt strangely emotional. He'd set a book out on the nightstand earlier but he didn't feel like reading like he always did before bed.

He'd attended many weddings, but this one had touched him in unexpected ways. He was only minutes older than Eli, but Gideon had always felt like his older *bruder*. And often Eli had resented him for treating him like his younger *bruder*. Well, in his defense Gideon felt Eli had sometimes acted like he was much younger. Eli didn't take things as seriously and he'd been careless with Emma and caused her so much grief.

But he was proud of Eli now, and he knew he couldn't treat him like the irresponsible *bruder* anymore the way he had for a time.

They didn't often talk about the way they were closer than he knew other males were with their *bruders*. His *mudder* called it their twin bond—they'd known what the other thought and felt without speaking. Today he'd felt the joy Eli felt as he walked to Elmer to get married.

And then Eli had looked at Emma, and Gideon had felt something move in him knowing that now Eli would share his thoughts and feelings with her—as he should. It was both a loss and a gift to know it.

There was a knock on the door.

"*Kumm*," he called.

The door opened and Leah walked in. "Thought I'd see how you were doing."

"Doing?"

She closed the door, and as she walked over to the bed he moved his legs so she could sit on the end of it. Then she just looked at him.

He shrugged. Talking about emotions didn't come easy for him. "I was just thinking about how Eli and I have always had a closeness because we're twins," he admitted. "We'll always be close, but his *fraa* will be the one he'll share his thoughts and feelings with now. And that's as it should be. I'm happy for them."

She patted his hand. "I know you are. They love each

other so much. And I think they'll have a stronger marriage now that they've gone through what they have."

"How about you?" he asked. "How are you doing?" He'd been so selfish, he realized, so focused on how miserable he felt being close to Hannah and having her refuse to look at him or talk to him more than she'd had to.

"It's one of those big steps you hope to see your *kinner* make," she said slowly. "Falling in love and marrying. Having *grosskinner*."

Tears welled up in her eyes and she smiled tremulously. "It was a very emotional day."

She reached into her apron pocket and pulled out a man's cotton handkerchief and stared at it. "I gave one of your *dat*'s handkerchiefs to Eli to carry in his pocket today. It made me feel like a part of your *dat* was with us."

She wiped her eyes then smiled at him. "I have one tucked away for you, too."

"I'm not *schur* I'm going to have use for it for some time."

"You're both hurting. But you'll make up. I have faith that you will. The two of you love each other too much not to."

"I hope you're right."

She tucked the handkerchief into her pocket and sighed as she stood. "Well, I'm tired even though I had a little lie-down earlier. I don't think I'll have any trouble sleeping tonight."

She chuckled. "Well, I suppose that'll depend on

John. He's sleeping in the portable crib in my room tonight. You get some rest."

Leaning down, she kissed his cheek. "Don't stay up too late reading."

"I won't."

But long after she left he found himself lying there, staring at the ceiling and thinking about Hannah.

His *mudder* had said he needed to talk to Hannah about getting married and staying at her *eldres* while they saved for a home of their own. She'd said that Hannah would probably rather do that than delay getting married, and he didn't have the right to decide things for her without talking to her.

Mudders were almost always right, he had to admit.

And *schur*, he'd like to have a nice big master bedroom in a big house like this. But sharing a room of any size with Hannah, being married to her was far, far better than being alone with his pride. Alone without her.

He'd find a way to get her to talk with him tomorrow.

Chapter Twenty-Nine

Emma turned from the stove as Eli opened the door to the kitchen, stepped inside, and washed up at the sink. "*Guder mariye, Mann*," she said, lifting her face for his kiss.

"*Guder mariye, Fraa*," he said, kissing her then rubbing his cheek against hers.

She laughed and reached up to rub the beard that was coming in. It was mostly a dark stubble after just four days of growing but still, it showed he wasn't shaving. Now the world would know he was her *mann*. A beard on an Amish man was like the wedding ring that *Englisch* wore to signify they were married. It had only been three days since he'd shaved but it looked *gut* on him.

John squealed and banged his hands on his highchair to say hello in his own way. Eli chuckled and walked over to kiss the top of his head, then let his *sohn* touch the growth on his face. John frowned and looked so intently at it that Eli burst out laughing.

"Someone's in a *gut* mood this morning," Gideon said as he walked into the kitchen. "*Guder mariye*, John."

John studied his face, looked at his *dat*, then Gideon again. He babbled at Gideon.

"*Nee*, I don't have a beard," he told John. "Maybe one day."

He nodded at Eli and then walked over and poured himself a cup of coffee. "*Guder mariye, Schwei.*"

"Did you make up with Hannah yet?" Eli asked him.

Gideon glared at his *bruder*. "I don't want to talk about it."

Emma shot Eli a warning look as she put a plate of bacon and dippy eggs on the table in front of him.

"Gideon? Two eggs or three?"

"Two. I won't be working in the fields all day like your *mann*. And *danki*, Emma, but I don't expect you to cook for me."

"Don't be silly." She fixed two plates, set his before him then sat with hers. She glanced over at John. He hadn't been real interested in the rice cereal he loved even after she mixed in some applesauce. She tried offering him another spoonful of it, but he closed his mouth tight and shook his head. Shrugging, she set the spoon back in the bowl and began eating her breakfast.

The door to the *dawdi haus* opened, and Leah walked into the kitchen carrying a plate of cinnamon rolls.

"I thought I'd share some of these." She set them down in the center of the table, poured herself a cup of coffee, then took a seat.

Eli and Gideon reached for them at the same time and bumped hands.

"There's plenty for everyone," she said, rolling her eyes at Emma. "Careful, they're hot."

Eli tossed his roll from one hand to the other and back again to cool it off a little then took a big bite. "Mmm. *Gut.*"

Emma finished eating and rose to put her plate and coffee cup in the sink. She began getting her things ready for her day at Hannah's shop.

"Are you *schur* I can't watch John so you don't have to take him to the shop today?" Leah asked her.

"*Danki*, but I think we'll both enjoy going in today. We've enjoyed being home, but it's time to get back to work." She grinned when Leah gave an exaggerated sigh and looked sadly at John. "You'll have plenty of *grossmudder* time when we come home," she reminded Leah.

Emma had packed her lunch the night before and made *schur* John's diaper bag had everything he'd need. She'd set them on the bench by the back door along with his stroller. A glance at the kitchen clock showed she was on schedule.

Then she glanced over and saw that Eli had leaned over to give John a spoon of the rice cereal he'd decided he didn't want more of, and John was smearing it all over his face and shirt.

"Oh my!" she cried and grabbed a dishcloth, ran some water over it, and rushed over to clean him up.

"Oops," said Eli. "Sorry."

"That's *allrecht*."

He hadn't had much experience feeding his *sohn* yet and didn't know to anticipate such behavior. She stripped off John's bib and his shirt, wiped his face, hands, and hair, and lifted him out of his chair.

"Eli, can you get a clean shirt out of his bag there on the bench?"

When she turned she saw Leah had already gotten it and held it out. "*Danki*."

Gideon rose, got his lunch tote from the refrigerator, and collected the things Emma had set out on the bench. "I'll put these out on the front porch and wait for Liz."

"*Danki*."

Eli clapped a hand on Gideon's shoulder as he passed him. "Have a *gut* day at work. And try to fix things up with Hannah."

Gideon shrugged off his hand and frowned at him. "I don't need you nagging at me, *Mamm*."

"Don't you talk to your *bruder* like that, Gideon," Leah scolded.

"*Ya*, Gideon." Emma joined Leah in glaring at him. "That's no way to talk to your *bruder*."

"Sorry!"

Emma started to fuss at him then felt something

wet on her arm. She looked down and saw cereal and applesauce on her dress. There must have been some on the chair when she got John out of his highchair. She handed John to Eli and rushed to the sink to clean the stuff off. But it just made things worse.

"I have to change my dress."

"Go ahead."

"Our ride's here!" Gideon hollered from the front door.

Torn, Emma tossed the wet dishcloth down and shook her head. "What a morning! I can't go in like this."

"Go change. I'll drive you to work. I'll tell Gideon to go on."

She ran upstairs, changed, and when she came down Leah was holding John.

"Eli's hitching up the buggy."

They walked to the front door, and when they went out onto the porch Eli was pulling the buggy around. Leah picked up Emma's lunch tote and diaper bag while Emma slipped the strap of her purse cross-body and grabbed the stroller.

"Have a *gut* day," Leah said and gave John a big kiss before settling him in his seat.

"We will, *danki*," Emma said as she climbed into the buggy.

Once they were on the road Emma leaned back and let out a relieved sigh. "Not the calmest start to a day."

He shrugged. "It's *allrecht*. Gives us a chance to talk on the way. And I have a few things to do in town anyway."

"Like what?"

"Just some errands."

He sounded a little evasive, but when she started to question him she saw that Fannie Mae was setting up her stand in front of her farm. Emma waved then turned back to Eli.

"Get some fruit and I'll bake you a pie tomorrow."

"What kind of fruit?"

"Whatever looks *gut*. She may have some early strawberries."

"I will."

"Enough for two pies. I know how much your *bruder* loves pie."

Eli nodded and then lapsed into silence. When several miles passed and he said nothing, just seemed to stare at the road ahead and brood, she bit her lip.

"What?" she asked finally.

"Huh?"

"Something's bothering you. Tell me what's wrong."

When he checked for traffic then pulled over and turned to her she searched his face.

"Something has been bothering me," he admitted. "Maybe we should have talked about this before."

* * *

Eli saw Emma pale and realized he'd scared her.

"Sorry, it's nothing bad," he said quickly. "I just realized we haven't talked enough about our future. You know you can stay home and not work if you want to. The farm is doing well, and there's no need to do outside work—"

"I love working in Hannah's shop, and John really enjoys all the people. And it's just two days a week now, maybe three when things get busier for Christmas."

He shrugged. "I know you said you didn't mind that the wedding was small. But we're not getting to do what couples in our community usually do after their marriage."

When she giggled he shot her a look.

"Emma." Then he laughed. "I'm not talking about that."

"Sorry." She pressed her lips together firmly and stopped giggling.

"Couples visit their friends on the weekends after the wedding, spend the night, collect their wedding presents."

"Our best friends were at the wedding and they gave us the best gifts—they supported us emotionally and helped us have a wedding," she said firmly. "Hannah gave me the material for my wedding dress and helped me sew it. Gideon helped pay for some of the wedding food and set up the benches and tables. That's more than enough for me. Isn't that more than enough for you?"

He gave her a thoughtful look. "I guess when you put it like that."

Traffic was already getting heavy in town when they arrived, but he was able to pull in front of Hannah's shop.

Emma put her hand on his arm and stopped him when he started to get out of the buggy. "It's felt so nice being part of the *familye* since we got married," she told him. "We are so lucky to be together, Eli, you and me and John."

He leaned down and kissed her. "I know. Have a *gut* day and I'll look forward to seeing you when you come home tonight."

She grinned. "*Danki* for the ride, but we'll make *schur* we catch one with Liz this evening."

Eli checked for traffic before he got out of the buggy and came around to help her get John and their things inside.

But when Emma approached the shop she realized it was dark inside. She peered in the window. Hannah wasn't in yet.

Emma rummaged in her purse and pulled out her key ring. "Hannah gave me a key."

She unlocked the door and they entered the shop. Emma went around turning on lights.

"Guess I'll be going." He backed toward the door.

"Why is it men are so uncomfortable in a quilt shop?" she asked.

"I'm not uncomfortable," he said.

"Then stay and keep us company until Hannah gets here."

"Fine." He looked out the shop window. "I'm surprised we got here before them."

"Liz has a lot of stops to make on the way here." She frowned. "I hope nothing happened."

Then she shook her head. "Gideon has a cell phone. He'd have called me."

Eli wandered around. He hadn't been in the shop since Hannah opened it. He'd come into town a couple of times to help her and Gideon when she was getting set up. Now it was filled with so much fabric and sewing goods. Quilts hung on the wall, and shelves were filled with colorful fabric, yarn, and sewing goods.

Emma put John in his crib and gave him his stuffed toys. Eli walked over and sat in the chair beside it. "He really does seem happy here."

"He's a happy *boppli*. Always has been. And he loves all the ladies who come in and fuss over him."

She glanced at the clock. "I'm going to go start a pot of coffee and put my lunch in the refrigerator."

He felt a moment of panic. "What if someone comes in?"

She laughed. "They can't, silly. I locked the door. It's not time to open yet."

"Oh."

Eli's cell phone signaled a text was coming in. He was still reading it when Emma walked back to the front.

"Did you get a call from Gideon?"

He shook his head. "Just looking something up."

When she continued to look at him curiously he searched for an excuse. "Weather. Just checking the weather."

She appeared to take what he said without comment. "Don't forget to get the fruit from Fannie Mae on the way home."

"I won't."

"Coffee should be ready by now. Want a cup?"

"Ya. Danki."

He walked to the window again and looked out. Still no sign of the van. It seemed to him that it was running a few minutes late.

Emma walked back in with two cups of coffee. "Relax. She'll be here soon. And you don't have to stick around. John and I have tended the shop by ourselves before."

He returned to the seat by John's crib. "You know what you said earlier? About being happy to be with *familye* since we married?"

She nodded and took a seat at the quilting table. *"Ya."*

"You really meant it, didn't you?"

"Of course. I love your *familye*." She smiled then sipped her coffee. "I think it was so sweet of Gideon to move his things to the downstairs bedroom to give us more privacy. He didn't need to do that."

"What would you think of him staying longer?"

"Longer? Eli, you need to stop worrying. He and Hannah are going to make up. They're too much in love not to."

"That's not what I meant. You'd really be *allrecht* if he stayed longer...and Hannah came to live with us too for a time?" He figured he'd better make *schur*.

"Well of course that would be fine." Now she gave him a really big smile. "Do you two think you can refrain from bickering the way you do?"

"We don't bicker."

"You do, too. I've been around when you two do."

"Girls bicker. Not guys."

She glared at him. "I'll have you know it's something both sexes do."

He grinned at her. "Are you bickering with me?"

Emma burst out laughing, and hearing her, John giggled and bounced in his crib.

"So glad we could entertain you," Eli told him as he shook his head.

Chapter Thirty

So close and yet so far, Gideon thought.

Hannah sat just inches from him in the van, but it felt like she was miles away.

Gideon noticed she'd edged over as close to the window on her side as possible. But she hadn't sat in another row because that would likely raise questions from Liz or other passengers.

He had to find a way to get her alone to talk to her and apologize. He'd tossed and turned last night trying to think of what to say to her to make things right again. Now as they rode to work he continued to wonder what he was going to do, what he was going to say to her when they got out.

But when Liz pulled up in front of Gideon's shop, Hannah fairly bolted out of the vehicle and hurried toward her shop pretending she didn't hear him calling her.

"Trouble in paradise?" Micah, the jewelry shop owner, joked as he stood unlocking his door.

Gideon forced a laugh and turned to unlock his own shop.

"Hey, sorry, bad joke. Is Hannah okay?"

"Just a little misunderstanding."

"Women, huh? Well, I'm sure you'll make up. The Amish believe in forgiveness, right?"

Gideon was glad to see the man didn't expect an answer and had already entered his shop. He walked into his, locked the door behind him, and headed to the back room.

As he started a pot of coffee he tried not to think about the fact that with Hannah giving him the cold shoulder since their fight at the pond he wasn't sharing morning coffee with her or the occasional lunch. Well, he was a big boy. It wouldn't hurt him.

And like Micah said, Hannah wouldn't stay mad long. She'd forgive him for mangling what he was trying to say that day at the pond.

When the pot finished percolating he poured a mug and took it with him to the front counter. He'd spend the time he usually took drinking coffee and occasionally having a donut with Hannah to do some paperwork.

But his mind wandered, and every time someone passed the shop he found himself hoping she'd come to speak to him.

When opening time came, Gideon was relieved to

unlock the door and turn the sign over. Then he sat carving a wooden toy. It kept him busy when the store was empty. When customers walked in, they always seemed to enjoy seeing him working on a toy. He'd learned his customers only really believed they were handmade when they saw him in action.

He sighed. It was entirely too quiet this morning. He needed things to be busy so his thoughts didn't constantly go around and around like a hamster on an exercise wheel.

When an *Englisch* couple walked in, Gideon was almost pathetically grateful. He tried not to be too eager to help them. Some customers didn't like that and wanted to browse in peace. Fortunately they had some questions and wanted help choosing a gift for a grandchild. As he wrapped and then rang up their purchase, they had more questions about where to eat lunch and what to see in the area.

He was truly sorry when they left. They were not only *gut* company when he was feeling down and alone, they were just the type of people he loved doing business with—so friendly, and they didn't ask intrusive questions about him being Amish.

More customers came in a short while later and things got busier. The next time he glanced at the clock on the wall it was lunchtime. Another solitary routine because of the rift between him and Hannah. He and Hannah hadn't been eating lunch together every day for the past week or so because their shops had gotten busier. So he told himself he didn't miss her as much as he would have if they'd still been having lunch almost every day.

But he wasn't any better at lying to himself than he was to other people. Food didn't taste as *gut* without her sitting on the opposite side of the counter sharing conversation and laughter. He ate his sandwich dispiritedly and decided to eat the apple and cookies he'd packed later when he felt hungrier.

He debated closing for a few minutes and getting some coffee and donuts midafternoon and surprising Hannah as he'd done a few times lately. But fear of being rejected kept him at the shop counter.

When the bell over the door jangled as someone walked in he looked up without enthusiasm. Then he brightened.

"Emma! John!" He hurried around the counter to greet them. "So nice of you to visit."

She pushed the stroller inside and shut the door. "We're taking a little break. Thought we'd stop by and say hello."

"It's *gut* to see a friendly face. Well, John. Don't you look handsome in your fancy clothes."

"Your *mudder* went to so much work to make him this nice outfit for the wedding. I'd save it for him to wear to church, but *kinner* grow so fast. I thought it would be nice for him to dress up for our first day back to work."

When John held up his arms Gideon bent to lift him from the stroller. He hugged him and looked at Emma. "Hannah barely spoke to me on the ride in."

She frowned. "I'm sorry."

John babbled at Gideon and patted his cheeks. "Thank you, John. I appreciate the sympathy."

"That's what he said?" Emma smiled.

"*Schur.* You didn't understand that?"

She shook her head. "*Nee.* We thought we'd see if you needed a break before we went back to Hannah's. I think John has an hour or two in him before he needs a nap."

"That's nice of you."

"Maybe you'd like to get coffee and something from the bakery and have a little afternoon break with Hannah," she suggested as she walked behind the counter.

He avoided her gaze. "*Nee.* I'm *schur* Hannah doesn't want to see me."

"She's unhappy, too," Emma blurted out then clapped a hand over her mouth.

His gaze flew to her face. "She is?"

"Don't you dare tell her I said that," she said quickly. "Hannah's my friend. She's been *wunderbaar* to John and me since I came back."

"I won't."

"Look, she's been quiet today and won't talk to me about it."

Gideon looked away again. "I'm *schur* Eli told you what happened."

She nodded. "He did. I just know if the two of you talked you could straighten things out."

"Easier said than done."

"Gideon," she said quietly. "Try."

He sighed. "I just didn't handle it right. I bungled what I wanted to say. I'm not as charming as Eli."

"Charm's overrated." She bit her lip. "You're not your *bruder* and besides, she's not in love with Eli. She's in love with you. So talk to her, fix whatever's wrong. And do it right away. Don't waste time. It's too precious."

She stroked John's hair. "Eli and I found out the hard way what not working things out can cost."

Gideon stared into John's deep blue eyes. She was right. He was miserable. He didn't want to waste another minute without her. He didn't care where they lived after they were married. He just wanted to be with Hannah. If Emma was right that Hannah loved him, that she was unhappy without him, then maybe she wouldn't care where they lived, either.

He had to find out.

"I think we'll take a walk," he said as he put John back in his stroller and headed for the door with him.

"You don't have to take him with you," she called.

He turned and grinned. "John's going to help me get Hannah to talk to me. She might be able to resist me, but she can't ever resist John."

* * *

Hannah glanced over as the shop door opened and Gideon wheeled John in with his stroller.

"Excuse me just a moment," she said to the customer

she was helping. She rushed over to Gideon. "Is something wrong? Where's Emma?"

"She's working at my shop. We need to talk. John told me to come talk to you."

Her jaw dropped. "Are you using John to get me to talk to you?"

"Why not? It all started with John."

"Are you blaming him for what you said?" she demanded. "A *boppli*?"

He shook his head. "I just want a chance to explain that I bungled what I wanted to say to you. It has to do with John, so I thought we should come see you together."

"I have a customer."

"We can wait."

He pushed the stroller over to the customer Hannah had been helping when he'd come in. "Ma'am? I apologize for interrupting you and Hannah."

"Why no problem, young man." She smiled at him. "What an adorable baby." She bent to coo at John.

Hannah stepped up. "You had a question about the quilt kit," she said, gesturing at the package in the woman's hand.

They discussed the merits of the kit, and the woman decided to look at others in the display. Hannah glanced over and saw that Gideon had moved the stroller over to the crib where John took his naps. She watched Gideon talk to John as he lifted him from the stroller and lay him in the crib. Her heart melted when he gently tucked the *boppli* quilt around John. He was so *gut* with John. He'd make a *wunderbaar dat* one day . . .

Then she had to hold back a giggle as she watched John pop back up like a spring and laugh at his *onkel*.

Hannah walked over to the quilt kit display to see if her customer had any other questions, and after a selection was made, they moved to the shop counter to complete the purchase. They chatted as Hannah rang up the sale. Since the woman was a regular customer and local, she tucked a flyer about quilting classes into the shopping bag. Then Hannah watched as her sole customer left the shop.

She met Gideon's gaze and knew she couldn't put off talking to him. He was patting John's back as the *kind* drifted off to sleep, then after a few minutes he walked over to her.

"What did you mean it all started with John?" she asked, folding her arms over her chest.

"In my own fumbling way I was trying to tell you that when I found out about John everything I had planned for my future had to change."

"Why? He's not your *sohn*."

"John deserved a *dat*, and if my *bruder* wasn't going to be one for him I was going to take that on."

Her respect for him grew beyond measure. Stunned, she sank down onto the stool behind the counter. "You never told me that."

He shook his head. "I had to wait to see what Eli would do. I'd hoped he'd step up and he did. But even then it didn't mean I could go on the way I planned. What I was trying to tell you that day by the pond was that when our *dat* died he left the farm to both of us with the understanding that we'd always take care of *Mamm*. We agreed that the first to marry would take over the farmhouse and Eli would always work the land because that's what he loves."

"You told me that."

"But I always thought I'd be the first to marry, since Eli didn't want to settle down for a long time."

Light dawned. "But then he did."

Gideon nodded. "How could I ask you to marry me when we'd have no place to live?"

"Many couples live with the bride's *eldres* until they can save for a place of their own," she pointed out. "Are you saying you don't want to do that?"

"*Nee—ya—*" he broke off when she glared at him.

He paced a few steps then turned to her. "I just want to provide for the woman I love. That's why I took you to the pond that day, to explain that we needed to wait so I could save up. All I did was mess things up between us."

"*Ya*, you did."

"After our fight, my *mudder* convinced me that I needed to talk to you, explain things better. She said you'd probably rather be married and the two of us save up together than wait."

"Your *mudder* is a wise woman."

"Does that mean you agree with her?" He approached her cautiously and reached for her hand. "You wouldn't mind our not having our own home when we marry?"

"Gideon, you haven't asked me to marry you. That

should come first, don't you think? Before we discuss where we'd live?"

He leaned forward, met her gaze. "Hannah, will you marry me?"

"*Ya*," she said and she smiled at him. "I will."

Gideon gave a big sigh of relief and leaned over the counter to kiss her. She didn't know how long the kiss might have lasted because she heard the bell over the shop door jangle and they sprang apart.

"Oops," Cassie said. She laughed as Hannah felt a blush steal over her cheeks. Mischief sparkled in her eyes. "Shall I go out and come back in a few minutes?"

"No of course not." She glanced at the clock. "You're early for the quilting class."

Cassie nodded. "I thought I'd do a little shopping first. Hi, Gideon."

"Hi." He glanced over at John sleeping peacefully. "I—uh—I'll just be getting back to my shop. I'll send Emma down for John."

"No hurry."

"We'll talk later," he told her meaningfully.

She nodded. "Later." She watched him leave, then realized she was being rude standing there staring after Gideon and ignoring Cassie. "Sorry, what did you say?"

Cassie laughed. "I said I'm looking at a woman in love."

Hannah felt herself blush again. She walked out from behind the counter. "I had better start a pot of coffee for the class."

"I'm sorry, I didn't mean to tease. He's nice. Before I got my license, I was an assistant to Rhonda, the Realtor for the sale of the toy shop."

Hannah nodded. "Gideon knew I wanted to start a quilt shop and let me know when this space came up for rent. He helped me set things up."

Cassie just smiled and said nothing.

"Let me know if you need any help finding anything," she said and escaped into the back room to start the coffee.

She'd just returned to the front of the shop when Emma walked in. She watched her glance at John and then their gazes met.

"So," Emma asked, her eyes sparkling with mischief. "What's new?"

"Doing a little matchmaking?" Hannah asked in a low voice so that Cassie couldn't hear.

"Did it work? Gideon wouldn't tell me anything, the meanie."

Hannah was still reeling a little at Gideon's proposal, but it was just too irresistible to tease Emma. She shook her head and forced an unhappy expression on her face. "I'm still so upset with him."

Emma's smile faded. "Oh no."

"I've asked you before—why is it that when someone's in love they want everybody else to be?" she asked Emma.

"I guess we just want everyone else to be happy, too." She sighed. "The two of you love each other so much. I know you do."

Emma looked so disappointed Hannah felt guilty. After all, Emma had just wanted to help two friends who'd had a disagreement. And it was so hard to conceal her inner joy over Gideon proposing. She decided it wasn't nice to continue teasing Emma.

A quick glance in Cassie's direction showed her that the woman was absorbed in a book about quilting. Hannah leaned forward. "Actually, Gideon and I straightened things out."

"Really?" Emma brightened.

She nodded. "Can you keep a secret?"

"*Ya!*" Emma said enthusiastically.

"Gideon asked me to marry him and I said yes."

Emma whooped and Hannah immediately shushed her. "Emma!" Hannah glanced at Cassie but she hadn't looked up.

"Sorry! Oh, I am so happy for you! You're going to be my *schwei*! I'm so happy! I can't wait to tell Eli."

"So much for keeping a secret," Hannah said drily.

"You can't mean I can't tell Eli!"

"*Nee*. But only Eli."

"And Leah."

"And Leah. I—" Emma broke off when several women came in.

"Quilting class," Hannah told her. "You can join us if you want."

"*Schur*, that would be fun. I'll stay until John wakes up."

Hannah welcomed the members of the class and waited while they settled into chairs around the table. It felt so strange to carry on with normal daily activities when she still felt the quiver of excitement over being engaged.

She'd started her day not speaking to Gideon and feeling discouraged about their relationship. Now she felt like she was walking on air.

Love. Who knew she could feel so happy?

Epilogue

Gideon took Hannah's hand, helped her from the buggy, then kissed her.

"*Kumm, lieb*, I want to show you something."

When he walked past the house and toward the path beside it, she looked at him curiously.

"I thought you invited me to supper with your *familye*."

"I did," he said, smiling at her. "We're doing something first."

Her eyebrows rose as he continued on to the path beside the weathered old barn.

"We're going to the pond?" She grinned. "Aren't you afraid of going there with me after what happened the last time?"

"Maybe I'll push *you* in this time."

"I didn't push you in. You got in my way when I was

trying to leave." But she couldn't help grinning as she remembered how he'd looked sitting there in the pond...

"Schur."

The pond came into view, but he kept walking toward the back of the property.

"I don't remember there being a path behind the pond," she said.

"Me either. But Eli said to keep walking."

"We're meeting Eli? Why?"

"I have no idea. He was very mysterious about it."

The path wound through the fields of corn due to be harvested soon. The deep green stalks rustled in the wind. Hannah inhaled the scent of ripening ears and hoped they'd have some for supper. She loved fresh corn on the cob.

She dug out a tissue from her pocket and wiped the perspiration from her forehead. The day was still hot, and she was having trouble keeping up with Gideon's long strides.

"Slow down," she said. "I'm burning up out here."

Then she heard something. A *kind*'s high voice.

"I hear John," she said. "Are we eating out here?" She hoped not. It was too hot for an outdoor picnic.

"I don't know any more than you do."

"Eli's probably putting us to work. After all, it's time to harvest." He looked at her. "Just think, we'll be married in just a couple of weeks."

She squeezed his hand, and when he stopped and kissed her again, she smiled.

They walked a little farther. John's voice got louder, but now Hannah could hear other voices, too—Eli's, Emma's, and Leah's.

Now she was really curious. Were they going to have to work for their supper? She didn't mind if they had to pluck a few ears of corn as long as they got to eat some for supper. There was nothing better than fresh-picked corn boiled and served slathered with butter.

Then they stepped into a clearing and saw Eli and Emma and John and Leah. John sat on a quilt on the ground, and he was stacking wooden blocks. When he saw them he grinned and chattered.

"Okay, Eli, we're here," Gideon said as he stopped. "Now, why are we here?"

"Well, you're not the only one in the *familye* who can plan," Eli told him. "I've been thinking. You don't have to buy land. I went into town sometime back and did some research at the county government offices. You and I and the men in the community...we can build you and Hannah a house here. I'll have my *bruder* and his *fraa* and their *familye* near. What could be better than that?"

"In the corn field?"

Eli chuckled. "We wouldn't be planting corn in this section anymore."

"But you need the acreage."

He shook his head. "*Nee*. I don't."

"Eli, you'll lose the money from the crops you could grow here," Gideon pointed out, not *schur* Eli had considered that. His *bruder* pretty much walked around in a happy daze these days.

"*Nee*," Eli repeated. "The farm will be just fine. And better yet, our *familyes* will all be together."

Gideon turned to her. He looked as stunned as she felt. "What do you think?"

She took a deep breath. "I think I need to sit down."

So she did, right on the quilt next to John.

"Think about it," Emma said. "The *familye* gets to stay close but have their own houses. Our *kinner* will grow up playing together, working on the farm together."

"We can start building after harvest," Eli said. "Get as much done as we can before cold weather sets in. Work on the inside during the winter. This time next year you could be moving in."

"A home of our own," Gideon said. "Here, on Troyer land. You're *schur* we can do this?"

"I checked. We can. So what do you say, Gideon? Hannah?" Eli prompted.

"I think it's *wunderbaar*," Hannah said slowly. "What do you say, Gideon?"

"I'd say this is beyond anything I could have dreamed possible. And maybe I need to sit down, too. My knees feel weak," he admitted with a laugh. He'd be calling Cassie to tell her there was no need to look for a home.

Leah smiled. "That's God for you. Always surprising us with something far better than we can dream."

Hannah watched John struggle to his feet. He wobbled then took an unsteady step forward. She gasped, turned to see if the others saw what she did.

"Look at him," Emma said so quietly her voice was almost a whisper. "Eli, look! John's trying to walk."

"Oh my." Leah chuckled. "Once Eli started walking

he was running me ragged in no time. You're going to have your hands full with this one, Emma."

John wobbled and fell down. But instead of crying he just laughed. He looked at his hands—of course he'd fallen forward into the dirt—and immediately stuck his fists into his mouth.

Leah swooped him up into her arms and started for the house. "I'm going to wash his hands. Supper in fifteen minutes."

Gideon stood and held out his hand to help Hannah to her feet. Then he turned and grabbed Eli in a bear hug. "*Danki* for thinking of this."

"*Danki* for helping me find my way," Eli said. Hannah saw him swallow hard as he looked at Emma.

"*Danki*, Eli," Hannah told him as she reached up to kiss his cheek.

She turned to Emma. "You knew and you kept the secret?"

Emma laughed and shook her head. "*Nee*, he knew better than to tell me before today." She glanced around and sighed. "It seems like such a *wunderbaar* idea. The four of us could have lived in the farmhouse and added on as we had more *kinner*. But this way you and Gideon get to have your own home."

Gideon turned to Hannah. "So what do you think, Hannah? Ready to plan a house together?"

She gazed up at him. "Oh, I'm so ready to plan a future together with you, *lieb*."

He cupped her face in his hands and stared deep into her eyes. "I can't wait to begin it."

"*Kumm*, let's go on and leave these two so they can have some privacy," she heard Emma say as they walked back to the house.

"Are they gone?" Gideon asked Hannah as he bent to kiss her.

"*Ya*," she said, smiling.

When they finally started back to the house dusk was falling. The old farmhouse looked warm and inviting, with light spilling out the windows. Hannah studied the way it spread out, with additions built on as the *familye* had grown through the years. One day their house might look the same as they had *kinner* and needed more space.

The thought made her heart beat faster.

They climbed the steps and walked into the kitchen. John was sitting in his highchair watching as his *mudder* and *grossmudder* put food on the table.

Then John looked over and saw them. He enthusiastically banged his hands on his tray to greet them.

"So, John, what do you think about Hannah and me living close by?" Gideon asked him.

John laughed and bounced so hard Emma had to reach out and steady the chair.

"I think John's happy you found a home," Eli told him with a chuckle.

"Just like John," Emma said simply, beaming at them. "Just like John."

Glossary

ab im Kopp—crazy
aenti—aunt
allrecht—all right
boppli—baby
bopplin—babies
braut—bride
breidicham—bridegroom
bruder—brother
bu—boy
buwe—boys
daedi—daddy
danki—thank you
dat—father
dawdi haus—a small home added to or near the main

house into which the farmer moves after passing the farm and main house to one of his children.

Deitsch—Pennsylvania German

Der Hochmut kummt vor dem Fall—Pride comes before the fall

dippy eggs—over-easy eggs

dochder—daughter

en alt maedel—old maid

Englisch, Englischer—what the Amish call a non-Amish person

familye—family

fraa—wife

grossdaadi—grandfather

grossdochder—granddaughter

grosseldres—grandparents

grossmudder—grandmother

guder mariye—good morning

gut—good

gut-n-owed—good evening

haus—house

hungerich—hungry

kapp—prayer covering or cap worn by girls and women

kind—child

kinner—children

kinskind—grandchild

kumm—come

lieb—love, a term of endearment

maed—young single women

maedel—young single woman

maed vun ehr—maid of honor

mamm—mom

mann—husband

mudder—mother

nacht—night

nee—no

newehockers—wedding attendants, sometimes called side sitters

onkel—uncle

Ordnung—the rules of the Amish, both written and unwritten. Certain behavior has been expected within the Amish community for many, many years. These rules vary from community to community, but the most common are to have no electricity in the home, to not own or drive an automobile, and to dress a certain way.

roasht—roast, a stuffing or dressing side dish made of cubes of bread, chopped celery, and onion

rumschpringe—time period when teenagers are allowed to experience the *Englisch* world while deciding if they should join the church

schul—school

schur—sure

schwardochder—daughter-in-law

schwei—sister-in-law

schwemudder—mother-in-law

schweschder—sister

sohn—son

verboten—forbidden, not done

whoopie pie—large soft cookie with marshmallow fluff filling

wilkumm—welcome

wittfraa—widow
wunderbaar—wonderful
ya—yes
zwillingboppli—twin
zwillingbopplin—twins

Note: While there are many similarities about Amish communities around the country each community makes its own rules. The Lancaster County, Pennsylvania, Amish community allows cell phones while some other Amish communities limit or ban them.

Recipes

FUNERAL SANDWICHES

- 24-count package sweet dinner rolls
- 24 slices Black Forest ham
- 24 slices Swiss cheese

Directions

Slice rolls in half. Place on 11×15-inch sheet pan. Layer 1 slice each ham and cheese on each roll. Replace tops.

Sauce:

- 1 stick butter, melted
- ¼ cup brown sugar
- 2 Tablespoons Dijon mustard
- 1 Tablespoon Worcestershire sauce
- 1 Tablespoon poppy seeds (optional)
- 1 teaspoon onion powder

Directions

Mix together with a small whisk. Brush tops of ham and cheese rolls liberally with sauce, then pour remaining sauce over all. Cover pan with foil and refrigerate for 4 to 24 hours. Preheat oven to 350°F. Bake rolls, covered, for 10 minutes, then remove foil and bake another 10 to 15 minutes until the tops are golden brown. Makes 24 dinner roll–sized servings. Serves about 12 if each person takes two rolls.

MARY'S BUTTERMILK BISCUITS

- 2¼ cups all-purpose flour
- 2¼ cups cake flour
- 1½ teaspoons salt
- 1½ Tablespoons baking powder
- 1 teaspoon baking soda
- 1 cup butter (very cold)—don't use margarine!
- 2 cups buttermilk
- ½ cup flour (for dusting the pastry mat and dusting while rolling)
- 2 Tablespoons butter (melted)

Directions

Preheat oven to 475°F. Combine the dry ingredients together in a bowl. Cut in the butter until the mixture is crumbly. Add the buttermilk and mix just until combined. The dough will be slightly sticky.

Turn the dough out onto a floured surface and pat it into a horizontal rectangle that is about 1½ inches thick. Fold the left side of the rectangle over the right side and pat it out into a vertical rectangle. Then fold the bottom half up to the top and press it out into a horizontal rectangle again. Repeat the steps above three times for a total of six folds. Be careful not to overwork the dough while you are doing this. The folding is what creates layers in the biscuits. Sprinkle a little flour on the layers if the dough starts getting sticky, but just pat gently and handle the dough lightly. After making those six folds, gently pat the dough into a rectangle that is about 1 inch thick. Use a sharp circle biscuit cutter and press down through the dough, then lift up. Do not twist the cookie cutter. Just push down, then pull straight up. Place biscuits on an ungreased baking sheet. Brush the tops of the biscuits with melted butter.

Bake at 475°F for five minutes, then reduce the heat to 425°F (without opening the oven) and bake for an additional 8–10 minutes. Allow the biscuits to sit for 2–3 minutes before serving. Serve warm. Makes about a dozen biscuits.

Buttermilk is recommended for the recipe, but if you don't have it it's easy to make by putting 1 tablespoon of vinegar in a measuring cup. Fill up the rest of the cup with milk and let it sit for 5 minutes. Now you have buttermilk!

ROASHT OR CHICKEN FILLING

- 1 stick (8 Tablespoons) butter
- 2 cups chopped celery
- 2 loaves bread, cubed
- 2 cups cooked and diced chicken
- 6 eggs, beaten
- 1 teaspoon salt
- pepper to taste

Directions

Preheat oven to 350°F. Melt butter in a skillet and sauté celery in it until soft. Set aside. Mix bread and chicken in large bowl. Add celery, eggs, and salt and pepper. Pour mixture into large baking pan. Bake 1½–2 hours. Serves 15.

CHOCOLATE CHESS PIE

- 1 stick (8 tablespoons) salted butter, melted
- 1 cup sugar
- 4 Tablespoons cocoa powder
- 3 eggs
- 1 (5-ounce) can evaporated milk
- 1 teaspoon vanilla extract
- 1 (9-inch) deep-dish pie shell (unbaked)
- Whipped cream (optional)

Directions

Preheat oven to 325°F. In a bowl, combine butter, sugar, cocoa, eggs, evaporated milk, and vanilla. Mix well. Pour the mixture into the pie shell and spread it evenly along the edges. Bake for 45 minutes. Serve with whipped cream (optional). Serves 8.

Book Discussion Questions

Spoiler alert! Please don't read before completing the book as the questions contain spoilers!

1. My parents were BOTH twins, so I've always been fascinated by the concept of twin siblings. Gideon and Eli are twins—something that happens more often in the Amish community than the *Englisch* one because the Amish have large families and the more babies a woman has the more likely she is to experience multiple births. Have you ever known twins? How were they alike? Different? Do you think you'd have liked to be a twin?

2. Gideon works as a maker of toys for children. What were your favorite toys when you were a child? How are the toys different today?

3. Hannah and Emma love working in a quilt shop Hannah owns. Have you ever quilted? Do you enjoy it? If not, what do you do for a hobby?

4. Have you ever thought about living in an Amish community? What do you think would be the hardest part of adapting to life in one?

5. Eli loves working on the farm his family has owned for generations. Were any of your ancestors farmers? Would you want to try farming? Why do you think so many people today think farming sounds like something some people say they'd like to try?

6. A baby born outside marriage is called an unforeseen blessing in the Amish community. What do you think of this?

7. Leah thinks both couples could share the farmhouse and add on as they have families. Do you think this could work? Have you ever had to live with a family member after you were married? How did that work?

8. The Amish believe God sets aside a partner for us. Do you believe this?

9. Have you ever visited an Amish community? Which one? What did you think about that way of life? Would you want to live there?

10. Eli comes up with a solution for the two couples. Would you want to live so close to a sibling and their wife or husband? Why or why not?

Look for the next heartwarming story in
the Hearts of Lancaster County series

THE AMISH FARMER'S
PROPOSAL

Available Spring 2022

About the Author

Barbara Cameron enjoys writing about the spiritual values and simple joys of the Amish. She is the bestselling author of more than forty fiction and non-fiction books, three nationally televised movies, and the winner of the first Romance Writers of America Golden Heart Award. Her books have been nominated for Carol Awards and the Inspirational Reader's Choice Award from RWA's Faith, Hope, and Love chapter. Barbara lives in Jacksonville, Florida.

You can learn more at:

> BarbaraCameron.com
> Facebook.com/Barbara.Cameron1

Want more charming small towns?
Fall in love with these
Forever contemporary romances!

THE SUMMER COTTAGE
by Annie Rains

Somerset Lake is the perfect place for Trisha Langly and her son to start over. As the new manager for the Somerset Cottages, she's instantly charmed by her firecracker of a boss, Vi—but less enchanted by Vi's protective grandson, attorney Jake Fletcher. If Jake discovers her past, she'll lose this perfect second chance. However, as they spend summer days renovating the property and nights enjoying the town's charm, Trisha may realize she must trust Jake with her secrets…and her heart. Includes a bonus story!

**FALLING IN LOVE
ON WILLOW CREEK**
by Debbie Mason

FBI agent Chase Roberts has come to Highland Falls to work undercover as a park ranger to track down an on-the-run informant. But when he befriends the suspect's sister to get nearer to his target, Chase finds that he's growing closer to the warm-hearted, beautiful Sadie Gray and her little girl. When he arrests her brother, Elijah, Chase risks losing Sadie forever. Can he convince her that the feelings between them are real once Sadie discovers the truth? Includes a bonus story!

A WEDDING ON LILAC LANE
by Hope Ramsay

After returning home from her country music career, Ella McMillan is shocked to find her mother is engaged. Worse, she asks Ella to plan the event with her fiancé's straitlaced son, Dr. Dylan Killough. While Ella wants to create the perfect day, Dylan is determined the two shouldn't get married at all. Somehow amid all their arguing, sparks start flying. And soon everyone in Magnolia Harbor is wondering if Dylan and Ella will be joining their parents in a trip down the aisle.

FRIENDS LIKE US
by Sarah Mackenzie

When a cancer scare compels Bree Robinson to form an *anti*-bucket list, she decides to start with a steamy fling. Only her one-night stand is Chance Elliston, the architect she's just hired to renovate her house. Bree agrees to a friends-with-benefits relationship with Chance before he returns to the city at the end of the summer. But as their feelings for each other grow, can she convince him to risk it all on a new life together?

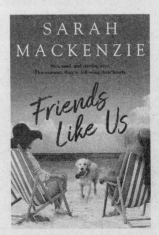

SUMMER AT FIREFLY BEACH
by Jenny Hale

Hallie Flynn adores her aunt Clara's beautiful beachside house, yet a busy job and heartbreak over the years have kept her away. But when her beloved aunt passes, Hallie returns to fulfill her final wish: to complete the bucket list Hallie wrote as a teenager. With the help of her childhood friend Ben Murray, she remembers her forgotten dreams ... and finds herself falling for the man who's always been by her side. But to have a future with Ben, can Hallie face the truths buried deep in her heart?

ONCE UPON A PUPPY
by Lizzie Shane

Lawyer Connor Wyeth has a plan for everything—except training his unruly mutt, Maximus. The only person Max ever obeyed was animal shelter volunteer Deenie Mitchell. But with a day job hosting princess parties for kids, the upbeat Deenie isn't thrilled to co-parent with Max's uptight owner...until she realizes he's perfect for impressing her type-A family. As they play the perfect couple, it begins to feel all too real. Can one rambunctious dog bring together two complete opposites?

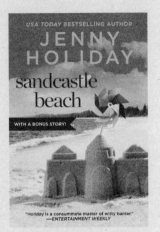

SANDCASTLE BEACH
by Jenny Holiday

What Maya Mehta really needs to save her beloved community theater is Matchmaker Bay's new business grant. She's got some serious competition, though: Benjamin Lawson, local bar owner, Jerk Extraordinaire, and Maya's annoyingly hot archnemesis. Turns out there's a thin line between hate and irresistible desire, and Maya and Law are really good at crossing it. But when things heat up, will they allow their long-standing feud to get in the way of their growing feelings? Includes the bonus story *Once Upon a Bride*, for the first time in print!

DREAM SPINNER
by Kristen Ashley

There's no doubt that former soldier Axl Pantera is the man of Hattie Yates's dreams. Yet years of abuse from her demanding father have left her terrified of disappointment. Axl is slowly wooing Hattie into letting down her walls—until a dangerous stalker sets their sights on her. Now he's facing more than her wary and bruised heart. Axl will do anything to prove that they're meant to be—but first, he'll need to keep Hattie safe.